# Claiming Quinn

## RAMONA GRAY

Adult Reading Material

Published by:
EK Publishing Inc.

Cover art by:
The Final Wrap

ISBN: 978-1-926483-93-1

# Chapter One

"Silas, man you have to go with us." His younger brother checked his reflection once more in the mirror before turning back to him.

"Seriously, Dude, if you don't come, the ladies will drop us in minutes." Gage gave him a pleading look.

Silas put his feet up on the worn coffee table. "Gage, I'm tired, my feet hurt and there's a show I want to watch."

Gage rolled his eyes. "God forbid you should miss your home improvement show."

Silas ignored him as Gage dropped onto the couch next to him. "I don't know why you watch those damn shows anyway, you already know how to do everything they do."

Silas grunted and leaned back against the couch.

"C'mon, Silas, please?" Gage said.

Silas sighed. He found it almost impossible to deny his younger brother anything he asked. He supposed it was because of the guilt he felt every time he looked at his sibling. Silas knew it wasn't his fault that their parents died in the car crash when he was twenty and Gage was only ten but it didn't ease his guilt.

He was in his first year of university, working toward his degree in architecture and enjoying his first taste of freedom from his parents' rules. He was only six months into it when his parents were killed. He left school and flew home immediately. It was nearly two weeks after his parents' funeral before the truth of it hit him. He was comforting Gage after another nightmare and as he held his crying baby brother, he finally realized that his parents were gone. They were alone.

He quit university and took a job with a local construction company. Their parents struggled to get by and the little money they left their two sons went toward their funeral costs. The last fifteen years were difficult but he and Gage soldiered through it together. On the better days, he liked to think that Gage was doing well. Even though he lost his parents at such a young age, Silas hoped he had done a good job of filling the void.

"Gage, I'm tired," he repeated. "It was a long day today, the weather is miserable and I don't particularly feel like going out in it again. Besides, don't you have midterms this week? You need to be studying."

Gage grimaced and ran a hand through his shaggy blond hair. "Yeah, yeah. I've got all day Sunday to study."

Silas frowned at him. "Gage, you need to take your classes seriously. You're this close to getting your BBA. Do you really want to throw it away for a bit of meaningless sex?"

"Stop lecturing me, Silas. I don't need to hear it right now okay?" Gage muttered.

"Gage - "

"I mean it, Silas!" Gage jumped off the couch and paced back and forth in the small living room. "Can't we just go out together on a Friday night and have a good time?"

Silas rubbed his forehead and Gage, sensing weakness, spoke quickly. "It'll be fun. You'll see. We won't be out that late. Angela said she would come if her girlfriends went, and her girlfriends will only go if they think you're there. I told them you would be. If we show up without you, they'll leave, and the guys will kill me."

"Gage, I have no interest in any of those girls. They're way too young for me," Silas replied.

"Yeah, yeah, I know. But they don't know that. They all think they have a chance with you. At the end of the night when they finally figure it out, they're more than willing to hook up with my friends. You're the ultimate wingman."

"Jesus, Gage." Silas shook his head. "Whatever happened to just going up to a woman and talking to her?"

"It doesn't work that way anymore, man. I mean, sometimes it does but c'mon, you've seen my friends. They're the nerdy types. We need a good-lookin' brute like you to reel them in first. Hell, you might even find yourself a nice, old chick to bang."

Silas laughed despite himself. "Well, how can I resist when you put it so eloquently?"

Gage held his fist out and Silas bumped it obligingly. "It'll be a night you won't forget, Silas. I promise you."

※ ※

"Quinn."

"My Queen." The tall, dark-haired woman dropped to one knee and bowed her head.

The queen, her blonde hair falling in a shimmering curtain to just below her knees, rested her hand on the dark one's head. "Stand, Quinn. You need not be so formal when it is just the two of us."

Quinn stood. She stared at the smaller woman clothed head-to-toe in a robe of soft blue silk. The colour matched her eyes perfectly and the queen wore it often.

In the flickering candlelight with her slender body hidden by the robe and her eyes glowing softly, the woman looked dainty and birdlike. Quinn knew better. She had seen firsthand the queen's fighting abilities and the sweet roundness of her face belied her sharp mind and cruel nature. Although she had not witnessed the queen's rise to power, she heard the tales of the ugly and brutal battles the woman had fought to gain the throne.

Now, the queen wrinkled her nose at her. "You smell, Quinn."

"Forgive me, my Queen. The weather has flooded many of the roads. Our wheels were caught in the mud and I spent most of the day digging out the wagons."

"Is that where you've been all day?" The queen

poured herself some sweet red wine and sipped delicately at it.

"Yes, my Queen."

"Do you believe that the queen's massina should be spending her time digging in the mud?" The queen's voice was deceptively soft.

"I believed that I should help your people. There were many wagons stuck and - "

There was a sharp crack and Quinn's head rocked back with the force of the slap. Quinn stared straight ahead. Her cheek was red and stinging but she made no move to rub it.

"Your only job is to protect your queen." The woman glared at her. "After so many years together, why must I remind you of this?"

"My apologies, my Queen. I will not forget again."

The queen sniffed and took another drink of her wine. "I trust you will not."

She returned to her chair by the large fireplace that dominated the bedroom and stared moodily into the crackling flames. Quinn remained by the door with her arms folded behind her back and waited patiently. Through the window to her left she could see the sky growing darker. It had been pouring rain all day and the distant booms of thunder were growing steadily louder. As lightning flashed across the sky the queen sighed.

"This is no ordinary storm, Quinn."

When Quinn didn't reply, the queen said impatiently, "Come – sit by the fire with me."

Quinn crossed the room and sat on the edge of the chair. She was tired and hungry and yearned for a hot bath but she did not allow any of her emotions to show on her face.

The queen finished her wine in two large gulps and set the glass on the small table next to her chair. "I spoke with the majii and she assured me there will be another orb three nights from now. I want you to go and bring back all those who appear. Male and female."

"Yes, my Queen."

"You will have to leave immediately. It is a two-day journey if you ride without stopping. Take Akia and the usual others, including Kila."

"Are you sure she is ready, my Queen?"

The queen snorted. "You question me, Quinn?"

"No, my Queen."

"Good. Then go and bring me my breeders."

Quinn rose and left the room silently. When the door to the queen's bedroom shut behind her, she leaned against the wall beside it for a moment. Her head was aching and she was bone tired. She sighed and pushed away from the wall, nodding to the guards who were standing watch outside the queen's bedroom. She had chosen them herself, both for their fighting abilities and their ability to keep their mouths shut about anything they witnessed or heard. She trudged down the hallway. She needed to gather the others and move out quickly if they were to arrive and set the traps before one of the other clans showed up.

❧ ❧

"Some weather we're having, huh?" One of Gage's friends, Silas thought his name was Craig, said politely.

Silas nodded. "Yeah."

He, along with Craig, Gage, Steve, Evan, and Kyle were standing huddled under the awning of a closed coffee shop. Silas glanced at his watch impatiently before nudging Gage. "When are they supposed to be here?"

Gage shrugged. "Any minute now. They were taking a cab here and then we're going to walk to the bar."

"Walk to the bar?" Silas glanced up at the sky. The rain fell in sheets and lightning was flashing across the sky every few minutes. "In this?"

Gage punched his arm as a cab pulled up in front of them. "You're not sugar, Silas."

The girls piled out, giggling and shrieking as they darted under the awning. A small blonde snuggled into Gage's arms. "Hi there."

"Hi, Angela." Gage grinned delightedly at her and kissed her cheek. "How are you?"

"I'm good." She glanced at Silas, looking him up and down quickly. "Hello, Silas."

"Hey, Angela." Silas blinked as a redhead with her breasts nearly falling out of the dark green dress she was wearing, pressed up against him.

"Hi, I'm Veronica," she said in a breathless little girl voice. "Like in the Archie comics."

"Hello, Veronica." Silas tried to take a step back and bumped up against the glass door of the coffee shop. Veronica pressed closer and rested one perfectly-manicured hand on his hard biceps.

"God, you're strong. Gage says you work construction."

"That's right."

"I love construction workers. So buff and tanned." She laughed – a high-pitched giggle that set Silas' teeth on edge.

He smiled politely at her before flashing Gage a warning look. Gage cleared his throat. "Silas, you know Angela and you've just met Veronica. These other lovely ladies are Andrea, Paula, Gemma and Lacey."

The women smiled at him as Gage stuck his hand out from under the awning and let the rain splash onto his palm. "What do you say we get to the bar before the whole damn street floods?"

Evan glanced at the dark sky, pushing his glasses up self-consciously. "Maybe we should wait until the rain slows down a bit."

"We'll be here all night then," Lacey pouted. "It's cold out."

"I don't mind." Veronica put her arms around Silas' waist and ran her fingers up and down the back of his leather jacket.

"We're not sugar, we won't melt." Silas said with another polite smile. He unwrapped her arms from his waist. "Let's go."

He stepped out into the rain, pulling his collar up as the others followed him. He strode down the street. Behind him he could hear the girls giggling and squealing as they slipped and slid in their high heels on the slick pavement. The street was completely dead. No cars passed by and there were no other people scurrying through the rain. Silas moved a little faster as cold rain dripped down the back of his neck and under his jacket.

A large boom of thunder went off directly above them and one of the girls screamed. Jagged lightning flashed and the top of the hydro pole in front of them exploded with a loud bang as sparks showered down. The street lights went out and they were plunged into darkness.

"Oh shit. Gage?" Angela said. "Take my hand."

"Sure, baby. Don't be afraid." Gage took Angela's hand as Silas turned to face the rest of the group.

"I think we should call it a night." He had to shout to be heard over the rising wind.

The girls gave small moans of dismay and Gage shook his head. "Nah, man, it'll be fine. The bar is a couple of blocks down. I bet they haven't lost electricity."

"Gage, this is - "

"What's that?" Veronica pointed to Silas' left. He stared curiously at the small glowing orb hovering twenty feet above the wet pavement.

Silas took a step back, joining the group as the orb grew steadily larger. The wind howled and he realized with sudden alarm that it wasn't just a wind from the storm. The orb was creating the wind and it was rapidly growing to tornado level.

"Back!" Silas roared. "Everyone get back now!"

He grabbed Veronica's hand and yanked her backward. "Move goddammit!"

She stumbled in her high heels and fell to one knee. He yanked her to her feet with a panicky roughness. There was a strange electricity in the air. He could feel the hair on his body standing on end and the orb was now five times its original size and crackling loudly.

"Silas, what the hell is going on?" Gage grabbed his arm.

"I don't know but we need to get the hell out of here now!" Silas shouted.

"What's happening? What is that thing?" Angela shrieked.

As if it heard her, the orb began to throb and pulse and Silas cursed and pulled Veronica back.

"Go now!" He pushed her down the street and grabbed Gage's arm. "We need to go! Right - "

The orb suddenly pulsed with a brilliant white light and the group threw their arms up to shield their eyes. Behind him, Veronica shrieked as she was lifted off her feet and sucked toward the orb.

"Silas!" Gage was being dragged toward the orb and Silas grabbed his arm grimly and dug his feet in. It was pointless. The wind was a howling, blasting tornado and he felt his own feet lifting off the ground. All around him the others in their group were being lifted into the air and sucked into the orb. There was another brilliant flash of white light, Gage's arm was torn from his grasp and both he and Silas were pulled into the light.

෧ ෨

"Silas. Silas, wake up, man. C'mon, open your eyes."

Silas groaned and blinked rapidly. His head was aching and throbbing. He blinked again as Gage's worried face swam into focus.

"You okay, buddy?" Gage helped him sit up and Silas touched his hand to his temple. It came away wet and he stared in disbelief at the red liquid on his fingers.

"You must have hit your head on a rock. I've been trying to wake you up for five minutes." Gage squatted beside him and gripped his shoulder. "How do you feel?"

"Like I've been hit by a truck," Silas groaned. The rain was still falling steadily but the wind had died down. He took a cautious look around. "Where the hell are we?"

"I have no idea." Gage helped him to his feet, steadying him when he swayed a bit. "But I don't think we're in Kansas anymore, Toto."

Silas continued to look around as Angela joined them. The entire wet and shivering group was standing in the middle of a field. In front of them was a large forest with tall and impossibly thick trees. Behind them was more field. He squinted in the darkness but it was impossible to tell how far the field went.

It was raining as hard as ever and thunder and lightning was crashing across the sky. It showed no sign of letting up as Steve pointed to the forest.

"C'mon, we should head for the trees."

"Are you sure that's smart?" Craig asked nervously. "We don't know what's in there."

"It's better than standing exposed in the middle of a field." Steve's brown skin was glistening with water. He shoved past him and started towards the trees. After a moment, the others followed.

It was even darker in the forest, but the trees

were so dense and their branches so thick that the rain could barely penetrate the trees and was reduced to a light drizzle.

"God, I'm so cold," Veronica moaned. Silas shrugged out of his jacket and handed it to her. She took it with a nod of thanks and slipped into it.

They gathered under a large tree and stared blankly at each other.

"Anyone have any goddamn idea what's happening to us?" Gage asked.

"Isn't it obvious?" Kyle pushed his thick black hair off his forehead.

"Isn't what obvious?" Craig asked.

"Time travel." Kyle touched the tree behind them, rubbing his finger along the bark and then staring at the pad of his finger.

"Shut up, Kyle," Evan said testily.

Kyle shrugged. "Then you explain it."

"I can't and neither can you. But we didn't just fucking travel in time through a giant glowing orb."

"I think we did." Kyle stared solemnly at them. "Shit like this happens all the time."

"It does not!" Paula said indignantly.

"Sure it does. People disappear under mysterious circumstances. Their family and friends say it was aliens but what do you want to bet it's some type of time travel."

Lacey snorted. "Or maybe it is alien abduction. Maybe that orb is some kind of alien life force that sucked us into space and dumped us on its planet."

Kyle shrugged. "Maybe. Anything's possible."

Lacey rolled her eyes. "I wasn't being serious, Kyle."

Silas wiped the blood from his face as Gage took a few steps into the forest. "Gage, stay with the group."

Gage frowned. "Did you hear that, Silas?"

"Hear what?"

"It sounded like singing. Everyone be quiet for a minute."

Silas listened carefully. Although he heard nothing, Gage frowned and moved deeper into the forest.

"Gage!" He said.

Gage shook his head. "I heard it. Can't you hear it?"

"No. Just stay here. Don't - "

Silas cursed as Gage broke into a jog and disappeared into the forest. "Goddammit, Gage!"

He chased after his brother and after a moment the others followed.

## Chapter Two

"Gage! Wait up!" Silas held his hand to his aching head and jogged faster. The blood was really flowing now and he felt sick to his stomach and woozy. Great. He probably had a concussion.

Behind him, he could hear the girls grumbling and complaining as they struggled to keep up in their high heels. He dodged around a tree and breathed a sigh of relief when he saw Gage standing motionless in front of him.

"Gage? Are you okay?" He stood next to his brother and peered anxiously at him.

"Yeah. Look." Gage pointed in front of him at the large pit in the ground. Silas frowned at the young woman who was standing in the pit, staring up at them.

"What the hell?"

"Please help me. Please." The woman's voice was soft and anxious.

Silas stared at her. Her blonde hair was long and wavy and she was dressed in an ankle-length blue skirt and a form fitting halter top that left her trim stomach bare. The halter top was cut low and revealed the tops of her small breasts. Her skin was pale and her light blue eyes stared pleadingly up at them.

"What are you doing in there?" Gage whispered as the others joined them at the edge of the pit.

"Please help me," the woman repeated. "I've been trapped in here for days."

"Did you – were you singing?" Gage couldn't stop staring at the woman and he paid no attention when Angela pulled on his arm.

The woman smiled. "You heard me?"

Gage nodded and Angela frowned a little at the look on his face before staring down at the woman. "What's your name?"

The woman ignored Angela completely. She was staring at Gage with a combination of delight and desire and Gage was returning her look unabashedly.

"Gage – knock it off." Silas shook his younger brother.

"We need to help her. We need to get her out of there." Gage took a deep breath and tore his gaze from the woman's face. "We should find rope or - "

"Guys, is it just me or is the chick glowing?" Evan was peering into the pit and the rest of them followed his gaze.

"Holy shit. She is," Steve whispered.

Silas stepped back. The woman in the pit *was* glowing. Glowing so brightly that the entire bottom of the pit was illuminated and soft light was flowing up to wash over their faces.

"She's so beautiful," Gage whispered. He took

another step forward as Angela gave Silas an alarmed look and tugged hard on Gage's arm.

"Gage, what's wrong with you?"

"Please help me. It's been days and I'm hungry and thirsty," the woman pleaded again.

Gage's eyes swept down her body, lingering on her breasts and then her hips. She began to glow even more brightly and her pale face reddened.

Silas frowned. Something didn't feel right. The woman looked too good - too clean - to have been in the pit for days. He took a few steps back, abandoning the group that was still gathered around the pit, and looked suspiciously into the trees. He squinted into the darkness that suddenly didn't seem as dark as it was before. There was a glow coming from the trees. He was sure of it. The hair on the back of his neck stood up and the throbbing in his head increased until it was a pulsing, blinding pain. He turned back to the group.

"Get away from there!" He suddenly yelled.

The group, except for Gage who was still staring transfixed at the girl in the pit, turned toward him.

"Get back now! It's a trap! Get - "

There was a soft whooshing noise. There were curses and startled screams as a large rope net hidden under the leaves that littered the forest floor swept the group off their feet and into the air.

"Gage!" Silas ran toward the gently swaying net. His foot hit something spongy and soft, something rough tightened around his ankle and the world was suddenly turned upside down. He swung back and forth, the tips of his fingers just brushing the ground as the others fought to escape the net.

"Silas! Silas – are you okay?" Gage stared at him, his face smashed up against the net. A foot rested against the side of his head.

"Just great," Silas groaned. The blood was rushing to his head and he could hear the blood from the cut on his temple dripping onto the ground in a steady patter.

Someone brushed by him. He caught a glimpse of long tanned legs and then a low voice was calling, "Kila! Kila – are you hurt?"

"No, Quinn. I'm perfectly fine. Get me out of here."

Silas watched as the dark-haired woman uncoiled a rope and dropped it into the pit. She wrapped one end around her arm and braced her feet. "Climb," she instructed.

He was rotated in the air by strong hands around his hips.

"Ooh, this one is big." A blonde, pale woman ran her hand down his chest. "Strong too. I'm going to claim him."

"Like hell you are, Fionn! I saw him first." Another blonde, she was shorter and curvier than the woman who was touching him came out of the trees and squeezed Silas' ass.

"You did not, Barkha! You're lucky he even got caught in the trap. He saw you glowing." Fionn glared at the woman.

Barkha shrugged and ran her hand up and down Silas' thick thigh. "I could not help it. You know I like the danens. Just thinking about having this one between my legs gets me going." Her pale skin began to glow and Fionn rolled her eyes.

"God, Barkha, you're such a tarnan."

Barkha scowled at her. "Take that back, Fionn. Take it back right now or so help me I'll - "

"Enough." Quinn's voice was quiet but the two women immediately stopped their bickering and bowed.

"Forgive us, massina," Fionn murmured.

"There will be plenty of time to claim him later. Right now we need to chain them and go."

"Are we taking the females as well?" A fourth voice could be heard and Silas strained to see around Barkha's ample hips.

"Yes, Akia, she wants them all." Quinn squatted beside him and poked at his blood-stained temple. "This one is injured."

Silas quickly grabbed her wrist and twisted hard. "Let us go, now."

Before he could twist again, two long and very sharp blades were pressed against his throat.

"Release her," Fionn snarled as Barkha pressed her blade deeper against his skin.

"Silas!" Gage yelled and struggled frantically in the net. There were grunts of pain and shouts of anger as his friends were kicked and jostled.

Silas released the dark-haired woman's wrist. She was staring at him with amusement in her dark grey eyes as she stood and indicated for the others to follow her, leaving him to swing helplessly. Working together, they released the net and it fell to the ground with a hard thump.

"You're on my hair!" Gemma screeched and Steve grunted as he was kicked in the stomach by

Paula.

"Quinn, what of the danen?" Kila asked.

"We'll cut him down and chain him quickly," Quinn replied.

Akia was already scaling the tree. She reached the branch that the rope was tied to and sawed through the rope with a knife she pulled from her belt. Silas collapsed on to his back with a loud grunt, hitting the back of his aching head on the hard ground. Before he could rise, Barkha and Fionn had their knives to his throat.

"Stay steady, danen," Fionn warned as Quinn straddled him and dropped to her knees.

She sat firmly on his sternum. Barkha handed her a large, thick leather collar and she quickly buckled it around Silas' neck. She rose up a little and smacked him lightly on the chest. "Turn over."

He stared unblinkingly at her and her eyes narrowed. "Turn over."

"If I don't?" He challenged.

She leaned over him, her breath warm on his face. "I'll kill one of your females. But first, you'll watch me cut out her eyes."

He grunted and she leaned back, smiling with satisfaction when he turned onto his stomach and chest. She took his wrists and locked leather cuffs around them. The cuffs were linked with a piece of heavy chain that was just long enough to allow him to move his hands to his hips but no further.

She patted him on his back. "Turn over and lay on your back again. Don't move. Watch him, Barkha."

She moved off of him and joined the others who

were opening the net. Silas stared at them. There were seven of them including Quinn. Correct that - eight. The one they called Akia had shimmied down the tree and joined the others.

With the exception of Kila, they were dressed similarly in short, blue cotton skirts that were cut into long strips so the fabric flowed easily around their legs. Their tops were leather bustiers with metal cups. On their upper arms they wore wide leather arm bands with metal studs hammered into them and leather wrist bands adorned each of their wrists. Knee-length leather boots completed their outfits.

They were of varying shapes and sizes with Kila being the smallest and Quinn the biggest. He guessed that she was around six feet tall and she had wide hips and large breasts. Exactly his type, he decided, if she hadn't just buckled a collar around his neck and chained his hands together.

"Listen to me!" Quinn stared at the squirming bodies in the net. "Quiet your tongues and listen."

Her tone brooked no refusal and they quieted as Akia and Fionn worked together to open the net.

"If you stay quiet and obey us, you will not be harmed. If you fight or if you try to run, I will kill you. Do you believe me?"

She squatted and stared at each of the prisoners. "Do you?"

"Yes." Craig cleared his throat. "We do."

"Good. We are going to open the net and each of you will lie still until you are collared and chained. For every unnecessary movement you make, I will cut off one of your fingers. Do you understand?"

"Yes," Craig replied again.

Akia and Fionn opened the net. All of them stayed perfectly still as one-by-one they were collared and chained. Kila helped Gage to his feet, her pale hands lingered around his waist and she smiled shyly at him. "Your name is Gage?"

"Yes." Gage swallowed as her fingers explored his chest through his t-shirt.

"My name is Kila." She pronounced it with a long e sound, and Gage repeated it. His hands were bound in leather cuffs and he clenched them tightly when she slipped her hands under his shirt and stroked the smooth skin of his chest.

"Get your hands off of him!" Angela glared at the blonde woman and Kila studied her carefully before looking at Gage once more.

"Is she your woman?" Her hands caressed his chest as Gage stared at her light blue eyes.

He hesitated and Angela scowled at him. "Gage!"

"No." Gage continued to look at Kila. "She isn't."

"You son of a bitch!" Angela tried to kick him and Fionn pulled her back and laughed.

"Quiet down, girl. It wouldn't matter anyway – we share the breeders."

"What do you mean breeders?" Gemma frowned. A woman with sandy brown hair and plump cheeks attached a chain to the metal hoop that was on the front of her collar.

"It will all be explained later." She smiled in a friendly way at Gemma but Gemma gave her a look of suspicion.

Kila was smiling at Gage. Her white skin radiated a soft glow and Quinn spoke sharply to her. "Enough, Kila. Remember who you are."

Kila flushed. Her glow cut out abruptly and she removed her hands from under Gage's shirt. "I remember well enough, Quinn."

"Good." Quinn turned around and rolled her eyes. "For Garna's sake, Barkha! You *are* a tarnan."

Barkha was emitting her own soft glow as she cupped and caressed Silas' dick through his jeans. "What? I am only touching the fabric of his pants. They wear such strange clothing when they get here, do they not?"

She continued to rub Silas as she spoke and Quinn stomped over and knocked her away. She fell hard onto her backside and glared up at Quinn.

"Garna! You don't have to be so rough, massina."

"Your orders were to watch him not fondle him." Quinn crouched over her and grabbed her chin. "Disobey me again and you'll find yourself working in the kitchens. Do you understand?"

"Yes, Quinn," Barkha said sullenly.

Quinn grabbed Silas' bound arms and heaved him to his feet.

*Jesus, she's strong*, Silas thought as he weaved a little in front of her.

"Garna, he's so big." Barkha stared up at him and glowed brightly.

"Barkha!" Quinn sighed with annoyance and Barkha cast her eyes to the ground, her glow dissipating immediately.

The darkness was still lit up and Quinn glanced around to see that everyone besides herself and Kila were staring at Silas and glowing brightly.

"Oh for the…" Quinn shook her head. "Have you all gone mad? He is only a man. If your queen were to see you this way – her own personal guard acting like wanton tarnans – she would have all of your heads."

She clipped a heavy short chain to the metal ring at the front of Silas' collar. "All of you are to stay away from him. No one touches him except for Naveen or myself."

"Who are you to make such rules?" Akia spoke. "Do you mean to claim him for yourself then?"

Quinn stared coolly at her. "I guess you'll have to wait until the claiming ceremony to find out. Until then – no one touches him. He's dangerous."

She gave the chain a hard yank and Silas had no choice but to follow her deeper into the trees.

## Chapter Three

"Garna, there are a lot of them this time!" A man ducked out of the tent and hurried towards them. He was on the small side and his back was bent with age.

"Welcome back, massina. Did any of them die coming through?" He asked Quinn curiously.

"No, Naveen." She glanced behind her at Silas. "But this one is injured."

Naveen peered around her. "Ooh, he's a danen."

Barkha winked at him. "He'll be popular at the claiming ceremony."

Naveen stepped closer to Silas and looked him up and down. "She will want him for herself."

"That's not fair," Barkha pouted. "We should have the chance to fight - "

"Enough, Barkha!" Quinn pulled Silas toward the tent that Naveen just exited. "Fionn, give the others some water. Naveen, come with me."

She led Silas into the tent and pushed him toward a small stool. "Sit down."

He sat down. It was awkward with his hands chained behind his back and he winced as she bent until her face was directly in front of his. "Naveen is going to examine you. If you try to harm him, I will hurt you in ways you've never dreamed of. Do you understand me?"

Silas stared into her grey eyes. "Who are you?"

She gripped his chin and squeezed it hard. "Do you understand me?"

"Yes." Silas pulled his head free of her hand.

"Good." She stepped behind him and nodded to Naveen.

"Hello, I'm Naveen." The man smiled at him in a friendly manner.

"Silas."

"It's nice to meet you." Naveen brushed back Silas' thick dark hair and studied the cut on his temple. He probed at it and Silas hissed in pain.

"Do you feel sick to your stomach? Light headed?" The old man questioned as he turned and rummaged through a leather bag on the floor of the tent.

"A little," Silas admitted.

The man nodded. "Aye, I'm not surprised. It is a nasty gash."

He looked at Quinn. "He'll need stitches."

"Can it wait until we return home?"

Naveen shook his head. "I do not believe so. The wound is not clotting very well. It would be best if I do it now."

He glanced down at Silas. "This will hurt I'm afraid."

Silas leaned away from the old man. "Are you a

doctor?"

Naveen smiled. "Well, in this world we're called kalans but it is the same thing. Mostly."

"What do you mean this world?" Silas frowned at him as Naveen rinsed the wound with water.

Naveen didn't reply, just hummed under his breath as he wiped away the streaks of blood from Silas' temple and face. He applied pressure with a soft cloth to the wound on his head for a few minutes, studying Silas' body and face as he did so.

"Garna. He's good looking isn't he?" He grinned at Quinn.

Quinn snorted. "He had all of them glowing like fireflies."

Naveen laughed. "Hell, I don't blame them. If I could glow I'd be glowing right now." He squeezed Silas' arm through his thin shirt. "He's strong too."

"Naveen," Quinn said and the old man blushed.

"I was just feeling the material of his shirt, that's all."

"Now you sound like Barkha."

Quinn spoke in a disapproving tone but Silas could hear the affection under it. Naveen was obviously someone she cared deeply about.

"Well, we'd better get this done," Naveen said cheerfully. "Hold his head, massina."

Silas stiffened when he felt Quinn's hands circle his head and hold it firmly.

"Sorry about this, Silas. I'll try to be quick." Naveen held a needle and thread in his hand and he poked the needle through the skin of Silas' temple.

Silas jerked with pain and tried to move his

head but Quinn held him still. "Easy, danen," she murmured. "It will be over soon."

Silas gritted his teeth and leaned his head against Quinn's firm abdomen. He could feel sweat breaking out on his forehead as Quinn moved one hand down his face and cupped his chin. She held him steady as Naveen continued to sew the gash closed.

As Naveen began to hum again, Silas hissed in pain. His chained hands latched onto Quinn's firm thighs. He dug in hard with his fingers but if it hurt she made no indication nor did she try to move away. He shoved his head against Quinn, trying subconsciously to move away from the pain. She used her other hand to squeeze and rub one large shoulder.

"Almost finished, danen. Take deep breaths." She continued to rub his shoulder and he closed his eyes and inhaled deeply.

"What does danen mean?" He muttered.

"Big one," she replied.

There was another sharp stab of pain and he twitched his head. Naveen frowned. "Hold him steady please, Quinn."

She strengthened her grip on his head. "For a danen you're kind of a bala."

Naveen snorted soft laughter and Silas frowned. "Bala means?"

"Baby." Quinn's full lips curved upwards and Silas squeezed her thighs again.

"You try getting stitches without anesthetic. Then we'll see who's a bala."

Naveen actually laughed out loud this time and

he patted Silas' head affectionately. "Oh, danen, you know not what you speak of. The massina carries many battle scars."

Silas frowned. They had a weird way of speaking. Forgetting the odd words that were peppered throughout their speech, they had an almost old-fashioned dialect with a slight accent that made them hard to understand from time to time.

As Naveen tied the thread and cut it, Quinn squeezed his shoulder. "Well done, bala."

She pulled free of his grip as Naveen rinsed the wound clean and peered out the opening of the tent. "The weather still hasn't cleared."

Naveen shrugged. "It can take a few days - you know that."

"Aye, I do. Although I wonder if there won't be two this time."

"That has only happened once before, Quinn, and it was many years ago."

She turned around and frowned at Silas' white face.

"Danen, are you okay?"

Silas swallowed thickly. "I think I'm going to throw up."

"Garna!" She grabbed a wooden bucket that was by the opening of the tent and rushed over. She had just enough time to shove it in front of him before he was leaning over and vomiting into it. After a few minutes he straightened, panting harshly.

Naveen wiped his mouth with a damp cloth and then used another to wipe the sweat from his brow and the back of his neck.

"He has a concussion I think." Quinn frowned.

Naveen gave her a quizzical look. "Concussion?"

"It's a," she gestured vaguely, "head injury. It's addled his brains a bit."

Naveen nodded. "Ah, like a kadeen?"

"Yes. He'll have to be watched through the night and woken every few hours."

Naveen held up his hands. "Count me out, Quinn."

She scowled angrily at him. "Are you a kalan or not, Naveen?"

"I am." Her anger didn't frighten him. "But I am also an old man who needs his sleep. I will be of no use to you if I am up every few hours all night."

Quinn rolled her eyes and he shrugged. "Ask Barkha to watch him. No doubt she will find that a very pleasing assignment."

Quinn snorted. "Aye, but I want him woken every few hours, not fucked every few hours."

Naveen laughed and wiped Silas' face and neck again. "Then I guess you're on kalan duty tonight, massina."

She sighed and crouched in front of Silas. "How do you feel, danen?"

"I have a bad headache," Silas mumbled. "Could I have a drink of water?"

"Yes." She gestured at Naveen who brought a tin cup filled with water. Quinn held it to his mouth and he drank greedily. The water was freezing cold and tasted amazing.

"Thanks," he said hoarsely. He was suddenly very tired and he wanted to close his eyes and sleep.

"Danen, take this." Naveen was holding a white packet of yellow powder in front of his mouth. It smelled like dead skunk and Silas wrinkled his nose and turned his face away.

"It smells awful."

"It will help with your headache. Take it," Quinn said sternly.

He swallowed the bitter powder and Naveen held another cup of water to his mouth to wash it down with.

"Naveen, help him to my bed. I will get the others settled and return shortly." She hesitated. "Do not let your guard down. He is injured and bound but remember his strength."

"I'll be careful," Naveen replied.

*Chapter Four*

Quinn entered her tent and studied the sleeping man in her bed. His face was still pale and the smell of the healing paste Naveen put on his wound radiated from him. She knelt on the ground beside him and pulled back the blankets. Naveen had removed his shoes and pants and a small pulse of desire went through her at the sight of his muscular legs covered in dark hair.

*He really was a danen,* she thought dimly. Another tremor of lust went through her. Perhaps because of her own height she had always liked the big ones. He was the biggest man she'd ever seen – in this world or the other.

She reached out with a trembling hand and stroked his chest. It was warm and hard and she eased up his t-shirt so she could study his chest and abdomen.

*Garna. He had an amazing body.*

She traced his flat stomach with the tips of her fingers. Naveen was right - she would take him for herself. When she was done with him there would be no shortage of women lined up for the chance to have him between their legs. He was going to be very popular.

He snorted in his sleep and she hastily pulled his shirt down before touching his forehead. It was cool to the touch and she shook his shoulder.

"Danen, wake up." There was no response and she shook him again.

"Danen, wake up." She spoke louder but his eyes remained closed. A thin thread of panic went through her and she straddled his prone body and smacked him hard on the chest.

"Danen! Open your eyes and look at me!" She demanded.

His eyelids fluttered rapidly and he uttered a low groan before blinking at her. She breathed a sigh of relief. Why she would be so concerned about a man she just met didn't seem to occur to her and she gave him a brief smile.

"How do you feel, danen?"

"My head hurts." Forgetting he was cuffed he strained to lift his hand to his forehead.

"Can you untie me?" He asked hoarsely.

She shook her head. "I cannot. Come, sit up for me."

"No. I'm tired." He pouted like a little boy and she sighed harshly and hooked her hand into the collar around his neck.

"Sit up, danen." Still straddling him, she pulled him into a sitting position and steadied him. "Do you feel dizzy?"

"A little," he muttered.

"Do you feel like you're going to throw up?"

"No. But it feels like there's a hammer pounding in my head." She could hear the dry click of his throat when he swallowed.

She reached for the water and poured him a glass. "Drink slowly."

She held the cup to his mouth, pulling it back a bit when he drank greedily at it.

"Slowly," she admonished before wiping the water from his chin. He stared hazily at her as her fingers lingered on his skin.

He had beautiful eyes, she decided. Light green with flecks of hazel in them. His nose was crooked, like it had been broken a few times, and his hair was thick and dark with threads of grey at the temple. He obviously worked outdoors. His skin was tanned and there were small lines around his eyes from years of working in the sun. His body was thick with muscles gained from a lifetime of labour, not from working out in a gym. She traced the dark stubble on his chin as his eyes flickered to her mouth and then to the tops of her breasts.

"You're so pretty," he whispered.

She swallowed back the tingle of pleasure that went through her and reached for the small white packet lying beside the bed. Keeping the powder in the middle, she unfolded the packet and held it to his mouth. "Open."

His nose wrinkled. "I don't want to take that again. It tastes horrible."

"I know." She stroked his face soothingly. "But you must. It will help with the pain. Open up, danen."

"My name is Silas," he said. "Why won't you

say my name?"

"Open up, Silas."

He pressed his lips together like a little kid and shook his head stubbornly.

"I can make you take it," she warned him.

Why she was so anxious to have him take the pain relief was beyond her. It was his problem if he wanted to be in pain. Except *she* didn't want him to be in pain. It made her feel guilty for some strange reason.

His eyes dropped to her mouth again. "One kiss."

"What are you talking about, danen?"

"Kiss me and I'll take the medicine." He smiled at her but she could see the cloudiness in his eyes.

"You're not yourself, danen." She squeezed his shoulder. "The blow to your head has confused you."

"I'm not confused." He smiled again at her. "One kiss, Quinn, or are you too chicken?"

A shudder went through her when he said her name and his grin widened. "You are afraid of me."

She bristled and set the paper packet on the floor of the tent. She threaded her fingers through the thick hair on the back of his head and tugged until his head was bent back.

"I am afraid of no one," she whispered against his mouth. Her soft lips pressed against his firm ones and they both shivered. After only a few seconds she moved her head back.

"There, danen, I have - "

"Again." The softly-growled word had her head bending and her mouth back against his before she realized what was happening. Although she was straddling him and his hands were still cuffed behind his back, he took control of the kiss. He sucked her bottom lip into his mouth before releasing it and licking her upper lip.

"Open your mouth," he demanded and once again she obeyed him immediately. He thrust his tongue between her lips and she moaned when he rubbed it against hers. The kiss seemed to go on forever, the seconds spinning into minutes as they explored each other's mouths.

Quinn pressed herself against his broad chest. Her clothing felt too tight and restrictive and she wanted to shed the heavy leather and free her breasts. She could almost feel the firm pull of Silas' lips on her nipples. She was actually reaching to undo her clothing when his rough voice brought her back to her senses.

"Release me, Quinn. I want to touch you," he muttered against her mouth.

She leaned away, breathing heavily and staring at a spot on the side of the tent. She was mortified by her behaviour and she took two deep breaths before forcing herself to look at the danen. His eyes were closed and she patted his shoulder.

"Danen? Are you awake?"

"Yeah. Kind of," he muttered. "You taste good, Quinn." He shifted under her and for the first time she clearly felt his erection.

She flushed and reached for the packet of yellow powder. "Open up, danen."

He opened his mouth and she poured the packet of powder onto his tongue. He closed his mouth and made a sour face as she reached for the cup of water. "Drink."

Once he was finished she pushed him back onto the pile of blankets that made her bed. He closed his eyes with a soft sigh. She crossed to the other side of the small tent and quickly shed her skirt and top before slipping into her nightdress. Shivering in the cool air, she returned to the bed and climbed under the blankets next to him.

He groaned and pulled at the restraints as she drew the blankets up over them both. "Danen, go to sleep."

"I'm not comfortable and I'm cold," he muttered.

She shifted onto her side and then helped him turn on his side until he was facing her. She had only one pillow and she was uncomfortably aware of just how close their faces were.

"Better?" She whispered.

He squirmed even closer. Although she knew she should stop him she made no objection when he threw one heavy leg over her hip and buried his face in the curve of her neck.

"Yes." His warm breath brought goose bumps to her skin.

He strained at the cuffs and she rubbed his back. "Do not do that, danen."

He muttered something she couldn't understand and then groaned. She kneaded the back of his neck until he relaxed against her.

"Go to sleep, Silas," she whispered.

"Okay."

He slipped into sleep but she continued to run

her hands over his broad chest and back for a few more minutes. Her pelvis was throbbing and her nipples were hard. She sighed harshly. It was ridiculous to be attracted to the danen. It had been many years since she was with a man but until she had the revenge she so desperately sought there was no point in even thinking about the danen.

৯৵ ৵৯

She woke him again a few hours later. Silas blinked and tried to focus. He thought his head wasn't throbbing quite as much and he didn't have that sickening rolling in his stomach when she helped him sit up and drink some water.

"Better, danen?"

"Yes." He looked around. "Where am I?"

"You don't remember?"

He thought back carefully. He remembered being led into the tent and having his wound tended to by a man named Naveen. He remembered the woman sitting beside him calling him a baby and he remembered throwing up and feeling like his head was going to explode. He thought that Naveen had removed his pants and boots before putting him in the bed. After that it was a blur.

"Sort of. This is your tent?"

She nodded her confirmation and he looked down at the nest of blankets he was in. "Your bed?"

She nodded again. "Are you hungry?"

"A little."

She crawled out from the blankets and crossed the tent. Her long dark hair which was braided earlier was now loose and flowing around her shoulders. Her bustier and skirt had been replaced by a plain, white shirt that fell to the middle of her thighs. A large scar twisted its way from her knee and up her thigh before disappearing under the hem of her shirt.

As she dug through a small leather bag, he said, "My brother. Where is he?"

She returned to the bed carrying a smaller leather bag in one hand. She slipped under the blankets and sat cross-legged beside him.

"The one called Gage?"

Silas nodded. "Yeah. Tell me where he is right now."

She smiled. "You are in no position to be making demands, danen."

"I want to know where he is."

"He's fine. Sleeping I would imagine." She brushed off his question and opened the bag. She withdrew a small pink plant and tore off part of the stalk. "Here."

He leaned away from it. "What is it?"

"It's good. Just try it."

"It doesn't look like food."

"It is. Trust me."

He snorted and she rolled her eyes and popped the piece into her mouth. She chewed and swallowed before opening her mouth and showing him. "See, danen?"

She tore off another piece and he opened his mouth and allowed her to place it on his tongue. He chewed gingerly and then grunted in surprise. "It's sweet."

"Yes." She rummaged in the bag and this time brought out something that would have reminded him of a bun if it hadn't been blue and shaped like a star.

"Try this." She tore off a section of it and he ate it slowly.

"Is it – is it bread?"

"Close enough."

She took her own section and ate it. Silas watched her chew and found himself fascinated with her mouth. Her lips were full and pink and she had straight white teeth. His eyes travelled over her face. She had a small, straight nose and high cheekbones. Her skin was tanned and her eyes were a smoky grey colour. She was, in a word, gorgeous.

He snorted angrily to himself as she gave him another piece of the sweet, pink plant. She had him trussed up like a turkey and wouldn't give him information about his brother. It didn't matter how gorgeous she was, the first chance he had he would throttle her pretty little neck.

Still, why was he so goddamn obsessed with her mouth? Why did he have a vague memory of those lips on his and of her soft moan? He shook his head to clear it and then groaned at the pain that ripped through his skull.

"Are you going to throw up again?"

"No. But remind me not to move my head."

She fed him more food and then gave him another drink of water. He swallowed it down eagerly and licked the drops from his mouth before discreetly tugging at the chain that connected the leather cuffs around his wrist.

She grinned at him. "The chain is heavy, danen. You will not break it no matter how hard you try."

He gave her a look of anger. "I want to know what's going on. Where are we? Who are you people?"

She closed the bag before setting it on the floor. "Everything will be explained to you tomorrow, danen. I promise you."

"My name is Silas." He spoke through gritted teeth. "I want to know right now."

She cocked her head and stared at him thoughtfully. "You're a man used to getting what you want, aren't you?"

He didn't answer and she pinched his cheek playfully. "Tomorrow, *Silas*. Go to sleep."

She started to push him back and he leaned forward. "I have to go to the bathroom."

"Can you not hold it until the morning?"

"No. But if it's too much trouble to uncuff me I can just piss in your bed," he snapped.

She sighed irritably and then untangled herself from the blankets. "Come then."

She helped him to his feet. He weaved a little and she steadied him. "Can you walk?"

"Yes," he grunted.

She tugged on the collar around his neck and led him out of the tent. They stepped outside. Silas took a deep breath of the cold air and looked around for his brother. They were in a large clearing and there were a number of tents scattered throughout it. Six horses were tethered to the ground and there was a wagon parked at the far side of the campsite.

"Where is my brother?" He said.

She turned and clapped her hand over his mouth. "Garna! Be quiet, danen!"

He glared at her and she stepped closer, tilting her head until her mouth was at his ear. "You need to keep your mouth shut. It's not safe. Do you understand?"

He snorted against her hand and she used her other hand to yank hard on his hair. "I mean it, danen," she hissed. "Your brother is fine. If you say one more word I will tie you to a tree for the night and see what remains of you in the morning. Do you understand?"

He nodded and she released his mouth cautiously. She grabbed his collar once more and pulled him toward the edge of the campsite.

He jumped in surprise when a soft voice drifted out of the darkness. "Massina? What are you doing?"

"Taking the danen for a piss," Quinn replied. "Has it been quiet so far?"

Fionn stepped out of the trees. "Aye. No sign of any other clans."

"Who is on watch next?"

"Dacia."

"Good."

Fionn stared at Silas who was shivering in the cold air. She studied his bare legs and when she glowed, Quinn smacked her hard on the arm.

"Control yourself, Fionn."

"Sorry, massina."

Quinn led Silas to the treeline and moved behind him. He waited for her to free him, his body beginning to tense as adrenaline filled his veins.

The moment she removed the cuffs he would take her as his hostage. She was tall and strong but she was also weaponless. Without her dagger, he could easily overpower her.

He jerked in surprise when instead of removing his cuffs she reached around his waist and yanked down the front of his underwear.

"What the fuck?" He grunted.

"Go, danen. I don't have all night," she replied in a whisper.

"Remove the cuffs."

She laughed. "Not a chance."

"I can't go like this. I'll piss all over my goddamn feet," he retorted.

"Oh for the love of garna." She reached around him with her breasts pressing into his back and held his cock in her hand, aiming it away from his feet. "How's that?"

Silas didn't reply. Her hand was surprisingly soft and he was trying desperately not to get an erection.

"I don't have all night, danen," she warned again.

He took a deep breath and concentrated. After a moment his urine flowed and he breathed a sigh of relief. He may have brought her out here in a desperate attempt to gain his freedom but he also did have to take a piss.

Quinn was immensely relieved that she was standing behind Silas. Her face was blushing brightly and her pelvis was aching and throbbing. Garna, his cock was huge in her hand. She could only imagine the size of it when it was erect.

His flow trickled to a stop and she gave his cock a quick shake before releasing it and pulling his underwear back over it. He turned around and she reached for the collar around his neck. He stepped back and arched one eyebrow at her.

"Are you going to wash your hands first?"

She tamped down the laughter that was bubbling up in her chest. "Let's go, danen."

He took a few steps forward and then stumbled to a stop. "What the hell?"

She followed his gaze up to the sky above them.

"The fuck? Why are there two goddamn moons?" He stared in disbelief at the two pale yellow globes in the sky.

He looked at her and she was impressed by the calmness in his face. "Why are there two moons? Where the hell are we?"

"Tomorrow, danen. It will all be explained tomorrow."

She led him back to her tent and he followed her quietly. He sat down in the nest of blankets and lay back with a loud sigh. He was more tired than he thought and his headache was coming back.

"Do you need more pain relief?" She asked.

He shook his head. "No."

She climbed in beside him and blew out the candle, plunging them into darkness. She tucked the blankets around them both and he shifted onto his side to face her. He moved closer towards her. She didn't protest and he shifted even closer until their bodies were touching.

"Are you cold, danen?" Her voice was slightly breathless.

"Yes." He wasn't that cold but he wanted to see what she would do.

She hesitated and then wrapped her arms around him. He shoved his large thigh between her legs and she twitched but made no attempt to move away. He pressed his face into her neck and closed his eyes. She might be holding him hostage but it was a long time since he felt a woman's body against his own and he had to admit that it felt good.

# Chapter Five

She woke from her dream reluctantly. In it she was on her back with her legs spread wide and the danen's muscular body wedged between them. His cock was sliding in and out of her, hard and throbbing and filling her tight pussy to the point of almost pain. She arched her hips again and again, moaning and lifting her head so that he could nip the tender flesh of her neck.

"Oh please," she sighed. She would never admit this and would go to her grave carrying the secret but she wanted to give up control in bed. She kept such tight control on every other aspect of her life, needed to in order to survive, that it was a relief to give it up in the bed. To allow a man to take control of her and allow him to use her body for his own pleasure was a shocking departure from her normal self. If the others were to find out –

A low groan forced her eyes open. She blinked in surprise at how close Silas' face was to hers.

"Good morning." He grinned at her and she realized with horror that she had both legs clamped around his large one and she was humping his hard thigh like a bitch in heat.

Before she could untangle herself, he pushed his body onto hers and pinned her down.

"Get off me, danen," she whispered weakly. Her entire body was throbbing and pulsing. Being pinned down by his large muscular body was making her so wet it was dripping down her thighs.

"No." He smiled again and rubbed his crotch against her.

A small moan escaped her mouth and his smile widened. "Open your legs."

She was squirming to open them before he even finished speaking. He shifted between them and let his full body weight rest against hers. She was finding it hard to breathe but she didn't complain when he leaned down and kissed her hard on the mouth. She opened her lips willingly and tangled her tongue with his. He kissed her until she was thrusting her pussy against his erection and running her hands restlessly over his broad back.

"Release me so I can fuck you," he demanded.

Without stopping to think about it she reached down and unhooked one side of the heavy chain from one leather cuff. The moment he was free he slid his hand around her throat and squeezed lightly.

She stared at him, feeling the cold chain against her chest through her sleep shirt and his warm, hard hand around her throat. She had made a mistake. She was helpless under the danen and he was about to choke the life out of her. Her need for him and her need to let him take control was going to end her life.

He growled low in his throat and then he was kissing her again, his hand leaving her neck to cup one large breast. She clutched at his shoulders as he pushed his hand under her sleep shirt and plucked at one erect nipple. He pulled and rolled it between his fingers until it was hard and throbbing and she was writhing under him.

He reached between them and shoved down his underwear. His cock was at the entrance to her pussy and thrusting in before she could even think of stopping him.

"Christ, you're fucking tight," he muttered.

He forced her thighs wider before shoving in more of his cock. She moaned in a combination of pleasure and pain. Her pussy clamped down on him and made him release his breath in a drawn-out hiss. He propped himself up above her and Quinn pressed her naked thighs around his hips as he forced his cock deeper. He was so big, so thick, and it had been many years since she had had a man between her legs.

She pushed at him experimentally and realized that she really was helpless under him. She was trapped beneath his large body and he was going to fuck her whether she wanted him to or not. The realization made her shudder with pleasure and a surge of wetness flooded her pussy. The additional moisture lubricated his cock and made it easier for him and he entered her fully with a loud grunt.

He stared down at her, his eyes hazy with lust and pleasure as her pussy stretched to accommodate him. "Fucking you feels so good, Quinn."

"Danen," she moaned.

"Silas. Say it," he demanded.

When she stayed silent he took her hands and pinned them above her head, driving hard into her. "Say it, Quinn."

"Silas," she whispered.

She bent her knees and braced her feet on the blankets crumpled beneath them. She thrust her hips at him and he growled his approval before kissing her. "Do you want me to fuck you?"

"Yes," she murmured. "Please, Silas."

"Please what?" He sucked on her lower lip as she wiggled under him.

"Please fuck me. Please," she moaned when he released her lip.

"I like it when you beg." He grinned at her. She felt like she should be embarrassed but he was easing his cock in and out of her in a slow, deep rhythm. Her embarrassment disappeared under a wave of pleasure so intense it was nearly painful.

"Ohh…" She moaned and pushed her hips at him in a silent plea to move faster. He refused, keeping the same slow rhythm that was driving her mad with need. She tugged at his hands. She wanted to run her hands under his t-shirt and feel that hard chest but he pushed her hands deeper into the blankets and shook his head.

"No, Quinn. I like you this way – pinned and helpless as I fuck you," he growled.

Her hips bucked against him in response and another slow grin crossed his face. "I think you like it too."

He licked her mouth. "Do you?"

"Yes." There was no point in denying it.

"Good."

He thrust into her hard and deep and she gave a low cry of need. Her hips were rising to meet him and her breath was coming in short, harsh gasps as she reached for her climax. Silas slammed in and out of her, his hard cock pounding into her aching pussy and driving her deep into the blankets. She was so close, so –

"Get off of her now, danen, or I'll slit your thick throat."

Quinn's eyes popped open as Silas ground to a halt inside of her. A sharp blade was pressed against his throat and he stared down at her, breathing heavily. She looked in surprise at Kila as the young woman pressed the blade harder against Silas' throat.

"Get off of her. I won't ask you again."

Silas eased out of her and kneeled on the blankets as Quinn scrambled to her feet, pushing her sleep shirt down as Kila glared at Silas.

"Put your hands behind your back, danen."

He complied with her order and keeping the knife at his throat, she quickly linked the chain to the cuff.

"You would rape the massina?" Kila sheathed her knife and raised her arm, her hand curling into a fist. As she brought her fist towards his face, Silas clenched his jaw. The blow he was expecting never came. Quinn had caught Kila's arm.

"Enough, Kila."

"Massina?" Kila frowned at her, taking in her flushed cheeks and the embarrassment in her eyes before looking down at Silas. Confusion crossed her face. "How did he free himself of the cuffs, massina?"

"Kila, I…"

"You released him," Kila whispered. She gave Quinn a horrified look. "Massina, what have you done? You – you never fuck the breeders. And to do so before the claiming ceremony?"

Quinn didn't reply and Kila took a step back.

"She will hurt you so badly if she finds out," the young woman moaned. Her voice began to rise. "If she finds out, if she - "

"Kila – be quiet!" Quinn hissed. She yanked Silas' underwear back up around his hips. The danen's large cock was still half-hard and glistening with her juices. She ignored the twinge of longing that went through her at the sight of it.

She cupped Kila's face and stroked it. "Listen to me, my sweet sandora. She will not find out. It was a – a moment of madness, nothing more. It will not happen again. You just need to keep quiet about this okay? Promise me, sandora."

"Quinn - "

Naveen stuck his head into the tent. "Massina, we need to get on the road. Are you - "

He frowned at the sight of the two women standing above the kneeling Silas. "What is going on?"

"Nothing, Naveen," Quinn said quickly. She grabbed her clothes and headed toward the opening of the tent.

"Help the danen dress. I'll change in Kila's tent."

Naveen nodded as Quinn left the tent with Kila

trailing after her.

❧ ❦

"Stop staring at me like that, Kila." Quinn dressed quickly, shivering a little with the cold.

"Why did you release him, Quinn? He – he is so big. He could have killed you," Kila said soberly.

"He didn't," Quinn replied. She rubbed her throat, remembering the way Silas had squeezed before releasing her.

"Quinn." Kila took her arm. "Please, look at me."

Quinn sighed and turned to her, willing herself not to blush.

"Why did you let the danen fuck you?" Kila whispered. "You – you've shown no interest in any man before this. I thought - "

"You thought what, sandora? That I do not like them? That I do not crave a man's touch from time to time? I may be the massina, I may serve the queen and do her bidding but it does not mean that I don't have my own wants and desires. My own - "

She stopped, breathing heavily as she stared at the young girl. She gripped Kila's head and rested her forehead against the young woman's. "Promise me you will not say anything, Kila. It was a moment of weakness on my part and it will not happen again."

"I won't, Quinn," Kila whispered. "Will you try and take him for yours at the claiming ceremony?"

Quinn shook her head immediately. "No, sandora. I told you, it was a moment of madness."

She hugged the young woman briefly. "Come, we must get going."

੭੭ ∾ふ

"Silas!"

Silas breathed a sigh of relief at his younger brother's call. "Gage, are you hurt?"

Gage shook his head as Silas walked carefully toward him. He stood in front of Gage, grinning happily at him.

"How about you? How do you feel?" Gage peered at his forehead as the others crowded around them. Like Silas, they all had their hands still cuffed behind their backs and Lacey made a groan of discomfort.

"Christ, my arms hurt. They made us sleep like this," she groused.

She blushed when Akia, standing behind them, laughed derisively. "They're always so weak when they first arrive. Are they not, Fionn?"

"Aye," Fionn agreed. "A few months of hard labour will toughen them up. It always does."

"What are you talking about?" Veronica asked suspiciously.

Fionn only smiled at her as Gage stared anxiously at Silas.

"Silas? How do you feel?"

"He's better." Naveen walked up behind them and pushed on Silas' broad shoulders. "Kneel, danen. I want to look at your head wound."

"It's fine," Silas grunted. "It doesn't need to be looked at."

Naveen rolled his eyes. "I will be the judge of

that. Kneel down."

Silas shook his head. "No. I won't - "

He grunted with pain and fell heavily to the ground. Quinn had kicked his legs out from under him and she reached down and twisted her hand into his hair. She yanked him to his knees and held a short, sharp blade to his throat.

"Stop it!" Gage ran forward but was stopped by Fionn's sword pointed at his chest.

"Stay where you are," she warned.

"When Naveen tells you to do something, you do it. You will not argue. Do you understand, danen?" Her hand still clutching his hair and her knife still at his throat, Quinn spoke into his ear.

"Yes," Silas grunted.

"Good." She stood behind him, keeping her hand wrapped in his short hair as Naveen examined the cut on his head. He applied more healing paste and then smiled at Silas.

"It looks better, danen. Do you still feel sick?"

Silas shook his head no, wincing when it made his hair pull in Quinn's grip.

"Good."

Naveen glanced at Quinn. "He should be fine to walk but if he tires we'll load him in the wagon for a bit."

She nodded before hauling Silas to his feet. Before she could stop him, he bent and whispered into her ear, "I really enjoyed fucking you this morning, Quinn. Do you think your friends would enjoy hearing about it?"

She stiffened and glanced quickly at the others before placing her own mouth at his ear. "Tell anyone about what happened between us this morning, danen, and I'll make you watch as I slice your brother's tongue from his mouth."

She stared up at his face, smiling when he paled, and patted his cheek. He pulled away from her touch and she traced her small dagger over his chest. "Be a good boy, danen, and no harm will come to your brother."

He jerked away from her as she replaced the dagger in the sheath strapped to her thigh. For the first time he noticed the sword hanging from a scabbard around her waist. The others had them as well and he frowned.

"Who are you people?"

She didn't reply and Naveen patted his arm. "Come, danen, all of you will have a bite to eat and then we will talk."

## Chapter Six

"Stop it! Do you know how much those shoes cost?" Veronica's shrill scream cut through the cool air and Barkha slapped her hard across the face.

"Garna! Shut your fool mouth!"

Veronica stared aghast at her as her cheek reddened from the slap. Silas doubted anyone had ever dared to raise a hand to the red-haired woman in her life and he had a feeling that adaptation wasn't Veronica's strong suit.

"You – you hit me," Veronica whispered.

"Aye, and I'll do it again if you don't keep your big mouth shut," Barkha snapped.

Dacia finished ripping the heels from Veronica's shoes and passed them to Barkha before grabbing Gemma's shoes.

"Why did you do that?" Veronica stared at her shoes in dismay as Barkha set them at her feet.

"After walking all day you'll thank me, foolish woman." Dacia grinned as she hacked off the heels on Gemma's shoes.

Angela was staring pensively across the clearing and Silas followed her gaze. Gage was sitting on the ground and Kila was sitting across from him. She was feeding him pieces of the blue bread that Quinn had fed him earlier and the two were staring delightedly at each other. Kila was glowing and Angela gave him a look of worry.

"What's going on with him?"

"I don't know." Silas gave her a sympathetic look as Kila brushed her hand across Gage's mouth, wiping away invisible crumbs. She gave him a drink of water and he swallowed it before smiling at her. Her glow brightened and Silas frowned at Naveen who was loading bags into the back of the wagon.

"Why do they glow?"

Naveen just smiled at him as he hopped nimbly into the back of the wagon.

"You really need to tell us what's happening. Where are we?" Steve demanded as Akia and Fionn moved the group behind the wagon.

"Do we chain them together, massina?" Fionn asked.

Quinn swung into the saddle of a massive black horse and shook her head. "No. They can walk behind the wagon unchained."

She stared at all of them. "I will give you your freedom to walk behind the wagon. You would be wise to stay with us. There are many things in this world that can kill you. Believe me when I say you are safest with us. And for the love of Garna, keep your voices down." She scowled at Veronica.

"Can you take off these cuffs?" Craig pulled at

the cuffs around his wrists.

Quinn shook her head. "No."

She glanced at Kila who was helping Gage to his feet. "Kila, we're leaving."

Kila led Gage toward the others. He fell into step beside Silas as Fionn climbed into the front of the wagon and the others mounted their horses. With a low whistle to the horses, the wagon started with a jolt and Silas and the others followed it on foot.

Naveen smiled at them from his spot in the wagon. "Listen closely, strange ones. I will do my best to explain what has happened to you."

The group crowded close to the back of the wagon as it moved slowly through the woods.

"The orb of light that you saw is a doorway. It sucked you in from your world and spit you out in ours," Naveen said cheerfully.

"What do you mean?" Craig asked. "Are you telling me we're on a different planet?"

"Not exactly," Naveen replied. "Think of it more as a different version of your earth."

"Told you it was time travel," Kyle said to no one in particular.

"This isn't time travel." Gage frowned at him.

"So to get back all we need to do is find another orb," Steve said thoughtfully.

Naveen shook his head. "I'm afraid not. There are many worlds and the odds of you being returned to your own world are very slim. Most likely you would be sent to another world. One that may not be as friendly as ours."

"Oh yeah, you're real friendly," Andrea snorted

and pulled on her cuffs.

"So what, you just track these orbs and take the people who fall out of them?" Kyle asked.

Naveen shrugged. "Yes. Although not all orbs deliver people. Some of them like the one you encountered takes people."

"How do you know which it will be?" Kyle asked.

"We have our ways," Naveen replied.

"What do you want from us?" Angela asked. She was walking next to Gage and she gave him a small smile. He returned her smile but his eyes quickly returned to Kila riding slightly ahead of them.

Naveen glanced at Quinn.

"Tell them everything," she instructed.

Naveen sighed. "You have to understand – in this world there are very few males. Only one in every fifty babies born is a male. Males are highly valued in this world. Wars have been started over them. Many years ago, when the orbs were first discovered the different clans made a pact to split the males that the orb brought. Each clan would have their turn in taking the people who fell from the orb."

Naveen glanced at Quinn. "It did not take long for the clans to turn on each other. Within a few years it became an all-out war to get to the orb first. The old pact was forgotten and now we all fight to reach the orb before the others."

"How do you know when the orb is opening?" Silas frowned.

"The weather gives us a clue. As well, our clan

is lucky. We have a majii among us who knows when the time of the orb draws near."

"How often does it happen?"

"There is no pattern to it. One month the orb appeared four times. Once we went for nearly five years without the orb appearing."

"What do you mean majii?" Veronica asked. She spoke quietly, staring nervously at Barkha who was riding beside the wagon.

"There is magic in this world," Naveen said simply.

"There's magic in ours," Gemma said.

Akia snorted. "Yes, card tricks and sleight of hand. Foolish magic."

Naveen cupped his hand and brought it to his mouth. He muttered an inaudible incantation, blew on his fingers and then opened his hand. A small ball of flame hovered above his palm and Silas gave a grunt of surprise as the women gasped.

Naveen closed his hand with a snap and the flame extinguished. "We have real magic in this world. Anyway, our clan reached your group first and it's lucky we did. There are so many strong males in your group. Our queen will be very pleased."

"What is your queen going to do to us?" Steve asked nervously.

"You will be treated well. I assure you." Naveen gave him a large smile.

"Tell him, Naveen," Quinn instructed. "It's better if they're prepared."

"Prepared for what?" Kyle asked.

"As I said before, males are rare in our world.

As you can imagine we are keen to procreate in the hopes of having more males."

Kyle's mouth dropped open and Steve stumbled and nearly fell. "Procreate? What do you mean procreate?"

Naveen frowned. "You do not know what this word means?"

"We know what it means," Silas said dryly.

"Breeders," Angela breathed suddenly. "That's what you meant when you said breeders."

Naveen nodded. "That's right. We will treat you well, feed you, care for you and in return you will help us with breeding."

"So we're going to be – be sex slaves?" Kyle said indignantly.

"I could think of worse things to be," Steve replied.

Lacey rolled her eyes. "Shut up, Steve."

"If you're from the world that we think you are then you're very valuable indeed. Your kind tends to give us more male babies," Naveen said.

"They are from that world," Quinn spoke suddenly.

"How can you be so sure?" Akia said.

"I just am," Quinn replied.

"What about us?" Angela asked. "If females are so plentiful why did you bring us as well?"

Naveen smiled at her. "There are many uses for you as well. Our clan is large and has done well for itself under the rule of our queen. There is always need for females to serve and clean."

"What?" Veronica nearly shrieked and then cringed when Barkha raised her hand threateningly at her.

"I am not going to be some kind of house slave," she said defiantly.

"If you prove yourself to be healthy and of good breeding stock then you can rise through the ranks. You can have babies, become protectors of our clan - the possibilities are endless," Naveen assured her.

"Lovely," Gemma muttered.

"What is this claiming ceremony you keep mentioning?" Gage asked Naveen.

Barkha, who had dropped back and was riding next to Silas, grinned delightedly. "We have a claiming ceremony every month. The eligible males are lined up and we're allowed to claim one as ours for the month. It's so much fun. There is food and games and everyone is given the chance to fight for the one they want!"

"Fight?" Craig asked.

"It's all in good fun." Barkha smiled. "Everyone is allowed to participate. Even those who are not good fighters can ask those of us who are to fight on their behalf."

"What are you fighting for?" Steve asked.

Barkha rolled her eyes. "Garna, you're a dumb one. We're fighting for you."

She reached out and rubbed her hand through Silas' dark hair. "We share the breeders. You're going to be very popular, danen."

Her skin was beginning to glow and Angela frowned. "What's with the glowing?"

"In our world, the women glow when they are um..." Naveen hesitated and Barkha grinned at Silas.

"When we find someone pleasing to us."

Gemma's mouth dropped open. "You mean when you're aroused you glow?"

Barkha shrugged. "What does aroused mean? Does it mean when we are hungry for a man?"

"Yeah," Gemma muttered.

Silas stared at Quinn who had ridden ahead of the wagon. Earlier this morning in the tent she had wanted him as much as he wanted her. At least he thought she did. But she hadn't glowed once. He would have noticed it if she had. His stomach churned. He was rough with her, pinning her down and fucking her like she belonged to him. He liked being dominant in bed and liked being the one in control, but he wanted his woman warm and willing.

*She wanted it. She begged you to fuck her remember?*

His cock hardened at the memory of her low voice begging him to fuck her. Her pussy had been soaking wet and if she wasn't turned on then she was one hell of an actress. Maybe her glowing ability didn't work.

"What if we don't want to be passed around and shared?" Gage asked. "What if we prefer to be with one woman?" He was staring at Kila as he spoke and Angela gave him a wounded look.

"Not possible," Barkha said cheerfully. "I already told you – we share the breeders. Of course, if the woman was to win the claiming ceremony for you each month then I guess you could be with only them."

She laughed. "That won't happen though. We

like variety." She stroked Silas' hair again. "Although I might make an exception for you, danen."

Akia snorted. "You know she'll take him for herself."

"You keep saying that." Silas stared at her. "Who are you talking about?"

"Why, the queen of course." Akia smiled at him. "She gets first pick of the breeders and she's going to be very fond of you. After she's done I fully intend to claim you."

"I'm claiming him first," Barkha pouted.

Akia laughed. "You'll never beat me, Barkha, and you know it. No one can beat me at the fights."

"Quinn could," Barkha muttered.

Akia glared at her. "No, she couldn't." She reached out and tugged on Gemma's long curly hair. "The rumour is the massina prefers the company of women. You're a pretty one. If you're nice to her perhaps she will take you to her bed."

Gemma stumbled away from her as Akia laughed and rode to the front.

"What if we don't want to be your sex slaves?" Craig asked.

Naveen blinked. "I – no one has ever refused the advances of our women before. Believe me when I say you'll be treated well. There will be some labour jobs but nothing you will not be able to handle. All we ask in return is that you provide your seed."

"Marvelous." Kyle rolled his eyes. "We're nothing but baby machines."

"Really Kyle? You're about to get all the pussy

you could ever want and you're complaining?"
Steve raised his eyebrows at him.

"Don't be so coarse, Steve." Andrea scowled at
him.

"Don't worry, baby, eventually you might get
your turn with me." Steve winked at her and
Andrea snorted in disgust.

"I'd rather sleep with a snake. You're - "

"Quiet!" Quinn's low voice rang out and the
group immediately quieted.

She drew her sword and the others quickly
followed suit.

"What is it, massina?" Kila whispered.

"Surround them now." Quinn dismounted and
quickly tied her horse to the wagon. Kila did the
same and within minutes Silas and the others were
surrounded by Quinn and the other warriors.

"Naveen, get down in the wagon," Quinn
muttered.

The old man immediately ducked down as
Veronica crowded up against Silas.

"Silas? What's happening?" She whimpered.

"I don't know."

Quinn was standing still and quiet. She cocked
her head as Kila whispered, "Massina, are they out
there?"

"Yes," Quinn murmured. "They're watching
us."

"Garna!" Barkha muttered. "Now what?"

Andrea stood on her tiptoes and peered over
Barkha's shoulder into the trees. "How do you
know - "

There was a soft whooshing noise and Silas

blinked in shock at the arrow that was sticking out of Andrea's throat. She made a soft gurgling noise and collapsed slowly to the ground.

"Andrea?" Angela said in a soft little voice as blood began to run out of Andrea's throat and seep into the ground.

Veronica shrieked, a loud wailing cry that made the hair on Silas' neck stand straight up. He shoved her towards the wagon. "Get under the wagon! Go!"

She ignored him and collapsed shrieking to the ground, curling up into a small ball in the soft dirt.

"Gage! Get under the wagon now!" Sage roared as wild shrieks were heard. A pack of women - at least he thought they were women - came bursting out of the trees. They carried spears and swords and they were screaming unintelligible sounds.

"Holy shit," Steve breathed, staring slack-jawed at the advancing women.

Their flesh was a light green and their jet-black hair was long and wild and knotted with bits of fabric. They were covered in piercings and they wore only a leather band around their breasts and short leather skirts.

Silas ran for Gage and knocked him to the ground. "Under the wagon! Now!"

Gage crawled awkwardly on his knees toward the wagon as Silas began to knock the others down. Veronica, tears streaming down her face, wormed her way under the wagon next to Angela. She buried her face in the blonde woman's shoulder as Angela stared at the advancing women.

Another arrow flew through the air and buried itself in Lacey's chest. She fell slowly to her knees, staring at the arrow in disbelief before collapsing forward. Angela screamed in horror, her face a mask of shock and fear.

The rest of the group had squeezed under the wagon and Silas took a running leap and heaved his large body into the wagon. He landed with a hard thud next to Naveen.

"Unchain me!" He hissed. "I can help them!"

Naveen shook his head. "No! I cannot!"

"Son of a bitch!" Silas flipped to his stomach and raised his head to stare over the top of the wagon.

The wild women were attacking Quinn and the others. He watched as Quinn, her face serene, thrust the sword in her right hand into the belly of one of the women before yanking it free and cutting off her head.

He stared wide-eyed as he watched Quinn cut a wide swath through the attacking women. She moved with a lazy, fluid grace that he never suspected in her. Watching her take down the women attacking her was almost like watching a dance.

She dropped to her knees, avoiding the sweep of the sword in the hand of the wild woman. With a powerful swipe, she cut the legs off the woman. The woman collapsed to the ground, blood jetting from the stumps of her legs. Quinn rose to her feet and plunged her sword through the forehead of the screaming woman.

"Holy fuck," Silas whispered.

He heard Barkha give a hoot of delight and turned to see her and Fionn thrusting their swords into the ribs of a green-fleshed woman at the same time.

"That one counts as mine!" Barkha shouted.

"It does not!" Fionn panted. "I stuck her first!"

"You did not!" Barkha ducked as a spear came hurtling towards her. Akia was slicing across the wild woman's throat with her sword and Barkha nodded her thanks before racing towards Dacia.

An arrow brushed by his face and Silas ducked back into the wagon. He lay on his back, panting and staring at Naveen.

"Stay down, danen. It is you and the other males they want," Naveen hissed at him.

Silas listened to the screams of pain and the nervous whinnying of the horses tied to the wagon. His heart was thumping in his chest and adrenaline was coursing through his veins.

"Naveen," he tried again, "unchain me."

Naveen shook his head. "No. The massina will kill me if I do. You need to…"

His voice trailed off and his face paled as he stared over Silas' shoulder. Silas looked up and gave a groan of dismay. One of the green-skinned women was peering over the wagon at him. She grinned with black and rotting teeth and raised a small wooden tube to her mouth.

Before she could wrap her lips around it, a hand appeared on the top of her head and gripped her hair. Her head was yanked back and Quinn slit her throat with her small dagger. Blood poured from the woman's throat and he squirmed away in disgust as Quinn released her grip on the woman's head and she fell to the ground.

She stared briefly at Silas before disappearing once more. Ignoring Naveen's muttered pleas, Silas sat up and stared out of the wagon again. Quinn and the others were winning. There were only a few of the wild women left and two of them had fled back into the trees.

Kila was grappling on the ground with one of them. The woman was straddling her and trying to plunge her knife into Kila's breast. Kila lost her grip on the woman's wrist and the woman raised her hand, the large and bloody knife gripped tightly in it. Silas' blood ran cold when he realized that Gage had squirmed out from under the wagon and was running towards Kila.

"Kila!" Gage screamed. He dove at the woman on top of Kila, knocking her onto the ground. The knife fell from her hand and she screamed in rage and rolled onto her stomach. She reached for the knife but Kila snatched it away from her. She jumped on the woman's back and drove her dagger deep between her shoulder blades. The woman shrieked in agony and Kila ripped the blade free before yanking the woman's head back and slitting her throat.

Panting, she rolled off the woman and smiled at Gage who was on his knees in front of her. "Thank you, Gage."

"Don't mention it." He grinned at her and then stiffened. Kila cried out at the small dart that appeared in his throat. One of the attackers was just lowering the wooden tube from her mouth when

Quinn's sword sliced across the top of her skull.

"NO!" Kila screamed and scrambled forward to catch him as Gage pitched forward.

"Gage! No!" She screamed again as his eyes rolled up in his head and he went limp.

## Chapter Seven

"There must be something we can do," Silas said frantically. He was kneeling beside Kila who was still cradling Gage in her arms.

"There isn't. I'm sorry, danen," Quinn said.

Kila looked up at her, tears swimming in her eyes. "There is, Quinn. You know there is."

"No, Kila. It's too dangerous."

"What is she talking about?" Silas asked.

Naveen knelt beside Gage and Kila and felt his throat. "His pulse is strong, massina. If we get the antidote he'll have a good chance of survival."

"What antidote?" Silas nearly yelled.

"It's too dangerous," Quinn repeated.

"Tell me!" This time Silas did yell and Kila flinched and cradled Gage closer to her body.

"The women who attacked us are called gorans. They're a clan of women who are after you for the same reasons we are. They use a poison to stun their prey, to put them into a dreamlike state so they are easy to take back to their camps. They have an antidote to their poison. If we could get the antidote your brother would still have a chance," Naveen replied.

"Then we have to go and get it!" Silas said angrily.

Naveen glanced at Quinn and she shook her head.

"Fuck you!" Silas shouted. "We're going after the antidote."

"We cannot, danen," she hissed. "It is too dangerous to go to their camp and retrieve it."

"Quinn, it'll take at least three days for the poison to kill him. I will go and retrieve the antidote and meet you back at the city," Kila said desperately.

"No, sandora. It's a suicide mission and you know it." Quinn crouched beside Silas and gave him a look of pity. "I am truly sorry, Silas. But we cannot risk the lives of our people to save your brother."

"Then let me go," Silas replied. "Tell me where their camp is and I'll get the antidote myself."

She sighed. "You would not survive. If you even made it to their camp they would capture you before you got anywhere near the antidote."

"At least give me the chance to try."

She hesitated and he felt a moment's hope before she shook her head again. "I cannot. I'm sorry."

He screamed in rage and sorrow as she stood and stared at the others. "We bury the dead and keep going. Move quickly."

ॐ ॐ

Silas stared miserably at the bottom of the wagon. Wrapped in blankets beside him, Gage was quiet and still. He watched his brother's chest rise and fall and closed his eyes for a moment. Panic was clawing at his insides and he took a deep breath. He had to figure out a way to get free and go after the antidote. He would have to take one of them with him to find the camp. Kila would probably go willingly.

He opened his eyes and squinted in the darkness at Gage again. His chest was still rising and falling evenly and Silas took another deep breath. After the attack the others had quickly buried Andrea and Lacey before continuing.

His group was in shock. They had stood quietly as Naveen muttered some type of prayer over the graves before Quinn herded them into the wagon. They hadn't travelled very far before Angela had a panic attack. She flailed and screamed until Barkha and Quinn held her down and Naveen poured a yellow liquid down her throat. It knocked the young woman out and Quinn allowed them to stop for the day. Silas spent the entire night sitting beside Gage in the wagon. Kila, her face pale and tears dripping down her face, sat with him until Quinn made her go to bed.

Quinn had knelt beside Silas and squeezed his shoulder. "I'm sorry, Silas."

"If my brother dies, I will not rest until I kill you."

"Aye. I would expect nothing less from you, danen."

Now, he pulled uselessly at the cuffs again. The

muscles in his arms bulged and sweat broke out on his forehead but the chain was solid. He swore under his breath and leaned against the wagon. The others slept on around him. Paula, Angela and Veronica were curled up together under a blanket and Steve, Craig and Kyle were stretched out beside them.

If he hadn't been such an idiot and taken Quinn prisoner instead of fucking her, Gage wouldn't be injured. He should have taken her prisoner and freed his brother and the others but instead he let his goddamn dick do all of the thinking and fucked her. They wouldn't be in this mess if he hadn't.

*Are you so sure about that? If you had tried to take off alone, all of you would be those green women's prisoners right now. You wouldn't stand a chance against them and you know it. You need Quinn and the others to survive.*

He stared blankly up at the double moons. If Naveen was right and they really were on a different world then –

*If he's right? There's two fucking moons, you moron!*

He closed his eyes and inhaled. Jesus, what the hell was happening? How the fuck could they have been transported to another world? That science fiction shit didn't happen in real life. It couldn't happen.

He snorted with surprise when a hard hand clamped over his mouth. He stared at Kila who was standing next to the wagon.

She put her mouth to his ear. "I'm going for the antidote. Will you come with me?"

Silas nodded immediately and she reached behind him for the chain. "I'm going to trust you, danen. You cannot do this without me. If you try anything your brother will die. Do you understand?"

He nodded again and she unclipped the chain. He rubbed his arms as she whispered, "Follow me and don't say anything. Dacia is on watch and we need to sneak by her."

He slowly and carefully climbed out of the wagon and with one last glance at Gage, followed her silently out of the campsite.

ॐ ॐ

"How do you know where the camp is?" Silas asked as he followed her deep into the woods.

She moved quickly and confidently in the dark and he stumbled after her.

"Keep up, danen," she warned him.

"Tell me how you know where the camp is," he insisted. "For all I know we could be walking in circles."

"When the gorans have gone after an orb in the past, they have always camped in the caves of Wintoria. It's about halfway between where the orb appears and their city."

"Does the orb always appear in the same spot?"

She nodded. "Yes."

"And you're sure that they'll camp in these caves?" Silas asked.

She shrugged. "I assume so."

"You assume so?" Silas grabbed her arm and pulled her to a stop. "You're risking Gage's life on a hunch?"

She frowned and yanked her arm free. "Our only other choice is to go back and watch him die. At least this way he has a chance."

"You're right. I'm sorry."

"It's fine." Her face softened. "We will get the antidote and save Gage. I promise, danen. Come, we must move quickly. It will take us a few hours to get to the caves."

෴ ෴

Silas wiped the sweat from his face. Despite the cool night air he was sweating profusely. Kila was keeping a quick pace and he was embarrassed to realize he was having a hard time keeping up. He really needed to work more on his cardio.

A light danced across his vision and he squinted into the darkness. He shook his head. Now he was seeing things. He armed the sweat off his forehead and kept going. Kila was a dark shadow ahead of him and –

The light flashed in front of him again and he stopped. He stared curiously at the bobbing light just a few feet ahead of him. It drew closer and his mouth dropped open in surprise when he realized it was a tiny female, barely bigger than his longest finger. She was pale and completely naked. Light green wings flapped behind her and she hovered in front of his face as she smiled and winked at him.

"What the hell?" He breathed.

She swooped forward and kissed the tip of his nose before hovering in front of his face. He held out his hand. She landed delicately in his palm and folded her hands in front of her.

"What are you?" He asked.

She smiled but didn't reply. Instead, she walked across his palm and stroked his thumb with her tiny hands. Her wings vibrated gently and he smiled. She was so tiny and pretty. He couldn't stop staring at the way her hands were stroking his thumb. She leaned forward and kissed the pad of his thumb before smiling shyly at him.

"You're a pretty little thing aren't you?" He whispered.

She nodded and stroked his thumb again. He leaned in to get a better look at her as she gripped his thumb and opened her mouth. He realized with numb surprise that her jaw was widening and large, razor sharp teeth were protruding from between her lips.

Before she could bite him, she was plucked from his hand. He stared in shock at Quinn as she crushed the tiny female in her hands. She dropped the lifeless body on the ground and gave him a look of annoyance.

"They're called poolas and her bite would have killed you in less than five minutes, danen. Nothing is as it seems in this world. You would do well to remember that."

He lunged for her but she was expecting it and sidestepped him neatly. His momentum carried him forward and he landed on the ground with a hard thud. The tip of her sword pressed against his back.

"Quinn!" Kila was running toward them. "Let him go. We're going after the antidote and you can't stop us." She drew her own sword and held it in front of her.

Quinn sighed. "You would draw on me, sandora? Does the boy mean that much to you?"

He does," Kila said defiantly.

Quinn sheathed her sword and stepped back. "If I had wanted to stop you I would have done so back at the camp when I watched you free the danen and sneak away."

Kila stared at her in confusion as Silas climbed to his feet.

"Massina, I - "

Quinn held her hand up. "Come, we will find the antidote and save your man."

"Thank you, Quinn." Kila hugged her hard and Quinn kissed her on the forehead.

"Do not thank me yet. We'll probably all die and die horribly at that."

## Chapter Eight

"Now what do we do?" Silas breathed.

They were lying on their stomachs, hidden among the trees. In front of them a large rock wall rose and disappeared into the darkness. There were two large openings in the rock. As they watched, a few of the gorans came out of the left one and crouched in front of the large fire that was crackling in front of the wall of stone.

"There are too many of them for us to defeat in combat," Quinn said.

"We need a distraction," Kila said. "While they're distracted we can sneak in and take the antidote."

"We have no idea which one of them carries the antidote," Quinn pointed out.

She stared thoughtfully at Silas and he frowned at her. "What?"

"What we need," she said slowly, "is something to trade for the antidote."

"We cannot trade the danen for the antidote, massina," Kila said in a horrified voice. "You know what they will do to him."

"What will they do to me?" Silas asked.

"We'll take him back before they do," Quinn said.

"How?" Kila asked. "How will you rescue the danen once he is in the caves?"

"What will they do to me?" Silas asked again.

"We wait until they're asleep," Quinn said. "I'll sneak into the caves and free the danen."

"It will be hours until they fall asleep," Kila said. "Especially if we give them the danen. They'll all want a turn with him and they won't wait until they return to their city. You know they won't."

"I don't like the sounds of that," Silas said.

"You shouldn't," Kila said. "There are more than twenty and once you lose your erection they'll be angry and will hurt you."

"Lose my erection?" Silas said. "I'd have to get an erection first to lose it. Let's call using me as a sexual sacrifice Plan B."

"It's Plan A," Quinn said as Kila gave them both a curious look.

"Plan A?" She asked and Quinn shook her head.

"Never mind, sandora."

She lifted her head and studied the group of gorans around the fire before sinking back into the grass. "Listen, danen, the only way we get the antidote for your brother is by trading you for it. You want to save your brother's life - this is the way we do it."

"Fine," Silas said.

She nodded but Kila grabbed her arm and hissed, "We cannot, Quinn. What happens if they capture you when you're sneaking back into their camp? If the danen is even still alive by the time they finish with him, they'll kill you and take him back to their clan. Gage will die anyway."

"If I'm still alive? I might be having second thoughts," Silas said.

Quinn reached into a small leather pouch that was lashed around her waist. Silas stared curiously at the small, bright green ball she withdrew from it. As she held the ball it began to glow and make a low humming noise.

"What is that?" He asked.

Kila gasped sharply. "Where did you get that, massina?"

"It's not important," Quinn said.

"What is it?" Silas asked again.

"It's a boden," Kila said. "It's very powerful and dangerous and if you lose control of it…"

She trailed off and Quinn carefully slipped the ball back into the pouch. "I'll be careful, Kila."

"How? You need a tremendous amount of control over it. If you mess up even one word of the enchantment, you'll be lost forever."

"I can control it," Quinn said. "I've had practice with a weaker boden and it wasn't a problem."

"Because it was weak! Because it was near the end of its life span," Kila said. "This one looks as though it's never been used. Where did you even find it?"

"Don't worry about it," Quinn said. "I told you

– I can control it."

"But if you can't?" Kila said.

"Then you put your sword through my heart and take the danen and the antidote to Naveen. Tell the queen I was killed by the gorans."

"I can't do that," Kila said in a horrified whisper. "Quinn, I – I cannot."

"Then give your sword to the danen and he will do it," Quinn said flatly. "If I lose control you can't let me live. You know that, sandora."

"This sounds like a really terrible plan," Silas said. "I don't even understand half of the plan and even I know it sounds terrible."

"It's the best one we have," Quinn said. "Kila, you will make the trade. Move slowly and do not touch your sword. They will dart the both of you before you even have a chance to tell them you wish to trade. Do you still remember their language from your studies?"

"Mostly," Kila said.

"Do you or don't you?" Quinn said sharply. "Your life depends on it, sandora."

"I know enough," Kila said. "What happens once I have the antidote?"

"Leave the danen with them and return to the forest. We will allow them to start the mating ritual. Once they are all gathered in one spot I will do the rest."

"This mating ritual thing – what happens when I don't get an erection?" Silas asked. "Will they kill me right away or give me a second chance to get a woodie?"

"Do not worry, danen, you will be freed long

before they start trying to get your dick to come out and play," Quinn said.

"Super," Silas muttered.

Quinn rose to her knees and hauled Kila up before hugging her. "Be very careful, sandora. Speak their language and do not reach for your sword. Do you understand?"

"I do. I'll be careful, Quinn."

Quinn studied Silas. "Keep your mouth shut and don't antagonize them. Understand?"

"I don't speak their language," Silas said. "Pretty sure I'm not going to piss them off."

"Don't say anything," Quinn advised. "They may cut out your tongue just because they find our language annoying."

"Thanks for the tip," Silas said.

Quinn stroked Kila's face before kissing her forehead. "Go, my sweet sandora. I'll be waiting for you here."

Kila took a deep breath before standing and tugging on Silas' arm. "I must chain you again, danen."

He allowed her to chain his wrists behind his back and didn't object when she curled her small hand into his leather collar. With one last look at Quinn, Kila led Silas toward the caves of Wintoria.

প্র প্র

Kila started speaking in the guttural language of the gorans before they even breeched the glow of the fire. The gorans jumped to their feet and Silas stiffened when they reached for the wooden tubes jammed into their leather skirts. Kila was repeating the same phrase. He guessed it was some kind of "we come in peace" message because the gorans regarded her suspiciously but didn't dart them.

There was a harsh hooting noise and they watched as a very large woman walked out of the caves. Her breasts were huge and barely contained by the leather band around them, and her thighs were as thick as his. Her stomach was a hard slab of muscle and she absently flexed her biceps as she walked toward them. Her black hair hung to her knees and was held back from her face by various sticks and long leather straps.

He stared at the ground as Kila spoke to the woman in a soft voice. He grunted but didn't object when the goran rubbed his chest. He waited, keeping his mouth shut as she touched his entire upper body before shoving her hand down the waistband of his jeans. Her hand wrapped around his dick and she made a hooting noise of pleasure before squeezing him.

He winced and Kila's hand tightened on his collar, keeping him in place as the woman squeezed him again before releasing him. She yanked her hand out of his pants and turned to the other women, hooting loudly and excitedly. The others moved a little closer as their leader studied Kila.

She spoke rapidly in her own language – he hoped Kila could understand what sounded like complete gibberish to him – and Kila nodded. She spoke slowly and clearly but Silas' pulse pounded when the leader scowled at her. She made a harsh noise of disagreement. Kila, showing more courage than he would have expected, shook her head and pointed at him before speaking again.

The leader of the gorans traced one hand down his chest before cupping him through his jeans again. He stared at the ground until she squeezed him tightly. He grunted in pain and raised his gaze to the woman's face. Her pupils were bright yellow and her irises the same shade of green as her skin. He held his breath as she leaned forward. She opened his mouth and examined his teeth before touching his thick hair and poking at his ears. When she stepped away Silas took a quick glance at Kila. Her face was pale but calm and only the tight grip she kept on his collar gave away her nerves.

The leader turned to the closest goran behind her and spoke quietly before gesturing at the caves. The goran ran nimbly to the cave, disappearing inside briefly before returning. She carried a small glass vial topped with a bit of moss. It was filled with a dark pink liquid and Silas watched eagerly as she held it out to Kila. Kila reached for it and the woman scowled at her before pointing at Silas. Kila released her hold on his collar and pushed him forward. She took the vial as the goran leader wrapped her large hand around Silas' collar. Kila backed away and disappeared into the cover of the trees.

His heart pounding rapidly, Silas stared at the goran leader. She was nearly as tall as he was. When she yanked him forward he wasn't surprised by her strength. She led him toward the opening of the caves and he scanned the trees around them. Quinn didn't appear and he tried to keep his panic level from rising. She wouldn't leave him to his fate, he was sure of it.

*Are you?*

No, he guessed he wasn't. But it was obvious that Kila cared about Gage and no matter what she would get the antidote to him. That's all that mattered.

The others were crowding around him now, reaching out to touch and poke his body. He tried to ignore the hands that were cupping and caressing his ass. The leader stopped him just in front of the caves and he leaned back when one of the others handed her a long, sharp dagger. She made another hooting noise and he flinched when she used it to slice open the front of his t-shirt. She cut the shirt off his body with precise motions. When it was lying in strips on the ground she caressed the front of his chest. She made an appreciative noise as she tugged on his chest hair. He winced and turned his face away when she leaned closer. She growled at him and bared her small and yellowed teeth. He tried not to grimace at the smell of her breath.

Four other women with their hands coated in some sort of red liquid – Christ, he hoped it wasn't blood - drew symbols on his naked chest and back as the others watched excitedly. His eyes widened with dismay when the leader stripped off the leather band across her breasts and shoved down her skirt until she was standing naked in front of him.

She reached for the waistband of his jeans and despite Quinn's warning to keep his mouth shut, he said, "Listen, not that I'm not into casual sex – it's great, really – but maybe we could get to know each other a little better before we start fucking."

The woman cocked her head and stared quizzically at him. Feeling desperate, he said, "You're, uh, you're an attractive woman – love the green skin, by the way – but I'm kind of seeing this other woman. Maybe you know her? Tall like you with dark hair – sliced up a whole bunch of your people earlier in the day?"

She scowled at him and he cleared his throat nervously. "Forget that last part. Anyway, I can't have sex with you because that other woman will be pissed and no one likes a pissed-off woman, am I right?"

He took a step back and pulled at the chain connecting his cuffs when the woman reached for him. She hissed like an angry cat and he made a loud grunt of surprise when a hard hand shoved him in the middle of his back. He pitched forward and landed on his knees with a painful thud. He was face-to-face with the woman's crotch and he stared at her pubic hair as she made another hooting noise of pleasure and ran her hand through his hair.

"Oh hell, no," he said. "Lady, don't take this the wrong way but I never eat pussy on a first date. It's a personal rule."

Her hand tightened in his hair and he tried to strain back as the others pushed him forward. Before they could shove his face into her crotch, there was a loud humming noise and the goran leader stiffened. She backed away as the trees lit up with a bright, green light and a figure emerged from the darkness.

Silas squinted at the figure as it moved forward rapidly. It was Quinn - at least he thought it was

Quinn - but her dark hair was now bright jade and her eyes shone with a hellish green light. The goran leader made a harsh shout and the others reached for their weapons. Silas shouted in warning when the goran closest to Quinn raised her wooden tube to her lips and blew harshly. Quinn held up her hand and the dart stopped in mid-air, spinning lazily before falling to the ground. The gorans made loud noises of surprise and fear and their leader screamed harshly at them. They hesitated a moment longer before charging forward with their swords and daggers drawn.

Silas tried to struggle to his feet and the leader knocked him flat on his back with one hard shove. He twisted around, watching wide-eyed as the gorans descended on the glowing Quinn. She stared serenely at them. He shouted hoarsely when she raised both her hands and a flash of green light shot out from her palms. The light washed over the gorans. Their flesh began to melt and they shrieked piercingly. They fell on the ground, writhing and screeching with smoke rising from their melting flesh as the goran leader and Silas watched in horror.

Quinn walked toward Silas without sparing a glance at the mass of wriggling, smoking bodies screaming into the night air. As she approached, the leader dropped her sword and fell to her knees. She stared silently at the glowing Quinn and Silas shook his head when Quinn reached out.

"Quinn, don't - "

Quinn placed her glowing palm on the forehead of the goran woman. She made a strangled yelp, her hands curling into fists around Quinn's wrist as Quinn's hand sank into her forehead. The goran's skull collapsed under the pressure, her forehead caving in as her eyeballs popped and green light poured from the empty eye sockets. She collapsed in a crumpled heap and Silas surged to his knees. The smell of burning flesh coated the air and a few of the gorans were still making dying moans that reminded him of animals trapped in a cage.

Quinn turned her gaze toward him and he made a low moan at the emptiness in her eyes.

"Quinn," he said as she walked toward him. "Quinn, it's Silas. Remember me?"

"I remember you, danen."

Her voice was different, gargled and sounding more animal than human. All the hair on the back of his neck stood up when she reached out and ran her fingers through his hair.

"Such a pretty man," she crooned.

She stared down at him and when she scowled he could feel his bladder wanting to let go.

"She will take you for herself," she said. "You belong to me but she will try and take you."

Silas cleared his throat. "Quinn, I don't - "

"You belong to me. Say it, danen," she growled.

"I belong to you," he replied quickly.

"I will kill her when she tries to take you," Quinn said. "I'll burn her eyes out of her head and feed her flesh to the pigs. Would you like that, danen?"

"Uh, sure," Silas said. "Quinn, why don't you tell that, uh, bobbin thing to take a hike and you come back to us, okay?"

She smiled at him, that terrible green light escaping from her mouth. "I like where I am, danen."

"Massina, listen to the danen."

Kila's soft voice came out of the darkness and Silas breathed a sigh of relief when she stepped out of the trees and moved cautiously toward them. "The boden must be removed before it takes further hold of you. Please, massina. Rid yourself of it now."

Quinn ran her hand through Silas' hair as she stared at the young woman. "You dare to tell your massina what to do?"

"Please, massina," Kila pleaded as her hand tightened around the handle of her sword. "Release the boden, quickly."

"You want the danen for yourself," Quinn said as her body trembled and the light surrounding her pulsed brighter. "You wish to have him between your thighs. Is that it, Kila?"

"No," Kila said. "It's his brother I want. You know that, Quinn."

"The danen is mine," Quinn said, her hand tightening painfully in Silas' hair. "I will kill all those who try and take him from me."

"No one is going to take him from you," Kila said.

"You lie," Quinn said.

"I don't," Kila said quickly. "The danen is yours. It is the boden who lies. Release it, massina, before it is too late."

Quinn bared her teeth at her before studying

Silas. She bent until her face was inches from his. The glow of her light made his eyes water and he blinked rapidly as she whispered, "I wish to fuck you, danen."

"Yes," he said, "but not until you release the boden."

She snarled at him and he said, "I won't fuck you until you get rid of the boden."

She hesitated and he made himself smile at her. "Please, Quinn. I want you, not the boden."

She released her grip and turned away. Kila drew her sword as Quinn bent at the waist. She made a harsh gagging sound, her entire body heaving. Silas struggled to his feet. They watched as Quinn gagged again before coughing repeatedly. Silas started forward and Kila grabbed his arm.

"Wait, danen."

Quinn dropped to her knees before making a loud retching noise. The glowing green ball shot from her mouth and landed on the ground in front of her. It glowed with a much duller light than before. Quinn picked it up with a trembling hand and shoved it into the leather pouch around her waist.

"Massina?" Kila said. "Is it you?"

"Aye," Quinn said hoarsely.

"How do you feel?" Kila asked as Quinn stayed on her knees with her head hanging down. Her hair was beginning to darken. The jade colour faded away to become her normal dark brown as she coughed again. She groaned and rubbed at her temples.

"I – I feel fine, sandora," she said as she craned her head to stare at them. "A headache and a little tired but - "

Her eyes rolled up in her head and she fell to the ground. Kila squatted and pressed her hand against Quinn's chest. "She's all right. Just fainted."

Silas stared silently at her and Kila gave him a weak smile. "That worked pretty well."

"Pretty well?" Silas said. "I was almost raped by a large green woman, Quinn melted over a dozen women using some weird green ball she swallowed and I came this close to wetting my fucking pants and you think it went *well*?"

"We have the antidote for your brother and we all live," Kila said. "It went well."

Silas snorted angrily as she stood and unchained him. "Can you carry the massina?"

He nodded and rubbed his arms before kneeling and picking up Quinn. "How far?"

"Not far. I just want to get her away from the smell."

Silas followed Kila's gaze to the goran women. They were reduced to a pile of green goo and bones and he swallowed down bile as he followed Kila into the forest.

಄ ೕ

She woke slowly. She kept her eyes closed and listened to the gentle lapping of the water, the murmur of Kila's voice and the deeper voice of the danen replying. She turned her head carefully. At least it no longer felt like someone was repeatedly slamming her head with a sledgehammer. She moved all of her limbs, grateful to have full control over them again. Ingesting the boden was necessary but the power and the almost complete lack of control over her own body had frightened her.

The weaker boden had given her power but wasn't strong enough to take control of her body. This one, humming with its full abilities, was too eager to stay within her. It was almost gleeful in its annihilation of the goran women. Frankly, she was surprised she expelled it. The urge to keep it within her and to let it feed from her was almost too much to resist. The only reason she released it… no, better to let that thought rest. It, much like the boden, was too dangerous to consider.

*Why? Why can't you admit that you released it because Silas said he would only fuck you if you got rid of the boden? It's been years since you've had sex and do you really think Kevin would care? He's been dead for over a decade.*

It wasn't about Kevin. She knew he wouldn't want her to stay celibate forever. It was about her revenge and she would never have it if she allowed her judgment to be clouded by the danen.

*Silas. His name is Silas.*

She sighed inwardly. Better to think of him as the danen. In fact, it was better to not think of him at all. If the queen even suspected that she wanted Silas she would use it to her advantage. She was the massina and the queen valued her for her protection and her abilities but it didn't mean she trusted her. The woman trusted no one. It was what kept her in power for so long.

"Massina? How do you feel?"

She opened her eyes and smiled at Kila. She

was kneeling next to her and Quinn didn't object when Kila helped her into a sitting position.

"Better, sandora." She studied the darkening sky. "How long was I out?"

"Hours," Kila said worriedly. "We've been waiting all day for you to wake."

"Garna," Quinn swore. "We must keep moving."

Kila shook her head. "It's almost dark. It's safer to stay where we are for the night."

"What about Gage?" Silas had joined them and he frowned at the two women. "What about my brother?"

"He will be fine," Kila said. "If we leave at dawn, we will be home before nightfall. The poison will not kill him before then."

"How do you know that for sure?" Silas asked as he scanned the growing darkness. "If you're wrong - "

"She isn't wrong," Quinn said. She stood and stretched tentatively before smiling at Kila. "I'm fine, sandora. I promise."

"We should leave now," Silas repeated.

"It's too dangerous to travel at night," Quinn replied.

"But sleeping out here in the open isn't?"

"I will keep watch while the two of you sleep."

"Quinn, you'll need rest as well," Kila protested.

"I have slept all day," Quinn said. "If I grow tired I will wake you. All right?"

Kila nodded before returning to the small smokeless fire burning near the water's edge. A crude spit had been built over it and the body of an animal was cooking. "I gathered some plants and killed a rappini. You need to eat."

"Thank you, sandora," Quinn replied.

The three of them sat around the fire and Kila sliced up the rappini, laying the pieces of meat to cool on the clean grass before collecting water from the lake in her waterskin. Silas frowned when she held out the leather bag to him.

"Shouldn't we boil it first?"

Kila stared at him curiously. "Why would we boil it?"

"Because it might make us sick. There are bugs and other bacteria in it," Silas replied.

"The water here is not like the water on your world, danen," Quinn said before taking the waterskin from Kila. She drank before handing it to Silas. He stared at her for a moment as if she might just start vomiting before taking a few tentative sips. He handed it back to Kila and she drank as well before dividing up the rappini.

Silas sniffed suspiciously at his portion. "What exactly is a rappini?"

"It's an animal that lives in the forest. It eats insects and frogs," Kila replied. "Eat, danen. It's only a rodent but it will sustain you."

"Mmm, rat," Silas muttered before closing his eyes and taking a bite of the meat. He chewed slowly before swallowing. "Not bad. It tastes like rabbit."

"Rabbit?" Kila asked.

"Furry creature with long ears and it hops," Quinn said absently as she ate her rappini.

"How do you know that?" Silas asked.

Quinn stared blankly at him for a moment. "You are not the first from your world to fall from the orb, danen."

"Exactly how many prisoners do you have back at your place?" Silas asked.

Kila scowled at him. "The breeders are not prisoners. They are treated very well, given the best of our food and protected always. They are vital to our existence and we treat them with respect. It is considered a great honour to be a breeder."

"Oh yeah? So, if a breeder decides he doesn't want to be a breeder anymore you just – what – let him go?"

"Of course not," Kila replied.

"Then he's a prisoner."

Kila sighed. "To be a breeder is a great honour."

"You sound like you're trying to convince yourself of that," Silas said.

Kila cleared her throat. "It is the way of our clan – of all the clans. If you are chosen as one - "

"If I'm chosen?" Silas said. "So now there's a selection process? I thought men were automatically breeders."

"Not necessarily. First they must be physically examined and a sample of their seed is taken to - "

"A sample of my seed?" Silas said. "What the hell does that mean?"

Kila glanced at Quinn. "Do you think he's simple, massina? He didn't appear so at first but - "

"I'm not simple," Silas replied. "I just want to know how you're planning on taking a sample of my seed."

Kila laughed. "Do I really need to explain?"

Silas glared at her. "What if I don't want to provide a sample?"

"Why wouldn't you?" Kila asked. "If you don't you will not be given the chance to be a breeder. As a breeder, you will be given the best food, a comfortable bed and a warm woman to – "

"Yeah, yeah, I get the picture," Silas said. "What happens to the women who are with us?"

"Are you matched to one of them?" Kila asked.

"If you mean am I married to one of them, no," Silas replied. "But that doesn't mean I want to see them being tortured or - "

Kila burst into soft laughter. "Tortured? We are not the cruel animals you think us to be, danen. Like we said before, the women will be treated well and will be given the opportunity to join our clan. They can become nannies for our young ones or clean quarters. They could even become warriors for the queen if they prove to be worthy."

She suddenly smiled proudly at Quinn. "Quinn once worked in the kitchens and now she's the massina."

"What exactly is the massina?" Silas asked.

"She is the queen's protector and she commands the queen's guard," Kila said. "Quinn has sworn an oath to protect the queen. There is no one stronger or smarter in our clan than Quinn."

Quinn smiled at Kila. "You speak in exaggeration, sandora."

"I do not," Kila said indignantly. She turned to Silas. "Our clan has done very well under the rule of our queen. We have more breeders than any other and our children grow healthy and strong. We have over a dozen male children – that is nearly unheard of. We have the best land for crops and traders always trade their best wares with us. Many have attempted to take over our clan. Quinn has stopped all of them."

"Not me," Quinn said. "There are many in the queen's guard who are strong and brave. It is because of them that we hold our own against the others, Kila. You know that."

"But it is you who leads them, massina," Kila insisted. "It is you who taught them to be strong and brave. They would die for you, Quinn."

"Don't say that," Quinn said sharply. "No one is dying for me, Kila."

Kila shrank back before giving Quinn a timid smile. "I am sorry, massina."

"No, I'm sorry," Quinn said. "I didn't mean to snap at you."

She handed the rest of her portion of meat to Silas. "Eat, danen. You will need your strength."

"Yeah," Silas muttered as he took the meat from her. "Can't let the breeders be too weak from hunger to fuck, am I right?"

Quinn didn't reply and Silas sighed heavily before eating the rest of the meat.

## Chapter Nine

Silas stared at the two moons. They were a dark yellow and shone twin beams of light across the dark lake. He shifted onto his side and cushioned his head with his arm before searching the edge of the forest. Kila was a sleeping lump across the dying fire and he could just make out the dark shape of Quinn standing next to a large stump. He had bathed in the lake after dinner, using a hunk of soap that Kila had in a pouch around her waist. Even though the water was cold it felt good to be clean of the marks the goran women had painted onto his chest and back.

The wind gusted and goosebumps broke out across his naked back. He kept his back turned while Kila and Quinn were bathing but was a little alarmed at how difficult it was. The urge to turn and see Quinn naked with her pale skin shining in the moonlight was almost too strong to ignore.

He sighed and turned to his back again. His brother was in some weird coma, he had almost been raped by a gang of green women and he was about to become some kind of baby-making machine. He was on a different fucking world for God's sake and all he could really think about was finishing what he had started with Quinn. He was losing his mind. Trying to get pussy was the last fucking thing he should be thinking about.

*Apparently you're about to have all the pussy you could ever want.*

Yeah, well, that might be a wet dream for some men but he'd always been a one-woman kind of guy. Fucking as many women as possible was never something he was into. The only reason he wasn't in a relationship was because he had put his life on hold to raise Gage.

*Oh yeah? Gage is in university now and hasn't needed you for a while. You could have found someone by now so why are you still single?*

He stared at the moons again. He was single because Gage did still need him. Maybe Gage thought he didn't but his brother was young and impulsive. Look at the way he was acting around Kila, a woman he barely knew.

*That's rich coming from a guy who was fucking a woman he barely knew less than forty-eight hours ago.*

His inner voice had a point but, Jesus, Quinn was smoking hot and he hadn't been laid in over a year. No warm-blooded man could have resisted her – not when he woke up to find her humping his leg in her sleep. He couldn't be blamed for taking what she wanted to give him.

*Are you sure about that? She didn't glow, remember?*

Unease spread throughout his stomach. She hadn't glowed but she wanted him. He could tell.

*Or you took advantage of a woman having a really great dream and you just happened to be right there.*

His unease grew. Had his need for control and his desire to dominate a woman – especially one like Quinn who was obviously strong and capable and powerful in her own right – made him just think she wanted him?

*Only one way to find out.*

He sat up and squinted into the darkness. He would ask her. Simple as that.

৵ ৶

Quinn stared silently into the darkness. Kila and the danen had fallen asleep nearly two hours ago and she scanned the trees, listening intently for any sounds. There was nothing but the rustling of animals and she relaxed a little.

She ignored her temptation to turn and stare at Silas. What good would that do? Just because she was ridiculously horny didn't mean she should wake him and lead him into the trees for a damn quickie. She tried to stop the image of Silas half-naked and bathing in the lake but it was impossible. God, the man had an amazing body. He politely kept his back turned while she and Kila were bathing but she couldn't resist peeking at him more than once while he bathed.

Kila hadn't failed to notice and she had flushed at the grin that widened on Kila's face every time Quinn turned to peek. She berated the others for acting like tarnans but she was no better. Just remembering him standing in the lake under the moonlight with the water dripping down his naked skin made her pussy ache and throb with need. She was wet and she was sorely tempted to venture a little further into the trees and take care of the problem. Maybe then she could concentrate.

They weren't out of danger yet. Naveen and the others would be in the city by now and the queen would know that she and Kila had risked their lives to save a breeder. Not that the queen cared if she lived or died but if something were to happen to Kila...

She shoved that thought out of her head. She would keep Kila safe and accept her queen's punishment. She rubbed wearily at her forehead. She was lucky the queen considered her valuable. Although even that might not be enough. She would probably lose her head tomorrow evening. While the thought of dying didn't bother her, not getting the revenge she sought made her stomach roll with anxiety. She had risked everything for the danen and his brother.

*That's right, you have. So why not take your reward for it? If the queen doesn't kill you tomorrow she will still take the danen first. You know as well as I do that you won't want him after that. Not once he's been with her. So take him for yourself now. Take him while Kila sleeps and no one will ever know. The danen will keep his mouth shut about it. If you're going to die tomorrow it would be nice to have that itch scratched first. The danen would be more than happy to fuck you.*

Her pussy throbbed with need and she shifted slightly and pressed her thighs together. Yes, she had no doubt that he would but it was too dangerous.

*It isn't. Garna, Quinn, we're probably going to die tomorrow! At least let's have a little fun tonight.*

She was tempted. God, was she tempted. The way Silas took control in bed made little shivers of delight run up and down her back. Kevin was well aware of what she liked in bed and had tried to be dominant with her but there was this feeling of something missing. It wasn't natural for him and his dominance had never felt truly real to her. He was playing a game of pretend and as hard as he tried he could never really give her what she needed. Back then she hadn't been nearly as strong as she was now, but she was always on the bigger side for a woman and Kevin was the same height as her. If she had really tried she probably could have overpowered him. The danen, on the other hand, was much bigger than her.

She shivered again as she remembered the way he held her down, the way he pushed apart her thighs and took her pussy with that thick, hard cock. She was helpless to stop him and goddammit, why did that have to turn her on so much? Why couldn't she be normal and not turn into a pile of submissive mush when the danen fucked her?

Speaking of the danen...

Without turning around, she said, "You should be sleeping, danen. We have a long walk tomorrow."

"How the hell did you hear me?" He grumbled. "I didn't make a sound."

"You make more noise than a graffin."

"What's a graffin?"

He was standing behind her now. She could smell his good clean scent and feel the heat of his naked upper body. It made her want to turn around and rest her face against his skin. He would be warm and hard and have exactly what she needed.

She clenched her hands into fists and stared into the darkness. "A very large, clumsy animal."

He snorted and she grinned a little. A graffin was very similar to a buffalo but she couldn't tell Silas that. She slipped up with the rabbit thing and the danen was smart. Only Naveen knew who she really was and she intended to keep it that way.

"Go to sleep, danen," she said again.

"I'm not tired."

She took a deep breath as her mind and her pussy screamed at her to take the danen. She couldn't. It was madness. "If you slow us down tomorrow I'll cut off one of your fingers. Go back to bed."

"It's not a bed. It's the ground," he said. He sounded remarkably unfazed by her threat to remove one of his fingers. "I can't sleep on the ground."

"Bala," she snorted.

"It's freezing," he said. "In case you didn't notice, the gorans took my shirt."

She had noticed. She had been noticing all damn night in fact, and his tanned skin and rock-hard abs were driving her batshit crazy. She took another calming breath. "You're lucky it was my clan who found you, danen. You will be given warm clothing and a bed. The gorans would have kept you naked and chained to the wall."

"Oh yes, lucky me," he said.

"If you do not wish to be a part of our clan just say the word," Quinn said. "I will deliver you to another clan. If not the gorans, perhaps the wathina clan? When you're not being fucked by multiple women you work in their mines. They lose a lot of men to cave-ins and are always on the hunt for others. I could trade you for some of their gold."

"Empty threat," he announced cheekily. "I've already figured out that my kickass body is winning me plenty of points with your people. You'd never trade me – there would be anarchy in the streets."

She tamped down her urge to laugh. It wouldn't do to let the danen know she was enjoying his company. "I could always tell the others that the gorans killed you."

"Kila would tell them the truth."

"You're wrong."

"Are there any clans in this world who don't treat men like pieces of meat?" Silas asked.

She thought for a second before shaking her head. "No. There is not."

"Lovely," he muttered.

"It could be worse," she said.

"So you keep saying but I'm not sure I believe you."

"It matters not whether you believe me. You're just another breeder."

"Ouch," he said. "Are you always this mean to

the guys you want to have sex with?"

She turned and checked to see that Kila was sleeping before glaring at him. "I do not want to have sex with you, danen."

"Bullshit," he said. "You think I didn't see the way you kept checking me out when I was in the lake? I thought you were going to wade in and offer to clean my dick for me."

She flushed bright red before hissing, "Keep your voice down or I'll chain you again and gag you with your own sock."

He grinned at her. "You know what I think, Quinn? I think you're the one who wants to be tied up."

"You know nothing about me."

"I know you liked it when I fucked you. I know you begged for my cock. I know your sweet little pussy was absolutely drenched when I was pinning you down and fucking you. You like being told what to do in bed. Admit it."

She licked her dry lips and shook her head. "I don't like it."

"You do," he said in a low voice before taking a step closer. Her breasts were almost brushing his chest now and she stared at his tanned skin as her pussy pulsed with need. "You want me to have control in bed. I want that too, Quinn."

He traced the line of her throat with one rough finger. "I want to pin you down and fuck you until you're screaming my name."

His hand dipped until he was tracing the swell of her breasts. "I want to watch these fucking amazing tits bounce while you ride my dick. I want you on your knees in front of me and my cock filling up your mouth."

"Stop it," she whispered as his fingers traced the fluttering pulse in her neck.

"Stop what? This?" He murmured before pushing one finger into her leather bustier and stroking the soft skin between her breasts.

She ignored her desire and yanked her dagger from her belt before holding it to his throat.

"Jesus, you're fast," he breathed.

"Don't touch me again, danen," she warned.

"You want me, Quinn."

"I do not."

"Liar."

She pressed the dagger a little deeper. "Call me a liar again and I'll cut out your tongue."

"That would be a damn shame. I'm dying to taste your pussy," he said with a wicked grin.

Her lips twitched upwards and his grin widened. "I'd be happy to eat your pussy right now if you'd like."

She made herself scowl at him. "I'm not interested."

"Li - "

"Danen," she interrupted, "you're very close to having your tongue cut out of your head."

"Why don't you glow when I touch you?" He asked.

Quinn stared at the blade she was pressing to his throat. "Perhaps you don't turn me on nearly as much as you like to think you do, danen."

He laughed, his chest reverberating against her breasts. She glanced nervously at Kila but the girl didn't move.

"I know exactly how much I turn you on, Quinn. Your glowing ability must be broken."

Now it was her turn to laugh. "That isn't how it works."

He pressed even closer to her, not noticing or not caring when a thin trickle of blood dripped from his skin under the blade. "Why don't I put my hand between your legs? If your pussy is wet, I'm going to sit on that stump right there and you're going to ride me until I come."

She stared at him, her nostrils flaring as warmth filled her body. "If I'm not?"

He grinned as his hand inched down her thigh to the hem of her skirt. "You'll be wet."

"Stop it, danen," she warned.

He ignored her and slid his hand under her skirt and up her warm thigh. He touched the edge of her panties and she inhaled sharply.

"Open your legs, honey," he coaxed. The endearment, one she had not heard in many years, weakened her resolve and she shifted her legs apart. He cupped her through her panties and she cleared her throat nervously.

"Not wet, danen."

He twisted his fingers under the crotch of her panties and glided them across her wet pussy lips before rubbing at her swollen clit. She moaned, the knife falling to the ground as she shuddered and twitched her pelvis against him. He pulled his hand free and showed her his glistening fingers. "You were saying, Quinn?"

He backed away from her and sat down on the

stump. She watched as his long fingers unbuttoned his jeans and he pulled out his erect cock. She licked her lips as he stroked it back and forth.

"A deal's a deal." He crooked his finger at her.

"I – I didn't agree to the deal," she whispered.

He continued to rub his cock, circling the head of it with his thumb. "Come ride me, Quinn. Don't you remember how good it felt when I was fucking you?"

She made a soft whispering sound of need and glanced at Kila again before she walked toward Silas.

"Take off your panties," he said in a low voice

She slipped them down her legs and stepped out of them. Her legs were shaking and her body was on fire with need. She couldn't stop staring at his cock and he held the base of it with one large hand as she straddled his thighs.

"You cannot tell anyone, danen. If you do, we both die. Do you understand?"

He nodded and reached under her skirt to squeeze her bare ass with one hand. "I won't say a word."

She gripped his shoulders and lowered herself down, biting her lip when she felt the head of his cock press against her pussy. She hesitated and he kissed her on the mouth.

"Keep going, honey. Slide your tight pussy down my cock."

She moaned and impaled herself on his cock. He kissed her again and swallowed her loud cry with his mouth as she stretched around his thick length.

"You're so damn thick," she murmured as she slowly settled onto him.

He brushed a strand of her hair back from her face and smiled at her. "You're so damn tight."

"We have to be fast," she said with another nervous look at the sleeping Kila.

"Sadly that won't be a problem," he said. "It's been a while for me."

"Me too," she admitted as she wrapped her hands around his thick neck. Her fingers brushed against the leather collar and she bit back her urge to remove it.

She squeezed his dick experimentally and he cursed under his breath. "Honey, you keep squeezing like that and it's going to turn from fast into embarrassing."

She couldn't help but grin at him and he returned it before cupping her face. "Hang on tight, Quinn."

She clung to him, her fingers digging into the back of his neck when he thrust roughly. He claimed her mouth again, sliding his tongue between her lips to taste her. She sucked on his tongue as his arm wrapped around her waist. He held her steady and shoved himself deep into her warmth.

"Jesus," he muttered. "You feel so fucking good wrapped around my cock, Quinn."

"Please, danen," she whispered. "Don't stop."

"Silas," he said. "Say it."

"Silas," she moaned before burying her face into his neck. He fucked her hard, bouncing her on his cock. She arched her back and clung to him. She widened her thighs when his hand moved between their bodies and slipped under her skirt. He rubbed at her swollen clit and tugged on it. She arched again with a soft, broken cry.

Her sword was still around her waist and bumping against their thighs and he touched it. She moved his hand away and he smiled at her before bouncing her on his cock again.

"Silas, oh God, oh," she panted into his ear. "I need more."

"What do you need?" He whispered. "This?"

He grabbed her wrists and yanked her arms behind her back, holding them with one hand as his other hand continued to rub her clit. She struggled to free herself, a little thrill of excitement running down her spine when he kept her completely immobilized.

"No," he said. "Be a good girl and come for me."

His hand tightened on her wrists and he tugged again at her clit. She clamped her mouth shut against the scream that wanted to escape as she came with a roaring rush of pleasure that made her entire body shake. She clenched down on him as she climaxed and he moaned harshly into her ear before arching into her. She welcomed the rush of wetness as he came deep inside of her. Her pussy squeezed him and he moaned again before releasing her wrists. Panting heavily, he rested his forehead on her upper chest and she stroked his thick hair before glancing at Kira. She still appeared to be sleeping and Quinn breathed a sigh of relief as Silas raised his head.

"Tell me that fell under the fast category and not the embarrassing category," he said.

She tried to stand and he clamped his arm around her waist. "Where are you going?"

"Let me go, danen," she said as she stared into the dark forest. "I'm supposed to be on watch, remember?"

"I remember," he said but kept her seated on his lap. "Listen, I'm clean. I've been tested recently and I'd offer to show you the results but I left them on my world."

She controlled her urge to smile and gave him a quizzical look. "Tested?"

"In my world people can get, uh, diseases from unprotected sex. We use a rubber - well, it's called a condom - to protect ourselves."

"I do not have any sex diseases," she said. "In this world that sort of thing does not exist."

"Are you certain? A lot of the, um, diseases aren't really that noticeable until it's too late."

"I'm certain," she said. "You will not get any hidden sex diseases from me or any of the others in my clan."

"I guess with your fiery need to procreate you never use anything like condoms," he said. His eyes suddenly widened. "Shit, what if you get pregnant?"

"I won't," she said.

"You don't know that," he said. He stared at her flat stomach as if he expected it to start rounding out any minute. She tugged on his hair.

"I will not get pregnant, danen. I promise you."

"You can't have children?" He asked.

"Something like that." She was definitely not telling him about the plant she took every month. No one but Naveen knew that she took it. The plain yellow plant was this world's version of birth control and Naveen had first given it to her when he saw the way she suffered each month during her menstrual cycle. It was strictly forbidden in her clan to ingest the plant – even the queen's massina was encouraged to bear children – and if anyone found out she'd be cast out from the clan.

"Release me, danen," she said. He hesitated and then let her go. She climbed off his lap and picked up her panties, shaking them out before sliding them on. "Go back to the fire."

He stood and buttoned his jeans before running his fingers across her bare upper back. She shivered all over before stepping away. "Don't touch me, danen."

"Don't touch you," he repeated.

She nodded and looked away from the hurt she could see in his eyes. "I enjoyed this but we cannot do it again. Ever. Do you understand?"

"Why not?"

"We just can't."

"Explain it to me."

"No," she snapped at him. "For Garna's sake, danen, just shut your damn mouth for once and do as I ask."

"So you just used me to scratch an itch, is that it?"

"Yes. As did you," she said.

He gave her a considering look before saying teasingly, "Maybe I don't want it to be the last time.

Maybe I'll let it slip that we fucked if - "

Her look of pure fury made the words die in his mouth. "This is not a joke, danen. It is forbidden to sleep with a breeder you have not claimed. If you tell anyone they'll kill us both. It matters not that I am the queen's massina or that you are a healthy breeder. They will slit our throats and feed our bodies to the pigs. Do you understand?"

"Yes," he said. "I'm sorry, Quinn."

"Go back to the fire," she repeated, "and forget this ever happened."

## Chapter Ten

"Holy shit," Silas said.

"Hurry, danen," Quinn said before tugging on the chain attached to his collar. As they approached the edge of the forest she chained his hands together again and attached the chain to his collar.

"It's a goddamn actual castle," Silas said. "How many people are in your clan?"

"We are a very large clan," Kila said proudly. "There are more than six hundred of us."

"Holy shit," Silas repeated.

Their home was at the foot of a large range of mountains. A river flowed in front of them and they quickly crossed the sturdy wooden bridge. Silas studied the fast-flowing water beneath the bridge. He guessed the river was about fifty feet wide. Once they were over the bridge, they followed a dirt path toward the giant stone wall that surrounded their home. Women were patrolling the top of the wall and one of them waved before shouting, "Hello, massina!"

"Open the gates, Barkha," Quinn shouted.

"Hurry!"

Barkha whistled piercingly. After a moment, the large wooden gates in the centre of the wall opened slowly.

"Let's go," Quinn said with nervous glance at the dark forest behind them.

Silas stared curiously as they walked past the walls. To the right, he could just make out a large wooden structure rising into the night sky. "Is that a water wheel?"

Kila nodded as they hurried past a stable full of horses. There was a blacksmith's next to it and Silas stared in utter fascination at the forge. It glowed with a dim light from the burning coals.

"Fuck, it's like I'm in the eighteenth century," Silas breathed.

"What?" Kila asked curiously.

"Kila, take the danen to the breeder's quarters, and then meet me at Naveen's," Quinn said as she pulled out the small vial of bright pink liquid.

"I want to see my brother," Silas said. He dug in his heels and refused to move when Kila pulled on the chain.

Quinn sighed irritably. "You can see him when he wakes, danen. Once he is fully awake Naveen will bring him to you."

"I want to see him now," Silas insisted.

Quinn glanced at Kila who nodded. "Let him, massina. It is his brother."

"Fine," Quinn said. "Move quickly."

Silas followed them down the dark streets to a large stone building. After the castle, it was the largest building in the village and he waited as

RAMONA GRAY

Quinn knocked on the door. It swung open and
Naveen gave them a beaming smile. "Massina, you
live! When you told me you were going after Kila
and the danen, I thought for certain that the three of
you would be murdered by the gorans."

Quinn laughed and let the old man embrace her.
"You know it'll take more than a clan of gorans to
kill me, Naveen."

"Aye," he said agreeably. "Did you get the
antidote?"

"We did," Quinn said as the three of them
followed him into the house and down the hallway.
Doors lined the hallway and he opened the third
door on the left before ushering them into the room.

"Gage!" Silas started forward and glared at
Quinn when the chain around his neck pulled taut.
She let it go and he stood next to the bed and stared
anxiously at his brother.

"His breathing is slower."

"Aye," Naveen said. "The poison is almost
through his body."

He took the vial from Quinn and stared critically
at it before pulling out the bit of moss that plugged
the opening. He sniffed the liquid before pointing
to Gage's head. "Massina, lift his head."

Quinn propped up Gage's head and Naveen
pried his mouth open before pouring the liquid
down his throat. He closed Gage's mouth and
rubbed his throat for a few seconds before nodding
happily. "There, that should do it."

"He isn't waking up," Silas said. "Why isn't he
waking up?"

"Give it time, danen," Naveen said. He moved

about the small room and lit the cluster of candles on the night table and the windowsill with flame he produced on the tips of his fingers. Silas stared at Gage in the flickering light as Kila knelt beside him.

"It will work, danen."

"What if it doesn't?" Silas said hoarsely. "What if we're too late?"

"He still breathes," Kila said. "It isn't too late."

She rubbed Gage's bare chest before pulling up the blanket and then standing. "He will be just fine."

Quinn joined them at the bed. "The danen needs to go to the breeder's quarters and we need to go to the castle. She will be looking for us and - "

"You are right, massina. I am looking for you."

Silas stared at the woman standing in the doorway. She was small and dainty with blonde hair that fell to her knees. Her slender body was wrapped in blue silk and Akia and a woman he didn't recognize were standing behind her. Quinn shoved him to his knees on the hard floor before kneeling on one knee and bowing her head. He could hear Naveen groan as he knelt to his knees as well. Without speaking, Quinn placed a hard hand against the back of his neck and forced him to look at the floor.

"My Queen," Quinn said.

"Rise, massina."

Quinn rose gracefully to her feet and Silas lifted his head a little. The queen's gaze had turned to Kila who was still standing.

"Hello, child."

"Hello, mother," Kila said. Silas' mouth

dropped open as Kila hesitated before walking forward and embracing her mother. The queen allowed her to press a soft kiss against her cheek then stepped away. She held out her hand and Quinn kissed her knuckles.

"You are late."

"I'm sorry, my Queen," Quinn replied. "We had some trouble with the gorans and - "

"I know what happened. Akia was very thorough in her explanation."

"I'm sure she was," Quinn said.

The queen stepped around her and studied Gage lying in the bed. "Did you give him the antidote, Naveen."

"Aye, my Queen. He will wake soon."

"Good."

Silas twitched when the queen touched his dark hair. He stared grimly at the floor as the queen ran her fingers over the back of his neck and the collar. "Look at me, breeder."

He raised his gaze to her face and her eyes widened before she smiled at him. "Aren't you a handsome one."

Her eyes were a very light blue, her skin was flawless and she was breathtakingly beautiful. Despite her exquisiteness, he preferred the warm loveliness of Quinn to the ice-cold beauty standing above him.

"Rise, breeder."

He stood clumsily and her eyes widened again. "A danen."

She ran an appreciative hand over his naked chest and he tried not to flinch when she traced the waistband of his jeans. He waited for her to just grab his junk and breathed a sigh of relief when she turned to Quinn.

"Why did you take the breeder with you?"

"I thought he would come in useful as a trading tool with the gorans, my Queen," Quinn said. "We traded him for the antidote and then I returned to the goran's camp and took him back."

"Did you?" The queen said thoughtfully. "You are very skilled, massina, but I find it hard to believe that you defeated an entire camp of gorans."

"We killed most of them when they attacked us," Quinn said. "It was not difficult to kill those who remained."

"I see," the queen replied. "What did I request you to do, massina."

"To retrieve the breeders from the orb and return to the clan."

"Did you do that?"

Kila took a step toward them. "Mother, I - "

"Hold your tongue, Kila," the queen said calmly. "Massina, did you do as I asked?"

"Yes, my Queen," Quinn replied.

"Did you? Or did you risk the life of my child?"

"Kila was never in danger, my Queen. She simply made the trade with the gorans and then waited for me to return with the danen."

Quick as a striking snake, the queen struck Quinn across the face with a hard blow of her fist. Quinn's head rocked back and she staggered on her feet as Silas started forward. He glared at Naveen when the old man placed a hand on his arm.

Naveen shook his head warningly and dug his fingers into Silas' flesh.

"They could have killed her when she made the trade," the queen said calmly. Quinn's cheek was already starting to swell but she stared steadily at the blonde woman.

"Forgive me, my Queen. It was a foolish mistake on my part and will not happen again."

"Aye, it will not. You will be punished accordingly."

"Mother, it was my idea to go after the breeder," Kila said. "Not Quinn's. I left without her permission and - "

"Kila, enough!" Quinn said sharply.

The queen struck Quinn again and then smiled at her. "Hold your tongue, massina. Return to your quarters and get some rest. Your punishment will wait until the morning."

"Yes, my Queen," Quinn said.

The queen turned to Akia and the other woman. "Put the breeder with the others." She held out her hand to Kila. "Come, child. A hot bath and meal is waiting for you."

Kila took her hand and gave Quinn an anxious look before following her mother out of the room.

❧ ❦

"Silas!" Steve, followed by Craig, Evan and Kyle, hurried over to him. "Jesus, man, we thought for sure you were dead."

It was early the next morning. Last night, Akia and the other woman had led him through the dark to a large stone building. Two women stood guard at the door and three more guards patrolled the hallway inside. They took him to a small room and pushed him inside before unchaining his arms and giving him a curt demand to stay. A woman dressed in a long cotton skirt and white shirt brought him food while a guard stood at the door. He thanked her and was a little bemused by her blush and the soft glow that emanated from her skin.

The room was small with just a bed and a chair but there was a bathroom attached to it. It reminded him the outhouse at his grandparents' cottage. There was a small table with a basin, pitcher of water and a towel. The toilet consisted of a wood plank set on top of an alcove in the stone wall. There was a round hole in the plank with a lid to cover the hole and he wondered briefly where the chute inside the hole led before deciding he didn't really want to know.

He ate the blue bread, the cheese and a meat he couldn't identify before pacing the small room. He had stepped out into the hallway and a guard immediately hurried over with her hand placed on the handle of her sword. The hallway was lit with a few torches but a great deal of the light came from the closed doors in the hallway. It seeped out from under at least half of them. The guard had ordered him to return to his room and when he'd hesitated she drew her sword and held it loosely at her side. Her point was clear and he returned to his room and stretched out on the bed. It was surprisingly comfortable and after a few nights of sleeping on the hard ground it hadn't taken long before he fell asleep.

Now, he studied the large room that he was standing in. A large fireplace was built into the far wall and three long wooden tables with chairs were lined in neat rows in front of it. Chairs and floor pillows were scattered around the rest of the room and guards stood in front of the two doors in the room.

"Silas?" Steve touched his arm. "You okay, man?"

"I'm good," Silas replied.

"What about Gage?" Evan asked. "Did you get the antidote?"

"We did and the old man gave it to him last night. He hasn't woken though."

"Well, it's good that you got the antidote," Craig said. "I'm sure he'll be fine."

"You don't know that," Kyle said morosely. "That Akia chick said the antidote only works eighty percent of the time."

"Shut up, Kyle," Steve said with a quick look at Silas. "Naveen said it would work."

New fear stabbed Silas' heart and he took a deep breath before looking around. There were about forty other men sitting and standing in the room and most of them were staring curiously at them.

"Who the hell is that?" Silas murmured.

"If you mean the big, blue guy, that's Vida," Evan said before craning his head to stare at the man. Vida stood a foot taller than the other men and his skin was a smoky blue colour. Silas noted the small black horns growing from each of his temples with a remarkable lack of surprise. Vida was wearing the same clothing they had given Silas this morning – a pair of grey pants and a white shirt – and he returned Silas' look unblinkingly.

"What is this place?" Silas asked.

"It's like the common room for the breeders," Steve said. "They feed us in here and we stay in this room unless we're working."

"Working? What kind of work?" Silas asked.

"Not sure," Steve replied. "We haven't been anywhere but this room and our own rooms since we arrived. Lloyd said that we won't have to do anything until we're given physical examinations and tested."

Evan shook his head. "Lloyd said they jack us off and collect our sperm. Is that really testing?"

"Wait, who's Lloyd?" Silas asked.

"Another guy from our world," Craig said excitedly. He turned and scanned the crowd of men before waving and shouting, "Lloyd – dude, come meet Silas."

A blond man with a thick beard and a thin and wiry body ambled toward them.

"Lloyd, this is Silas. The guy we were telling you about," Craig said.

"Nice to meet you." Lloyd held out his hand and Silas shook it.

"You're from our world?" Silas said.

"I am. Been here about five years now. I think. Time kind of gets away from you here," Lloyd said. "Got sucked in by that glowing ball of light just like you fellows did."

"You're from Texas," Silas said.

Lloyd nodded. "Was it the southern drawl that gave it away?"

"My family lived there for a couple of years when I was a kid," Silas said. He glanced at the guards in the room. "You ever try and escape?"

"Nah," Lloyd said. "Ain't no point to that. These women got skills when it comes to fighting."

"Do they watch us all the time?" Silas asked.

Lloyd nodded. "Yep. Listen, I'll tell you what I told your buddies – there ain't no way off this rock so you might as well settle in and get used to your new life. It ain't half-bad to be honest."

"If we escaped and found another orb," Kyle said, "we could use it to return home."

"I told you before, that ain't possible. Even if you managed to escape and even if you didn't die while you were waiting for an orb to show up, there's no guarantee that it would take you back home," Lloyd said patiently.

"You can't possibly know that," Kyle said.

"All the men in this room came from the orb and we're the only ones from our world. It's like Naveen said – there are many other worlds. I've got it good here and if I can't get back to my world I sure as hell don't want to get zapped to a completely different one," Lloyd said.

"Got it good?" Kyle scoffed. "We're nothing more than goddamn sex slaves."

"That's a problem because why?" Lloyd said. "You're a young, healthy male – you honestly going to tell me that you ain't up for fucking a different woman every month?"

"Some of us aren't man whores," Kyle said

bitterly.

Lloyd laughed. "To each their own, I guess. But I ain't got a problem with what we're doing and neither do most of the other men here. In the five years I've been here no one's ever tried to escape."

"Not even the big blue guy?" Silas asked.

"Nah, Vida's what ya call a pacifist," Lloyd said. "He's big but he don't like to fight. Hell, I don't know why he would. He's real popular with the ladies here. They like 'em big. He gets at least twenty women fightin' for him at every claiming ceremony."

He eyed Silas. "Although you might become the new favourite for a while."

"What exactly is the claiming ceremony?" Silas asked.

"It's a big party they have once a month. It's actually a lot of fun. There's lots of food and wine and they're not stingy about sharing it with us. Tell you what, if I actually could get back to our world I'd make damn sure that I had the recipe for their wine with me. It's fucking delicious."

"But what happens at the ceremony?" Silas persisted.

Lloyd stretched lazily before moving toward one of the large pillows on the floor. "We got some time before breakfast. Have a seat and I'll get you up to date on how this place works."

Silas and the others joined him on the floor and Lloyd grinned at them as he reclined on the pillow. "So this place is like a real - oh, what's that word – utopia? Yeah, utopia. They work, eat and play together and you rarely see disputes between them.

The women have their own building. It looks a lot like this one only bigger. It has a common room for socializin' and eatin' and a big kitchen. There's another room where they all sleep unless they're with a man that month. If they win a breeder, they join us at night in our rooms for the month."

"So any of the women here can sleep with us?" Silas asked.

"Nope. They got a set of rules. The woman has to be at least twenty-one to participate in the breeding and once they're over forty they're out. They have a real hard time getting pregnant here and I guess they don't want to waste our sperm on the older ones. O'course, that rule don't apply for the queen. She's close to fifty at least and she gets her choice of man every month."

"She ever pick you?" Steve asked.

Lloyd shook his head. "No. She picks Vida a lot or some of the bigger men." He grinned at Silas. "She'll take you, sure as shit."

"What do you know about the queen?" Silas asked.

Lloyd glanced at the guards at the doors before lowering his voice. "She's a right bitch. Meaner than a nest of rattlesnakes as my dad would say. Rumour is that she took over the throne about twenty-five years ago. She wasn't royalty or anything like that. She just decided she wanted to be queen so she took it. She's dangerous. If she picks you make sure you stay real respectful. You don't, she'll feed you to the pigs."

"Why would she do that? I thought we were important," Craig said.

"Oh we are but that bitch is straight up crazy. Anyway, if a woman does get pregnant, they're moved to another building. It's like a hospital and nursery and living space rolled into once. They're allowed to socialize with the other women if they want but they don't have to. They got their own kitchen and common room. After the babies are born they got their own little rooms like we do so they can have time with their babies. But the other women are always on hand to help. They got tons of them who act like nannies and help care for the babies."

"So they don't raise their own babies?" Evan asked.

"They do but they got lots of help if they need it," Lloyd replied. "Babies and children here are real precious. They protect them and care for them like they're goddamn gold which, seein' how difficult it is for them to even get pregnant, I suppose they are."

"Do you have any kids here?" Silas asked.

Lloyd nodded. "Yep. I got five of the women pregnant since I've been here. Three of them are boys." He spoke with a tinge of pride. "It's what makes me so popular at the claiming ceremony."

"You've had sex every month with a different woman for five years and only impregnated five of them?" Kyle said in disbelief.

"I told you – it's real difficult for them to get pregnant," Lloyd replied. "Five is a high number, trust me."

"Do you get to see them?" Silas asked.

"Oh yeah," Lloyd replied. "Not on the regular

but occasionally their mamas will bring them to me when I'm working. Let me hold them and shit."

"What kind of work do you do here?"

"They mostly use us for manual labour, shit like that. But they're real careful with us. They don't make us do a lot or anything they think will put us in danger. If we have any special skills they'll use us for that."

"What do you mean?" Silas said.

Lloyd scanned the room before pointing to a short, chubby man. "See that guy there? He used to be a teacher on his world. They use him in the school to teach the kids."

"What did you do before?" Evan asked curiously.

"Me? I was an accountant," Lloyd said. "Not much help in this place. They don't have any type of currency."

"You're kidding me," Silas said.

"Nope. Everything is strictly by trade. Each week traders come knockin' on their door. They set up shop and the women trade with them for any supplies they need that they can't make on their own. Frankly, I don't think it's much that they need. They have a real nice setup going on here."

"What do they have to trade?" Evan asked.

"From what I can tell they mostly trade services. You seen that big water wheel when you were comin' through the gates, yeah?" Lloyd said.

The others nodded.

"Well, they use that to grind their grain in the mill. It must be a real uncommon thing in the world because most of the traders who come to this place exchange their goods for having their grain ground up."

He scratched lazily at his beard. "They do real well on the food side of things here. They've got grain crops and a couple of small orchards just outside the walls. There's a giant garden within the walls and they also grow food in greenhouses with nothing but water."

"They use hydroponics here?" Steve said. "You're fucking kidding me."

"I ain't," Lloyd said. "It's not the same type of food we eat but it's food."

"How the hell do they know about hydroponics?" Steve said to the others. "They don't even have electricity or plumbing for fuck's sake."

Lloyd laughed. "It's a bit weird. They're way behind us in some things and way ahead of us in others."

"How do they grow food so well?" Silas asked. "They're right up against a mountain. The soil must be rocky for miles."

Lloyd shrugged. "I ain't no farmer but from what I can tell the grain they grow does real well in rocky soil."

"What kind of grain is it?" Kyle asked.

"No fucking idea. They've got some food that's the same as ours. They got apples in their orchard, and strawberry plants and a nest of raspberry bushes growing right next to the breeders' quarters. They grow lots of vegetables in the garden that are the same as ours – carrots and lettuce and cucumbers and shit like that. But they also have a bunch of food I ain't never seen before. The plants they grow in water have a pink stalk and are sweet as hell. Loena - she's the woman I'm sleeping with this month - says it has tons of nutrients and if they had to they could survive on it alone."

"What about animals?" Silas asked. "They have pigs here?"

"Yep, they look just like the pigs on our world. They also got chickens and goats. But that's about it when it comes to similarities in livestock. They do have a herd of what they call graffins. They're like a big shaggy cow – or buffalo maybe – and they're dumb as shit. They use them mostly for milk but I've seen them butcher one when it stops giving milk."

He made a face. "The meat's kind of tough and stringy. We mostly eat pork here and whatever they hunt in the forest. I've tasted meat that's kind of similar to deer and other stuff that reminded me of bear, but I don't think they have either of those animals here."

"What about the claiming ceremony?" Silas asked.

"Hold your horses. I'm getting' to it," Lloyd said. "So, the women here all have jobs of a sort. Some are nannies, some are gardeners, some are housekeepers. The queen's got about fifty of them who live in the castle and take care of her and her daughter."

"How many women live here?" Craig asked.

"I don't know an exact number but if I had to guess, I'd say about six or seven hundred. Apparently they're one of the biggest clans."

"What about these other clans? Do you see them much?" Steve asked.

"Nah. Some of them do some trading with us but from what I can tell, most of the clans stick to themselves. Unless they're tryin' to take this one."

"Does that happen a lot?" Steve said.

"It's happened about three times since I've been here. Only once was it a real issue. The first two were small and the queen's army pretty much destroyed them in half a day. The third one was a huge mass of those green women – they're must have been close to three hundred of them – and they attacked us for three days straight. They got real close to the walls but on day three the massina led the others out beyond the wall and killed the ones that remained. There was only about a hundred left at that point and, Jesus, it was like watching lambs being slaughtered. We was watchin' from on top the wall and those green women are tough but they're no match for the massina and the rest of the army."

"How big is the queen's army?" Kyle said thoughtfully.

"Oh at least a couple hundred, maybe two fifty," Lloyd said. "They're all tough as shit and you don't want to cross any of them. They won't kill you but they'll make sure you never try anything again."

"Why do they glow?" Craig asked abruptly.

Lloyd laughed. "Ain't that the coolest thing you ever saw? At night, this place is lit up like goddamn Times Square. Hell, last night Leona was glowing so brightly my eyes were waterin' while I was fucking her."

"Do all the women glow?" Silas asked.

"Yep."

"You're sure?"

"O'course I am. You'll see it for yourself when you're fuckin' one of them. Or even just walking down the street. Half the women start glowin' when they're just starin' at you."

"You've seriously had sex every single night since you got here?" Steve said.

Lloyd shook his head. "Nah, they give us breaks every other month. I love fucking but not even I could keep up with that pace."

"So you have a month of sex and a month without," Kyle said.

"Yes. Mostly. Sometimes they'll make you go two months in a row but not that often. They don't want to wear us out. We also have to see Naveen every month just to make sure we're in good health."

"How come Naveen isn't a slave?" Kyle asked.

Lloyd shrugged. "He's what they call a kalan which is basically a doctor. Plus, he can do some kind of magic shit. He can shoot flames from his goddamn fingertips. During that fight with the green women he brought down a bunch of these ugly, giant-ass birds to attack them just by muttering a few incantations. I think that stuff makes him more valuable than a breeder. I get the feeling that he's the kind of guy who'd rather take it up the old poop chute than fuck a woman anyway. If you know what I mean. Don't matter anyway. He's got to be pushing seventy and probably shooting blanks."

"The claiming ceremony," Silas prompted.

"Right, right," Lloyd said. "At the beginning of every month they hold the claiming ceremony. Any woman who's eligible for breeding gets to bid on a man who's available for sex that month. Once they've put their bid in they're paired up to fight."

"They actually fight?" Kyle said.

"No. Well, yeah, but they use wooden swords to fight. No one gets hurt. The winner of the fight then fights the winner of another fight and so on until they're down to two women. The one who wins the final fight gets the man for the month."

"If some of the women are just housekeepers or gardeners and the others are in the army, how is that fair?" Steve asked slowly. "A housekeeper wouldn't have a chance of winning."

"They don't," Lloyd said. "But they can ask one of the women in the army to fight on their behalf. Lots of them do that otherwise it would be nothing but the queen's guard who get to fuck."

"What about Quinn?" Silas asked.

"The massina? She's tough, that one. After the queen, she's the next in command." Lloyd glanced again at the guards. "A lot of the women here are afraid of the queen and for good reason, but I ain't talked to one that didn't respect Quinn. She's tough but fair."

"Why are they afraid of the queen?" Kyle asked.

"I told you – she's batshit crazy. The reason the women get along so well in this place is because the queen doles out punishment to those who don't. And it ain't easy on them."

"What kind of punishment?" Craig asked.

"Public beatings mostly."

"You're kidding," Evan said uneasily.

"I ain't. Any of the women break the rules the queen has them punished."

"Who does the punishing?" Silas asked.

"Mostly that Akia bitch," Lloyd said sourly. "Although occasionally I've seen Quinn do it but I get the feeling that the queen uses Akia because she likes to do it. The men who've been with her says she's a real ball buster in bed too. Most of the women don't keep the men chained when they're fucking but I ain't talked to a man yet who said Akia left them free. She likes keeping them chained up and in her control."

"Have you slept with her?" Kyle asked.

"No, thank God," Lloyd said. "I ain't got nothin' against dominant women but that bitch is as crazy as the queen. Loena says Akia's been angling to be the massina for years."

"What exactly is the massina?" Craig said.

"She's like the general of the queen's army. Like I said, she's second in command to the queen and she also acts as the queen's personal bodyguard when she leaves the clan."

"Does that happen often?"

"Not that I can tell. The queen's only left once or twice in the five years I've been here. Mostly the massina just defends us against attacks from other clans and trains the other women to fight. They're always doing practice fights in the courtyard in front of the castle. I'd say she advises the queen too but I get the feeling there ain't no one the queen listens to. Not even the massina."

"How long has Quinn been the massina?" Silas asked.

"I don't know. She's been the massina for as long as I've been here," Lloyd said. "God, what I wouldn't give to have that woman in my bed. She's a looker."

"Who has she slept with?" Silas asked.

"The massina?" Lloyd laughed. "She don't sleep with no one. It's real strange actually and I'm surprised that the queen hasn't forced her to. Almost all the women of breeding age fuck the men sooner or later. I suppose the queen doesn't want her getting pregnant. She'd be difficult to replace. When she fights in the games it's a real thing of beauty. Like watching a real pretty dance ...ballet maybe."

"I thought you said she didn't sleep with anyone," Silas said.

"She doesn't. The women can ask others to fight for them, remember? The massina gets asked a lot. She don't always agree to fight but when she does... it's somethin'."

"The other women agree to fight her?" Evan said curiously.

"Oh hell, yes. They love fighting against her. It's like a point of pride to fight the massina. They never win but I think they just like to tell the story about how they fought her."

"What about the women who were with us?" Kyle asked. "Are they even still alive?"

"Oh I'm sure they are. They take anyone who comes through the orb, even the females. They treat them well from what I can tell. They usually become housekeepers or nannies but there's a couple of them who joined the army. They can breed too if they're healthy. They're pretty lucky. The other clans just straight out kill any females who come through the orb."

The far door opened and about a dozen women came in carrying platters of food. They placed them on the long tables as the men began to move toward the tables. Lloyd stood and stretched. "Breakfast time, fellas. C'mon."

## Chapter Eleven

"What's going on?  Do you know?" Silas asked the man standing next to him.

After breakfast, all of the men had been led out of the building to the courtyard just in front of the castle.  It was filled with women but they were eerily quiet.  They stood in small groups, whispering amongst themselves or staring uneasily at the front of the castle.

"Punishment," the man said in a low voice before moving away.

Shit.  Silas had no doubt who they were punishing.  He scanned the crowd for Quinn but there were so many women he didn't have a chance in hell of spotting her.  He did see Naveen and he bellowed the man's name before waving frantically at him.  The other men frowned at him as did several of the guards but he ignored them and called Naveen's name again.

The old man wandered toward him, nodding to the other men before stopping in front of Silas. "Good morning, danen."

Naveen was uncharacteristically somber and Silas' pulse thudded heavily. "My brother, Naveen. Is he…"

"He's fine, danen," Naveen said. "He woke this morning. He was groggy but lucid and ate and drank a bit."

"Thank God," Silas breathed. "When can I see him?"

"He needs more rest but I'm sure by tomorrow he'll join the rest of you. How is your head?"

"It's fine," Silas said as Vida appeared silently beside him. He glanced at the big man as Naveen gave Vida a strained smile.

"Good morning, Vida."

"Naveen," Vida replied. His voice was low and gravelly. Now that he was close to the man Silas could see the small sharp fangs that were his eye teeth.

He held his hand out. "I'm Silas. It's nice to meet you."

Vida stared at his hand before shaking it briefly. "Vida."

He lapsed into silence and Silas turned back to Naveen. "Have you seen Quinn?"

Naveen's face paled and he cleared his throat. "She is in her home."

"Her home?" Silas frowned. "I thought the women lived together."

"They do but the massina has her own quarters next to the castle. When she is not on duty she lives there." He pointed to a small stone building nestled on the left side of the castle.

"What are they going to do to her?" Silas asked

in a low voice.

"She will be punished," Naveen said.

"It wasn't her fault," Silas said. "Kila and I went after the gorans on our own. Quinn had nothing to do with it. If you would let me talk to the queen, I'm sure I can make her understand that -"

"Stay away from the queen, danen," Naveen said sharply. "Do you understand? To approach her without invite is asking for punishment or death."

"Quinn is about to be punished for something that isn't her fault," Silas said. "How is that fair?"

Naveen laughed bitterly. "Nothing is fair when it comes to the queen. Keep your mouth shut while Quinn is being punished, danen. The massina is strong and she can handle what's about to happen."

"This isn't right, Naveen," Silas said.

"No, it is not," Naveen replied. "I must go. They will bring you to me later and I will examine your head. All right?"

He left without waiting for Silas' reply. Silas stared up at Vida. "How long have you been here?"

The big man remained silent and Silas nudged him. "Vida?"

"Many years," Vida replied shortly.

"Are you happy here?"

"Does it matter?"

"If you could leave, would you?"

"Be quiet," Vida said abruptly. "It is beginning."

The queen emerged from the castle. She was followed by a truly miserable-looking Kila. Her eyes were swollen from crying and her face was pale but she stood stoically next to her mother. Today the queen was draped in pink silk and her hair was wound in a braid around her head. She studied her subjects and Silas grunted when Vida's hard hand pushed on his back. Everyone was kneeling and he dropped to one knee as the queen walked down the steps and stood next to a small stone wall. Two chains were embedded within the wall and she smiled haughtily at the crowd as they rose to their feet.

"Good morning."

"Good morning, my Queen!" The crowd shouted as one.

"You all know why you are gathered here this morning. One of you has disobeyed my rule. What happens when there is disobedience?"

"Punishment!" The crowd roared.

The queen smiled before staring at the small stone building next to the castle. The door opened and Quinn walked out. She was wearing dark pants and a plain white shirt and her dark hair was in a high ponytail. The crowd watched curiously as she stood next to the queen.

"Massina," the queen said, "do you admit that you willfully disobeyed your queen?"

"Yes, my Queen," Quinn replied. Her reply was lost in the loud gasps of the crowd and the queen scowled.

"Enough," she said and the crowd quieted instantly.

"Will you accept your punishment in front of those who watch?" The queen asked.

"Yes, my Queen," Quinn said.

Taller than everyone but Vida, Silas had no problem seeing Quinn's face. It was pale but composed. As her gaze swept across the crowd they locked eyes for a moment. He tried to smile at her but it came out as more of a grimace. Her expression didn't change and she bowed her head when the queen stroked her hair.

"The wall, Quinn."

She walked toward the wall and smiled briefly at Kila when the young woman reached out and squeezed her arm. Quinn faced the wall silently as the queen called Akia's name. Akia joined the queen. She was holding a short but thick piece of wood that was sanded smooth. It reminded Silas of a miniature baseball bat and a thick thread of unease trickled down his back.

"What are they going to do to her?" He muttered to Vida.

Vida just shook his head and Silas watched anxiously as Akia approached Quinn.

"Your shirt, massina," Akia said. "Remove it."

Quinn unbuttoned her shirt and dropped it to the ground, revealing the smooth skin of her back. Akia prodded her in the middle of the back with the bat and Quinn pressed her naked upper body against the wall before reaching up and wrapping her hands around the chains above her.

"My Queen?" Akia said.

"We will start with ten," the queen replied.

Akia bowed before standing next to Quinn. She raised the bat and with a viciousness that made Silas wince, slammed the small wooden bat into Quinn's back. Quinn shuddered but didn't cry out and Silas cursed under his breath. Akia hit her a second and then a third time and Silas started forward. His arm was taken in a hard grip and he glared at Vida.

"Let me go."

"She'll kill you," Vida said in a low voice. "You and the massina if she thinks there is a reason for your concern."

Silas paled and stopped struggling. Vida released him and he stared at the ground, trying to block out the horrible thudding sounds as Akia hit Quinn repeatedly. By the time she reached ten, Silas' stomach was rolling with nausea and sweat was dripping down his forehead. He raised his head and made a low groan. Quinn's back was a fiery red and he could see her skin already beginning to swell and bruise. She was still standing stiffly against the wall, her hands wrapped so tightly in the chains that they dug into her skin.

"My Queen?" Akia was breathing heavily and swinging the bat in a low arc.

"Five more," the queen said serenely.

"Fuck," Silas snapped. "She'll fucking kill her."

"The massina is stronger than anyone else in the clan," Vida said.

This time Silas couldn't look away as Akia slammed the bat into Quinn's back. He held his hands in tight fists, flinching each time the bat connected. Quinn's flesh rippled under the onslaught and he could hear her ragged breathing across the silent crowd. She remained completely silent, not even a whimper crossed her lips. He was both impressed and horrified by her silence.

When Akia was finished, she returned to the queen's side. Silas had never hit a woman in his life but he could have cheerfully slapped the smug smile off the woman's face. The queen pointed at the crowd and Naveen scurried forward. He touched Quinn's shoulder and spoke into her ear before helping her unwrap the chains from around her hands. She pressed her forehead against the wall, breathing heavily as Naveen eased her arms into her shirt. She winced but remained silent as Naveen buttoned her shirt and took her hand. He led her past the queen and stopped when the woman held up her hand and studied the crowd.

"Do you see what happens when you disobey me?" She asked. "Not even the queen's massina is exempt from punishment. I am to be obeyed in all things. It is me and only me who protects you from the dangers outside of these walls. Without me, you are nothing and have nothing. Do you understand?"

"Yes, my Queen!" The crowd replied. Their voices were hushed and they watched uneasily as the queen placed her hand on top of Quinn's head.

"Massina, look at me."

Quinn raised her head and the queen smiled benevolently at her. "Will you disobey me again, massina?"

"No, my Queen."

"Good. Naveen, take her to your quarters and treat her injuries. I require my massina returned to me in perfect health."

"Yes, my Queen," Naveen said.

As the crowd watched he led Quinn out of the

courtyard. Silas glanced at Kila. The young woman looked like she was going to vomit and her eyes were watery with unshed tears. The queen reached for her hand and Kila took it numbly. Without speaking, the queen turned and ascended the stairs of the castle with Kila in tow. They disappeared inside and the crowd glanced apprehensively at each other.

"Go on now, all of you." Barkha had joined Akia at the bottom of the castle stairs and she clapped her hands briskly. "Get back to work."

The crowd slowly dispersed and Silas watched as Barkha glared at Akia before stomping away from her. Akia laughed and tapped the bat against her leg, watching as Silas and the other men were herded back to the breeders' quarters.

మ ళ

"Naveen?" Barkha called as she led Silas into his home. "I have brought the danen as you requested."

"Thank you, Barkha." Naveen came hurrying out of a room, drying his hands on a piece of linen. He was juggling five white pouches and he dropped them into a bucket in the hallway with a wet plop. The strong smell of mint and something else Silas couldn't identify clung to Naveen and the pouches. "Put him in the exam room, please."

Barkha nodded before giving him a hesitant look. "Naveen, the massina?"

"She'll live," Naveen said.

Barkha's body relaxed. "Akia was brutal this morning. I have never seen her hit someone so hard before."

"Are you surprised?" Naveen asked. "You know she hates Quinn."

"Aye, I know," Barkha replied. "Do you need me to stay while you examine the danen?"

She gave Silas a quick look, her skin already beginning to glow. Naveen shook his head. "No, the guards are just outside. Besides, the danen will not hurt me. Will you?"

"No," Silas said.

"Are you sure I shouldn't stay?" Barkha asked. She rubbed her hand up and down Silas' arm as her glow brightened.

"I'm positive, Barkha," Naveen said. "I am only examining his head, not preparing him for testing."

"Have you chosen someone for his testing yet?" Barkha asked.

Naveen laughed. "No, you little tarnan. The testing is not for a few days."

"Keep me in mind, will you?" Barkha said. "I haven't tested a breeder in ages."

Naveen laughed. "Go on, Barkha. I will ask one of the guards to get you when I'm finished with the danen."

Barkha nodded and took Silas to a room before leaving. Naveen had followed them in and the moment they were alone, Silas said, "My brother, Naveen. Can I see him?"

"Aye, I guess that would be fine. Let me look at your head first and then I'll take you to him."

Silas sat down on a chair and Naveen cleaned the cut on his forehead with some water before prodding it. "How do you feel? Any more headaches or nausea?"

"No," Silas said. "How is Quinn?"

"In a great deal of pain," Naveen said shortly as he mixed together some powder with a bit of water, "but she will live."

"I want to see her," Silas said.

Naveen wiped some paste onto the cut on his forehead. "She is sleeping, danen. She needs her rest."

"I just want to see her for a minute," Silas said.

Naveen washed his hands. "I will remove the stitches in a few more days. Come, you can see your brother now."

Silas followed him down the hall and into Gage's room. Gage was propped up in the bed. He was pale and sweaty but awake and he gave Silas a weak smile.

"Gage!" Silas hurried forward and hugged him.

Gage winced and patted his back. "Careful, man. I'm as weak as a goddamn kitten."

"How do you feel?"

"Okay. Pretty tired. Naveen said it's because of the poison and that it should dissipate after another day or so. How are you doing? How are the rest of the guys?"

"They're fine, we're all fine," Silas said. "Jesus, you fucking scared me."

Gage smiled again at him. "I'm okay, Silas. How is, um, Kila doing? Have you seen her at all?"

Silas frowned at him. "You're asking about Kila? What about Angela?"

Gage flushed a little. "What about her?"

146

"Aren't you two dating?"

"No. She hadn't agreed to go out with me yet. You know that, man."

"Doesn't mean you should just forget about her."

"I haven't. Naveen said that she and Veronica were fine. They're being treated well."

"Kila is the queen's daughter. Did you know that?" Silas said.

Gage's eyes widened. "No."

"Stay away from her, Gage. The queen is," he glanced at Naveen who was watching them with bright interest, "crazier than a shithouse rat."

Naveen snorted laughter. "Do not say that in front of others, danen. Your tongue will be removed from your head."

He moved closer to the bed. "Your brother is right, Gage. You would be wise to stay away from Kila."

Gage didn't reply and Silas took his hand and squeezed it. "Gage, stay away from Kila."

A stubborn look crossed Gage's face and he shook his head. "I'm not a kid anymore, Silas. You can't tell me what to do."

"Jesus, Gage, this is not some kind of fucking game," Silas said. "We're on a different world and shit here is different. We need to be very careful until we can escape."

"You cannot escape," Naveen said cheerfully before taking Gage's hand from Silas and pressing his fingers against his pulse. "There are worse dangers outside of these walls. I thought you would realize that by now."

Silas didn't reply and Naveen smiled at Gage. "Your pulse is getting stronger by the hour. Rest some more and I will bring you food in a little bit. All right?"

"Thanks, Naveen," Gage said. He patted Silas' arm. "Don't worry about me, Silas. I can take care of myself."

"You almost got yourself killed trying to save a woman you just met," Silas said. "You're not thinking straight when it comes to Kila."

Gage just shrugged. "I like her."

"You don't even know her."

"Can you go, Silas? I'm pretty tired," Gage said suddenly. "We'll talk about it later, okay?"

"Yeah," Silas said. "Just get some sleep, okay?"

"I will. Bye, Silas."

Gage closed his eyes. With one last worried look at his brother Silas joined Naveen in the hallway.

"Naveen, what happens if the queen finds out that Gage likes Kila?"

Naveen gave him a grave look. "You must make sure that never happens, danen. You and your brother are here for one purpose only and it matters not if Gage falls in love with Kila. He can never have her for anything more than sex."

He patted Silas' arm. "Kila knows the rules. It's obvious she is fond of Gage but she will not allow him any closer than is wise."

"I hope you're right," Silas said.

"I am," Naveen said confidently. "Kila knows better than anyone of the cruelty of her mother.

Come, it's time to return to the quarters."

"I want to see Quinn just for a minute," Silas replied.

Naveen hesitated. "I don't think that's wise, danen."

"Please, Naveen. I want to apologize to her. It's my fault she was punished."

Naveen sighed and Silas waited anxiously as he glanced down the narrow hallway. "Fine, but only for a moment."

"Thank you."

He sucked in his breath in a horrified gasp when they entered Quinn's room and he saw her back. Her flesh was swollen and dark bruising covered her from the top of her back to the bottom. Akia had been brutal in her beating and had left no space uncovered.

"Jesus Christ," Silas whispered. He felt more than a little sick to his stomach as he stared at Quinn. She was lying on her stomach with a sheet pulled to her waist. He couldn't stop staring at the bruised and swollen flesh of her back.

"It's only going to get worse as the day goes on," Naveen said solemnly. "Although the poultices I've been using will help reduce the swelling."

"Have you given her anything for the pain?"

"Aye, she's had quite a bit of the yellow powder you found so foul," Naveen said. "As much as I can give her without killing her."

He glanced at the sun out the window. "You have seen her, danen. Come, you must leave. I need to prepare more poultices for the massina's back."

"Let me stay with her while you're doing that. Please, Naveen."

"I can't leave you alone with the massina," Naveen said with a frown. "Not when she is injured so badly."

"I'm not going to hurt her. I promise," Silas said.

Naveen studied him carefully before nodding. "Aye, I do not believe you will. Fine, you can stay with her for a bit. But if you do hurt her I will make sure the queen allows me to feed you to the pigs myself."

"I won't hurt her," Silas repeated as the old man slipped out of the room.

He crouched beside the bed and touched Quinn's arm. "Quinn? Are you awake?"

Her eyelids fluttered open and she stared hazily at him. "Silas?"

"Hi."

"Wh-what are you doing here?"

Her voice was slurred and her eyes were hazy from the drugs that Naveen gave her.

"I wanted to make sure you were okay."

Her eyes slipped shut and he rubbed her arm. "I'm sorry, Quinn."

"It hurts, Silas."

"I know it does, honey. I'm sorry." He hesitated and then stripped off his shirt before sliding into the bed beside her. He stroked her dark hair. "What can I do?"

"Help me turn to my side," she muttered.

He helped her ease onto her side, his stomach

churning at her small grunts of pain. He rubbed her upper chest. She smelled strongly of mint and other spices and he smoothed her hair back from her face. "Better?"

"A little," she sighed. She wormed closer to him and he carefully pulled her into his embrace. He rubbed the back of her neck and pressed a kiss against her forehead. She sighed and rested her head against his broad chest as she eased her arm around his waist and clung to him.

"You shouldn't be here, Silas," she whispered.

"Do you want me to leave?"

"No," she said. "I'm so tired."

"That's the drugs Naveen has given you. Sleep, Quinn. It will help," Silas said.

She nodded and continued to cling to him even after she fell asleep. He rubbed the back of her neck again and stared silently at the wall. He stayed perfectly still and kept his eyes closed when Naveen returned.

"Danen, turn onto your back," Naveen whispered.

Silas kept his breathing slow and even and Naveen sighed. "I know you are awake, danen. Turn onto your back and bring the massina with you. I need to put more poultices on her back."

He put his arm around Quinn's hips and shifted onto his back, bringing her with him. She moaned but didn't wake. When she was sprawled across his body with her legs entwined with his and her face buried in his neck, Naveen rearranged the sheet around the both of them before placing the white pouches across her back. They were warm and steaming in the cool air and Quinn groaned again in her sleep at the weight of them.

"What are those?" Silas asked.

"They'll help heal her faster," Naveen said. "Can you stay like this for a while, danen?"

"Yes," Silas said.

Naveen touched Quinn's hair affectionately before giving Silas a careful look. "Falling for the queen's massina is just as dangerous as falling for the princess. Remember that, danen."

He left the room before Silas could reply.

## Chapter Twelve

"It is looking much better, massina," Naveen said happily as he studied her naked back.

It was three days later and Quinn sat up in the bed, pulling on her shirt as Naveen patted her shoulder. "You are a fast healer."

"That's good," Quinn said absently. Her back was still aching dully despite the yellow powder she ingested earlier and even the pressure of her shirt caused some pain.

She stood and slipped into her pants as Naveen frowned at her. "Where are you going, massina?"

"Back to my home."

"You should stay another night. It is better but if you leave the queen will put you back to work."

"I know," Quinn said before yanking on her boots. She winced at the flare of pain in her back. "I've been here long enough, Naveen. I've shown too much weakness as it is."

Naveen snorted. "Weakness? Massina, you took fifteen blows without a single cry of pain. There is no doubt of your strength. Do you remember much of the last couple of days?"

She shook her head and Naveen said, "I'm not surprised. I gave you a lot of pain meds. Both Kila and the danen came to see you. Do you remember?"

"No," Quinn said. She didn't remember Kila's visit but she had a hazy memory of being in Silas' arms and his low voice whispering in her ear.

"How is Gage?" Quinn asked.

"The breeder is better. I sent him to the quarters yesterday. Kila was here twice to see him as well."

Quinn gave him a startled look and Naveen nodded. "Aye, she was. Both times I covered for her with the guards and made it appear like she was here to see you. But I fear her affection for the breeder will not remain secret for long."

"Garna!" Quinn said. "What is she thinking?"

Naveen shrugged. "She fancies him."

"She'll get him killed."

"She's young and impulsive," Naveen said. "She asked me to allow her to be the one who tests him."

"Fuck, did you say yes?"

"Of course I did. I cannot deny a direct request from the princess."

"Do not tell anyone you're letting her test him," Quinn said.

"I won't," Naveen said. "It will be easy enough to keep it secret. We're testing all the new breeders tonight and I can slip her into his room without the others knowing."

"You haven't tested any of them yet?" Quinn gave him a look of surprise.

"I have not. I was busy taking care of you and the breeder," Naveen replied.

"Who have you chosen to test the danen?" Quinn asked casually.

Naveen gave her a shrewd look. "No one as of yet, massina. Although I have been deluged with requests from many. Akia has been the most persistent."

"She is not to touch him," Quinn snapped.

"Did you have someone else in mind?" Naveen asked.

"No," Quinn muttered.

Naveen leaned closer. "Perhaps the massina wishes to test the breeder herself?"

Quinn hesitated and Naveen said solemnly, "There is nothing wrong with taking a breeder for yourself, massina. Many find it strange that you do not."

"You know why I don't," Quinn said. "I can't let her have any power over me."

"Aye, I know. But taking the danen for a month doesn't mean anything."

"She'll take him for herself so this whole conversation is pointless. You saw the way she looked at him," Quinn said. "I'm surprised she's not doing his testing."

Naveen laughed. "Like the queen would ever lower herself to do the testing. Should I put your name down for testing the danen, massina?"

"No," Quinn said. "You should not."

☙ ❦

"You fellas excited about your big night?"

Lloyd asked as he joined them at one of the tables in the common room.

"I'd be more excited if I knew exactly what was happening," Craig said.

"I told ya," Lloyd replied. "You get your tallywacker pulled by a hot chick."

"Lovely," Kyle said. "I don't suppose we get any say in who pulls our dick?"

"Nope. Naveen chooses who does the testing. It's no big deal. Just try and last as long as you can. They like men who have stamina, if you know what I mean. Hey, ya big smurf," he said cheerfully to Vida when the man joined them.

"What is this smurf you keep calling me?" Vida asked as he sat next to Silas.

"Uh, never mind," Lloyd said. "What's up?"

Vida glanced above him. "Nothing is up."

Lloyd laughed and nudged Kyle. "Vida takes everything real literal like."

The blue man glared at him. "It is Vee-da, you idiot. How many times must I tell you that?"

Lloyd grinned nervously. "Right, sorry. Anyway, you should be happy. Once you're tested you'll finally get out of this room and get to see all the lovely ladies on a regular basis. Plus, you'll get to participate in the claiming ceremony. It's only a couple days away."

"What if you don't want to participate?" Kyle asked.

"Jesus, boy, I already told you a million times – you ain't got a choice. You worried that you're gonna get an ugly chick? Don't be – most of the ladies here are real fuckin' lookers."

156

Kyle shook his head as Lloyd reached across the table and poked Silas. "You're going to cause a real battle at the claiming ceremony. I guarantee it."

He grinned at Vida. "Finally got yourself some competition, big guy."

Vida just grunted and Lloyd stood up. "I gotta go. Loena buttered my biscuit but good last night and I need to get in a nap before tonight. Later, boys."

He sauntered away as Vida glanced at Silas. "Are you certain you're from the same world as him?"

Silas nodded and Vida shook his head. "Until you and your friends arrived I believed all men from your world were babbling idiots."

Silas gave him a curious look. "Do they speak English in your world, Vida, or did you learn it here?"

"We speak this language although we do not call it 'English'," Vida replied.

"What's the name of your world?" Craig asked.

"Medina," Vida said. There was a note of longing in his voice.

"Does everyone look like you?" Ethan asked.

Vida nodded. "Yes, although I am big even for my kind. Our women are big as well, not like the females in this world."

"Quinn is pretty big," Ethan said.

"True," Vida said. "She would do well on my world. The women of my world are all warriors like her."

"Are they blue?"

Vida shook his head. "No, they are the loveliest shade of purple. They match the sky."

"Purple sky," Craig said with a small shake of his head. "How many moons?"

"Only one. Over half of my world is covered with water. This world is a desert," Vida said with a note of bitterness in his voice.

"I take it your people like to swim," Craig said.

"We do," Vida said before folding forward one of his ears. The others stared at the gills in shocked silence. "We breathe under water as well as we breathe above it."

"Holy shit," Gage said. "You've got goddamn gills."

"How long have you been here?" Kyle asked.

"Many years. At least twenty-five, by my count."

"Fuck, how old are you?" Gage asked.

"Sixty-five," Vida said. "I am in my prime."

The others stared silently at him and he gave them a curious look. "What?"

"Sixty-five isn't exactly young on our world," Silas said. "You look around my age and I'm in my thirties."

Vida shrugged. "We can live to be well over a hundred. It is considered tragic if we die before then."

"What was this place like twenty-five years ago?" Craig asked.

"Very different. The queen had just taken power and the clan was in chaos. Many did not support the way she overthrew the previous queen but she had a big enough army that she was able to contain them."

"How did she contain them?"

"She murdered all those who opposed her."

"Shit," Kyle breathed.

"The clan was rather large even back then. But by the time she was finished it was half the size."

"Jesus, she's a fucking lunatic," Kyle said.

"She is insane but the clan has flourished under her rule. When I first arrived, there were only ten breeders and now there are nearly fifty. It was dirty and smelly and there were no clear rules. The queen changed all of that. It was she who started the trading, she who found the majii who can predict the orb's arrival and she who brought order out of chaos."

"Yeah by murdering anyone who stood up to her," Steve said.

"That is true," Vida replied.

"Has it always been like this with the breeders?"

"If you mean the claiming ceremony each month, yes," Vida said. "For a time the queen decided the women could fight with real swords but it resulted in too many deaths so she switched back to wooden swords."

"Isn't that nice of her," Kyle said.

"How long has Quinn been the massina?" Silas asked.

"Ten years or so," Vida replied.

"What did she do before that?"

"She was in the queen's army. There was an attack on the walls by a clan called the warkins. They brought many warriors and after a week of attack were successful in breaking down the gate.

The current massina panicked and failed to lead her warriors properly. It was Quinn who pulled them together and saved the clan from being overtaken. She led them to victory and personally saved the queen's life when a group of the warkins invaded the castle. The queen is a vicious warrior herself but there were over a dozen of the warkins and she would have been killed if Quinn had not saved her."

Vida rubbed absently at one of the dark horns protruding from his temple. "After, when the warkins were dead and order restored the queen killed the current massina and made Quinn the new massina. She has been the queen's protector ever since."

"How many of the women have you slept with?" Evan asked.

"Many," Vida grunted. "There are nearly twenty young ones who have come from my seed."

"So, delicate question but how do they keep from inbreeding if you've been here twenty-five years?" Steve asked curiously.

"They keep careful records of lineage. A woman named Zeeda runs the trading and supply store and keeps track of the births and the deaths. Although it is easy enough to tell who I fathered – most of the girls are at least a light purple and the two boys share my colouring," Vida said with a small grin.

"If you could leave this place, would you?" Silas asked abruptly.

Vida gave him a thoughtful look before nodding. "I would. The babbling idiot is correct in that it is not a hardship to live here. We are treated well but I would leave."

"Why?" Craig asked.

"I miss my home. I miss the skies and the mountains and the water," Vida said.

"Do you have family?"

"No," Vida replied. "At least none who would miss me."

"Yeah but even if you did find an orb they keep saying there's no guarantee it would take you home," Steve pointed out.

"Perhaps not but I would take the chance," Vida said before standing. "I grow tired of talking with you. Good luck in your testing tonight."

ॐ ॐ

"Massina?"

Quinn came out of the small bedroom as the front door of her home opened. Kila stepped inside and closed the door before beginning to cry.

"I'm so sorry, massina."

"Hush, sandora. It isn't your fault," Quinn said.

"It is. It's entirely my fault. It should have been me up there being punished," Kila sobbed. "I tried to make mother change her mind but she refused."

"I'm glad she refused," Quinn said. She moved toward Kila and opened her arms as the young woman sobbed brokenly. "Come here, my sweet sandora."

Kila nearly threw herself into her arms and Quinn winced at the sharp pain in her back. Kila stiffened and dropped her arms. "Garna, I'm sorry!"

Quinn smiled and stroked Kila's hair. "Stop apologizing. Come, we will have some tea and you can fill me in on what's happened the last few days."

"Sit down and rest, Quinn. You are still pale," Kila said.

Quinn sat down at the small table as Kila placed dry leaves in a clay kettle before filling it with water that was bubbling over the fire. She sat it on the table and grabbed two mugs and the jar of dried pink stalks. As the tea steeped she sat next to Quinn and took her hand.

"What have I missed?"

"Nothing, really. Akia has been acting massina in your absence and she's being a total fleeta about it."

Quinn smiled a little. Fleeta was this world's version of bitch and she wasn't surprised that Akia was being so miserable to the others.

"She's made us do about a thousand exercises in the last few days and most of them are completely useless. The new breeders are being tested tonight."

"Aye, Naveen told me. He also told me that you specifically requested to test Gage and that you visited him twice."

Kila blushed and stared at their clasped hands. "I like him, massina."

"I know you do, my sandora, but it's very dangerous for both you and the breeder."

"She won't find out," Kila said.

"Do not be so sure of that, Kila."

"I'm going to bid on him at the claiming ceremony," Kila said defiantly.

Quinn sighed. "Kila, it is not - "

"It will be my first one and I want him to be my first," Kila interrupted. "Gage is kind and sweet and I know he will make it special. I want it to be special, massina."

"There is nothing wrong with wanting it to be special but you know that the breeders are shared by everyone. It is your mother's rule and you have seen what happens when you break the rules."

"Why does it have to be this way?" Kila said bitterly. "Why can the breeders not have their own choice on who they wish to breed with? When I am queen things will be different. I promise you, Quinn."

Quinn frowned at her. "Kila, you have never disagreed with the breeding rules before. Why now?"

"You know why," Kila said.

Quinn sighed. "You cannot let your mother see your affection for the breeder."

"His name is Gage."

"If she knows that you have feelings toward Gage she will use that against you. Do you want to see him injured or even killed because of that?"

Kila paled and rubbed at her forehead before straining the tea and pouring it into their mugs. "You know I do not."

"Then you must keep your feelings for Gage hidden."

"I hate her," Kila said suddenly.

"Hush, Kila. She is your mother."

"You are more of a mother to me than she ever will be," Kila said. "I love you, Quinn."

Quinn squeezed her hand. "I love you too, Kila. Will you do me a favour?"

"Aye, if I can."

"Bid on more than just Gage the night of the claiming ceremony. It will lessen your mother's suspicions if you do."

Kila sighed. "All right."

"Do you promise?"

"Aye, I promise."

"And for garna's sake, do not let anyone know you are testing Gage tonight."

"I won't, massina. Will you test his brother?"

"Of course not. Why would you think that?" Quinn asked.

Kila grinned at her. "I do not sleep as deeply as you think I do, massina."

"Shit," Quinn said as Kila giggled.

"You sounded like you enjoyed yourself with the danen that night in the forest."

Quinn flushed red and Kila laughed again. "I did not look, massina, I promise you. But it was difficult to drown out the noise."

"You can't say anything, Kila," Quinn said.

"Of course I won't. Will you bid on the danen at the claiming ceremony?"

"Your mother will take him for herself, you know that."

"But if she doesn't will you bid on him?" Kila persisted.

"No. I will not give her anything to use against me," Quinn said.

"Taking the danen once will not make her suspicious," Kila said.

"It might," Quinn said.

"Do you care for the danen?"

"I barely know him," Quinn said.

Kila shrugged. "That doesn't mean you can't care for him. I've never seen you show any interest in the breeders, so obviously there's something you enjoy about the danen. You've never even taken Vida and he's made it perfectly clear that he would enjoy your company."

"Vida is a good man," Quinn said slowly, "but I have no interest in him."

"Is it the blue skin or the fangs?" Kila asked. "Fionn has been with him several times and she says he uses his fangs in the most delightful way. She says he's very skilled at both lovemaking and pussy eating."

"Kila!" Quinn gave her a shocked look and Kila laughed.

"I may still be an innocent but it doesn't mean that I don't listen in when the others discuss the breeders."

"I have no interest in Vida," Quinn repeated. She had no interest in any man that had been with the queen and the queen chose Vida often.

*What happens when she takes Silas? Will you lose interest in him as well?*

Her stomach tightened with jealousy. The thought of Silas being in the queen's bed made her stupidly angry and she tried to calm herself. There was no point in being upset about it. The queen would take Silas and yes, she would lose interest in him after that. She couldn't be with any man that had been with the queen. Not after what she did to

Kevin. She had her time with Silas and she needed to forget him.

"Quinn? What's wrong?"

"Nothing, sandora," Quinn said. "Just a little tired. Let us talk of other things now, shall we?"

આ ✖

"Kyle? You okay?" Silas touched the younger man's shoulder. They were standing in one of the many rooms in Naveen's home with Evan and Steve. Craig and Gage had already been taken by Naveen to different rooms.

"I'm fine," Kyle said.

"Kyle, I know you're not on board with this and I get it, I do, but you can't fight them. You saw what the queen is like when her rules are disobeyed."

"Yeah, I know," Kyle replied. "It isn't that I don't want to have sex with different women. Hell, I like sex as much as the next guy. It's just having our choice taken away that's bugging me. We're nothing more than baby-making machines to these chicks and frankly it's kind of degrading."

"Yeah, I know, but there isn't much we can do about it right now. After we've been here for a while we can start formulating a plan to escape. But for now, we just need to go with the program."

"I will," Kyle said morosely. "Honestly, it's been a while since I've had sex and I'd be lying if I said there wasn't a part of me that was looking forward to tonight and the stupid claiming ceremony. Lloyd wasn't lying when he said these chicks are good looking. I want to have sex - I just

166

hate that I don't have a choice in who it's with."

"Suck it up, buttercup," Steve said cheerfully. "This is our life now and I for one, am planning on enjoying it."

"Shut up, Steve," Kyle said before rolling his eyes.

The door opened and Naveen smiled at Silas. "Danen, you're next."

❧ ❧

"Massina, what are you doing here?" Fionn smiled at Quinn when she entered the hallway.

"How is the testing going?" Quinn asked.

"Fine. Naveen just took the danen to the exam room. Two of the breeders have already been examined and are being tested now."

"Good," Quinn said. She clapped Fionn on the back before heading down the hallway. She turned the corner and rested her ear against the main examining room. She could hear Naveen speaking to the danen in low murmurs and she ducked into an empty room when she heard Naveen walk toward the door.

"This way, danen," Naveen said. "You will be tested shortly."

She held her breath and prayed frantically that Naveen wouldn't choose the room she was hiding in. She released it in a harsh rush when their footsteps faded and waited until she heard a door close before creeping back into the hallway. She hesitated, torn between leaving, and her desire to know who Naveen had chosen for Silas' testing. Her choice was made when Naveen stepped out into the hallway and shut the door behind him.

"Hello, massina," he said in a low voice. He didn't seem at all surprised to see her and she blushed a little.

"Good evening, Naveen. How is the testing going?"

"Good," he said. "The princess is with Gage and Belda is with the one called Greg."

"Craig," Quinn said absently. "His name is Craig."

"Such strange names they have," Naveen said with a soft laugh. A glow was beginning to emanate from beneath one of the doors and low groans could be heard.

"I see Belda has begun the testing," Naveen said.

"Who is testing the danen?" Quinn asked.

Naveen smiled at her. "I have not chosen anyone for the danen as of yet, massina."

Quinn bit at her bottom lip. "Why not?"

"I wanted to give you the opportunity to change your mind. Have you?"

Quinn hesitated before nodding briefly.

"Good," Naveen said happily. "The danen is chained to the chair. Do not unchain him for the testing."

"I know the rules," Quinn said.

"Aye, you do," Naveen said. "The bowl is in the room. Make sure you collect as much of his seed as you can please."

"Fionn and Matina saw me come in."

"I will give a believable reason for your absence. Do not worry," Naveen said.

"Thank you, Naveen," Quinn said. She squeezed the old man's shoulder as he walked by and he gave her an affectionate look.

"Aye, you are welcome, massina."

ॐ ॐ

Silas shifted on the chair before tugging at the chains that bound him to it. After the physical exam, Naveen brought him to this room and asked him to remove his clothing. Once he was naked and sitting in the chair, the old man chained his arms and patted his shoulder. "It won't be long, danen."

"Who is it doing the testing?" He asked but Naveen only grinned at him before setting a wooden bowl at his feet and leaving the room.

He shifted again. The room was dark and cold and goose bumps were rising across his skin. Despite his talk with Kyle he was feeling anxious and unsettled. He had told Kyle that he had to accept whoever it was that tested him but he probably should have given himself the same damn pep talk.

He had only been with Quinn once but already the thought of another woman touching him was making his balls shrivel. He swore inwardly. He hadn't wanted a relationship for years and had been content with just one-night stands. Now when he was facing a life time of one-night stands, he was lusting after the one goddamn woman he couldn't have.

*Not one-night, buddy.*

He sighed. Fine one-month stands. It didn't negate the fact that the only woman he really wanted was Quinn. She had gotten under his skin in a way that no other woman had and his one bout of sex with her wasn't nearly enough.

*She might choose you for the claiming ceremony.*

She wouldn't. She never took anyone for the ceremony. Part of him rejoiced at the fact that at least he wouldn't have to watch her fight for another man, while the other part of him pouted that she wouldn't choose him either.

*Hey, Silas? I don't mean to interrupt your little pity party but you've got bigger problems right now. Mainly the fact that some chick is going to come in here and if you don't get an erection you're going to be in a world of hurt.*

He took a deep breath. Very true. If he couldn't provide them with a goddamn semen sample they'd have no use for him. He'd just have to close his eyes and pretend it was Quinn touching him. He had a bad feeling that it would be the only way he would even get an erection. Jesus, he was in so much fucking trouble.

The door opened and he strained to see who it was in the dim light from the hallway. The door closed, plunging them into darkness before he could get a good look. He sat stiffly in the chair as the woman approached him.

She didn't say anything and he jumped when she ran her hand across his bare chest. He inhaled when her fingers traced his abs and cleared his throat.

"Uh, hey, I'm Silas. What's your name?"

More silence and he tried not to flinch when her

soft hands touched his thighs. Despite her touch his cock remained stubbornly flaccid. Feeling anxious, he tried again. "So, um, do you do this often? Testing the breeders, I mean?"

Still no answer and he grunted when the tips of her fingers touched the head of his cock before she curled her hand around him and stroked back and forth. He conjured up an image of Quinn, tried to pretend it was her in the room with him and her hand that touched him. It didn't help. His dick stayed limp and he tried to keep the nerves out of his voice.

"I've never, um, done anything like this before so maybe you could not judge me too harshly. I'm not used to being chained to a chair while a strange woman starts wanking me."

The woman released his cock and Silas cleared his throat again. "I just need, uh, some time."

"Tell me, danen - are you always this talkative before a hand job?"

Quinn's low voice, laced with amusement, drifted out of the dark. Silas released his breath in a harsh rush. "Jesus, Quinn. Why didn't you tell me it was you?"

"We're not technically here to talk to you, danen," she said. Her hand drifted across his abs again and this time his cock stiffened immediately. She touched his cock and he moaned with pleasure as she laughed. "That's better."

"What are you doing here?" He said.

"I thought that was obvious," she replied as she stroked him.

"Jesus, that feels so fucking good," he muttered.

She released him and he cursed under his breath. "Don't stop."

She straddled him. There was the rustle of clothing and he jerked again when he felt her nipple brush against his mouth.

"Suck, danen," she demanded.

He sucked at her nipple, circling it with his tongue before nipping at it with his teeth. She moaned and clutched his head. She dug her fingers into his scalp before guiding him to her other nipple. He sucked eagerly at it and she arched her back then tugged his head back.

"Kiss me," he demanded.

She dropped her mouth to his and they kissed deeply, their tongues dipping and darting into each other's mouths. After a few minutes, she lifted her head and took a gasping breath.

"I want to fuck you," he said.

"We can't. I need to collect your seed," she said.

He muttered another curse and she rubbed the back of his neck before sliding from his lap. He missed her soft weight immediately and pulled uselessly at the chain. "Unchain me, Quinn."

"I cannot. It is against the rules."

He hesitated, remembering what had happened to her the last time she broke the queen's rules. "How's your back?"

"I – what?"

"How's your back?" He repeated.

"Fine. Much better."

"I doubt that," he said. "It's only been a few days. Can I see it?"

"No," she said. "Be quiet, danen. We're not here to talk."

"I know," he replied. "Are you feeling well enough to do this?"

She laughed. "It is my hand I'll be using not my back, danen. Maybe my mouth."

His cock twitched and he released a harsh breath. "Fuck, yes. Use your mouth. Please."

She knelt in front of him and he wished desperately that he could see her. The room was pitch black and she was nothing more than a dark shadow in front of him.

"Quinn, a light, please," he pleaded. "I want to watch you suck me off."

She squeezed his naked thighs. "Not this time."

"Quinn, just one candle, please. Light one goddamn candle I'm begging – oh sweet, fucking hell!"

Quinn's mouth – her wet, deliciously hot mouth – had slid over his cock. He arched desperately, his arms rattling the chain uselessly as he made a low pleading noise.

She sucked him lightly for a few moments before raising her head. "Do you like that, Silas?"

"Yes," he said hoarsely. "Keep sucking."

"Don't come in my mouth," she said. "If you do we'll both be in trouble."

"I won't," he promised immediately.

She rewarded him by sucking his cock back into her mouth. As her tongue slid up and down his shaft, she cupped his balls with her right hand and held the base of his dick with the left. He moaned, his hips rising and falling with the rhythm of her mouth. He liked being in control but there was something exciting about being chained and helpless while Quinn sucked his dick.

He closed his eyes and let his head fall back as Quinn licked the ridge around the head of his cock. He groaned and trembled violently when she took over half of him into her warm mouth and sucked in a deliciously firm rhythm. After only five minutes he was shuddering and close to the edge.

"Quinn, I'm so close," he moaned.

She immediately released him. He made a truly pathetic whimper of disappointment that quickly turned into a groan of pleasure when her hand stroked him back and forth. The edge of something smooth bumped against his dick and Quinn rubbed harder and faster.

"Fuck!" He shouted as his climax roared through him. He was barely aware of Quinn pumping him with rough, brisk strokes or the low sound of approval she made. He collapsed against the chair, panting heavily and twitching. Quinn stroked his naked thighs with her warm hands and he cried out when her mouth surrounded the head of his dick one last time.

She released him with a soft pop. "Sorry, danen. I wanted at least a small taste."

He groaned and yanked at the chains that bound him to the chair. "Unchain me, Quinn."

"I can't."

"You can," he insisted. "Unchain me so I can make you come."

"Silas, we can't do that. If we were caught, the - "

"I'll eat your pussy," he said. "I'll make you come in less than five minutes, I promise."

She hesitated and he leaned forward. "You know you want my tongue in your pussy, Quinn. Unchain me."

She sighed with regret. "No, Silas. The risk is too great. Naveen's home is filled with others right now."

"I'll be quick," he wheedled. "No one will find out."

There was a knock on the door and they both stiffened. It opened a crack and Naveen said in a low voice, "Massina, are you finished? The others will be done soon and it's best if you leave before they do."

"Aye, Naveen, we're finished," Quinn replied. She reached out and ran her fingers through Silas' hair. "Do not tell anyone I was the one who tested you."

She traced the line of his jaw then walked toward the light from the open door. "Here."

She handed a bowl to Naveen and a trickle of embarrassment went through Silas when Naveen said, "That is an impressive amount. Well done, massina."

"Goodnight, Naveen."

She left the room and Silas squinted at Naveen. "Unchain me."

"I will return shortly and release you," Naveen replied cheerfully before shutting the door and plunging Silas into darkness again.

## Chapter Thirteen

"So how do we know if we passed?" Craig asked.

Lloyd shrugged before tearing a piece from the blue bun he was holding and shoving it into his mouth. "If you got a stiffy and shot some of your boys out last night during the testing then you passed."

"Are you serious?" Kyle said. "That's all you had to do to pass?"

"Well it ain't like they got microscopes to see if your boys are swimming, do they?" Lloyd said with a laugh. He took a swig of water and wiped his mouth. "Maybe Naveen does some hocus-pocus shit to it. I don't really know. But as long as I've been here if a guy blew his wad during testing he passed."

"Have there been guys who haven't?" Gage asked. He was sitting next to Silas at the table and he grinned cheerfully at his brother. Based on Gage's mood Silas had a fairly good idea who had tested him last night.

"There was one since I've been here," Lloyd said. "Couldn't shoot his load no matter how hard they yanked him. Hell, he couldn't even get his tent to pitch."

"What did they do to him?" Kyle asked apprehensively.

"They kept him for a couple of months, used him for manual labour like the rest of us and tried pullin' his tallywacker on a weekly basis. Rumour is that he never busted a nut once so eventually they traded him."

"Traded him to who?" Gage asked.

Lloyd shrugged again. "Just one of the traders. Don't know for sure what happened to him after that but I overheard one of the warrior ladies talkin' to another chick and she said he'd be sold to another clan."

He swallowed a large piece of pork before studying Evan. "Who popped your weasel last night?"

"She said her name was Dora," Evan replied. "She was nice."

Lloyd laughed. "Dora works in the castle and she's got a face like a dog lickin' piss off a nettle. She's one of the rare ugly ones in the clan."

Evan flushed. "It was dark. I never saw her face."

"Lucky for you," Lloyd said. "You'da never got your general to stand if you'd seen it."

There was a grunt of disgust from Vida who was sitting on the left side of Silas. "Show more respect to Dora or I will remove your tongue."

Lloyd paled and took a quick look at the others.

"All right, all right there, big fella. No need to get testy. I didn't know you had such a hard-on for her."

He cleared his throat before nudging Steve. "Who'd you get?"

Silas tuned out Steve's reply as Vida scowled at him. "I dislike that human very much."

"Are you – do you have a relationship with Dora?" Silas asked.

Vida shook his head. "Breeders do not have relationships with the females of this clan. But I have been with Dora a few times and she is sweet and kind-natured. Do you believe because she is ugly that the human should be allowed to treat her so disrespectfully?"

His big hands were curling into fists and Silas shook his head hastily. "No, of course not."

"Good." Vida relaxed his hands before biting into a purple piece of fruit. At least Silas thought it was fruit. He had tried it yesterday and it had a slightly grainy taste and reminded him vaguely of pears.

"Silas, who did you get?"

He glanced at Lloyd. "Don't know, she never said."

"Never said?" Lloyd frowned at him. "Did she talk?"

"Not a word."

"That's real weird. I ain't never heard of a woman refusing to talk during testing. Hell, in my test I had Fionn and let me tell you – that girl's got a filthy mouth. I almost shot my wad just from the shit she was whisperin' in my ear."

"Mine didn't say anything either," Gage said quickly.

"You serious?" Lloyd asked.

Gage nodded and Lloyd shook his head. "That's some weird fuckin' shit right there."

"Five minutes," one of the guards suddenly called.

Lloyd popped the last piece of pork into his mouth before standing. "Well, boys, looks like your vacation is over. You'll be put to work with the rest of us."

෨ ෨

"Shoveling shit?" Craig moaned. "I'm getting my degree in engineering and I'm shoveling pig shit?"

"Could be worse," Vida grunted. "You could be cleaning the pits."

"What are the pits?" Silas asked as he pushed past one of the large hogs and tossed the shovel of manure into the wheelbarrow. He studied both the shovel and the wheelbarrow, surprised all over again at how many things in this world were similar to their own.

"Where the human waste from the castle and other buildings collects," Vida said. A small grin crossed his face. "I believe the babbling idiot human is cleaning it today."

Craig slapped a pig on the hindquarters. It squealed angrily and took off across the pen. "You know what? Cleaning out the pig shit is just fine with me."

Silas grinned a little before throwing another

shovelful of manure into the wheelbarrow. He stuck his shovel into the ground and stared thoughtfully at the forest beyond the pen. The clan kept two extremely large pens with simple shelters against the elements just outside of the walls. The one they were currently standing in had at least a hundred pigs, maybe more. The second one was smaller and it had a herd of about twenty large, shaggy-haired creatures. One lifted its snout to the sky and made a sound that was half-moo and half-bellow. He nudged Vida. "Those are the graffins, right?"

Vida nodded. "Stupid creatures but the humans here use their bodily fluids in the most creative ways. They give it to the young ones to drink and they make a rubbery substance that is rather tasty."

"Cheese," Craig said absently as he shoveled shit. "In our world it's called cheese."

"Cheese," Vida repeated slowly. "I enjoy the taste of cheese very much."

Silas continued to stare at the forest as one of the guards standing outside the pen frowned at him. "Back to work, breeder."

"There is no point in thinking of escape," Vida said to him in a low voice. "They would catch you and even if they didn't, you wouldn't survive long. The forest is full of strange creatures."

Silas decided he was probably right. If Quinn was telling him the truth, he was almost killed by a naked woman no bigger than his finger. He picked up another shovelful of manure as Vida winced.

"What's wrong?"

"Nothing," Vida replied shortly. He rubbed at

one of the horns growing out of his temple as Silas gave him a once over. The big man's blue skin was looking cracked and irritated and his eyes were bloodshot. There were deep grooves in the skin around his eyes and his thick hair and horns looked dull. Silas could feel heat radiating from him in a slow wave.

"Are you sick?"

"No."

"You look sick."

"I'm not."

"Vida?"

Silas' head snapped up at the sound of Quinn's voice. She was standing just outside of the pen, dressed in a plain white shirt and leather pants. Her dark hair was braided and she held her sword loosely at her side.

"Good morning, massina," Silas said.

She ignored him and continued to stare at the blue man beside him. "It's time."

A look of relief crossed Vida's face and he stuck the shovel into the ground and hurried across the pen to the gate. Silas followed him and pretended to shovel as he strained to hear their conversation.

Quinn was studying Vida and she touched the dry, scaly skin on his forearm. "I should have taken you yesterday. I'm sorry, Vida."

Vida shrugged. "You needed time to heal. Do you feel better, massina?"

He eyed Quinn's body with obvious appreciation and Silas tried to ignore his immediate jealousy. He liked Vida well enough but he didn't like the way he was looking at his woman.

*Quinn's not your woman.   Stop thinking that way, idiot.*

He drifted a little closer as Quinn favoured Vida with a rare smile. "I'm fine, Vida."

"I am glad to hear it, massina," Vida said in a low, seductive voice. "If there is anything I can do to help you heal do not hesitate to tell me."

More jealousy flooded through Silas and he scowled at Vida's back.

"That's kind of you," Quinn said.   Without looking at Silas, she said, "Is there something you wanted, danen?"

"No," Silas said as Vida glanced over his shoulder at him.

"Then get back to work or I'll have them move you and your shovel to the pits," Quinn said coolly.

She opened the gate and Vida followed her out of the pen.   Silas watched as she and two other women took Vida past the graffin pen and toward the river.   When they reached the edge of it Vida stripped out of his clothes.   The two women immediately glowed brightly at the sight of his naked body.   Silas was slightly mollified by the fact that Quinn didn't glow at all.

*She doesn't glow for you either.*

He ignored his inner voice as Vida dived into the river.

"What's he doing?"   Craig wandered over and stared curiously at Vida.

"Swimming," Silas said.

"Get back to work."   One of the guards watching them reached over the fence and prodded

Craig in the arm.

"Yes, ma'am," he said before saluting her.

She grinned a little and Craig winked at her. She began to glow and gave his body a slow perusal. "I find you handsome, breeder. Perhaps I will bid on you at the claiming ceremony tomorrow night."

Craig leaned against the fence. "I don't have a problem with that."

She laughed and touched his arm again. This time she let her hand linger on his biceps and Silas rolled his eyes when Craig flexed his arm. He burst into loud laughter when the woman shrugged before flexing her own arm. Her muscles bulged and Craig blushed when she said, "I don't mind fucking breeders who are not as strong as me."

Silas laughed again and Craig gave him a dirty look before glancing at the river again. "Why are you letting him swim in the river?"

"The blue breeder needs water to live. Without it he'll die," the woman replied.

"Why doesn't he just swim to freedom?" Craig said in a low voice to Silas.

"Why would he?" The woman asked. "He is treated very well here and even one as big as he is would not survive alone in the forest. Now, continue with your work or when the massina returns she'll move you both to the pits to clean."

❧ ❧

"You know, this really isn't all that bad," Evan said cheerfully as he sank into the steaming water.

"Speak for yourself," Craig said from the tub

next to him. He sniffed at his armpit before grabbing the soap and rubbing it vigorously over his skin. "You didn't have to clean up pig shit all day."

"Hey, it wasn't exactly easy weeding the crops," Evan replied. "Most of their weeds have these thorns that are as big as my thumbs. Dora gave me leather gloves but I still got stuck a few times. Hurt like a son of a bitch.

"So you saw Dora, huh?" Gage said. "Is she as ugly as Lloyd said?"

Evan shrugged. "She's not gorgeous or anything but she's sweet. She said she was going to bid on me at the claiming ceremony and ask one of the queen's guard to fight on her behalf. I'm cool with it."

Gage glanced at Silas. "You're quiet."

"Just tired," Silas said.

Just before dinner, about half the men had been led from the common room to what was obviously a communal bathing room. A dozen metal tubs were lined up in two neat rows of six. There were no faucets but each tub had a hole plugged with a small metal piece of rod. Below each hole in the tub there was a larger hole in the floor. Each tub was filled with steaming hot water and all of the men had stripped eagerly and climbed into a tub.

"Lutan, will the other men bathe after we're done?" Craig asked the man in the tub beside him.

The dark-haired man shook his head. "Nah, they're the breeders this month so they have a bath every morning. If we're not breeding they only let us bathe every couple of days. Except for Vida. He gets a bath every day. He didn't used to but the massina made a special rule for him. She also convinced the queen to let him go swimming in the river once a week. He swims unbelievably fast. I thought for sure he'd try to escape but he never has. Between you and me, I think the massina has a thing for the blue guy. She's always getting him special treatment."

Ignoring his jealousy, Silas stared at the tub to his right. Vida had climbed in about ten minutes ago, submerged completely in the water and hadn't reappeared since.

"I thought the massina didn't sleep with the breeders," Gage said with a quick look at Silas.

"She never bids at the claiming ceremony," Lutan said, "but I think she gets up to it with Vida even though it's against the rules. They're just really careful not to get caught."

"Why does he get to go swimming and bathe every day?" Evan asked curiously.

"He needs the water," Lutan replied. "He gets all cracked looking and dries out like a croken in the sun if he doesn't."

"Croken?" Evan said.

"It's a sea creature," the man said. "Shaped like a star. You don't have them where you're from?"

"Maybe," Evan replied, "but if it's the same thing we call them starfish. What was your world like?"

Lutan shrugged. "Much more advanced than this one but at least they don't have vampires."

"Vampires?" Steve said. He sat up in the water and leaned forward. "You have vampires on your world? Like creatures with fangs that drink blood?"

"Yes. You have them too?" The man said.

"No. They're just a myth in our world. A made-up creature to scare people."

Lutan sunk lower into the water as he shuddered noticeably. "They were real on our world. Horrible creatures and their numbers were outgrowing ours. Pretty soon there won't be any humans left for them to feed from. I've been here for nearly four years. For all I know it could have happened already."

"I guess you're glad to be in this world instead of yours," Evan said.

The man shrugged. "Yes and no. I miss my family. I didn't have a wife but I was close to my mom and dad. Of course, if I hadn't been sucked into that orb I would have been dead anyway."

"What do you mean?" Gage asked.

"I was being fed on by a vampire when the light appeared and sucked us both in."

"A vampire got sucked into this world?" Craig stopped scrubbing his upper body and stared wide-eyed at the man. "You're kidding me."

"No. Spit us out into the same field I imagine it spit you into. The vampire was lying dazed a few feet away from me and I took off running for the trees. He caught up to me just at the treeline and started feeding again. That was when the massina and the others showed up."

Silas paused in washing his face. "Quinn was there?"

The man nodded. "The queen always sends the massina to the orb."

"What happened?" Silas asked.

"The vampire attacked one of the women – I

think it might have been Medina or Fionn, maybe – and the others started stabbing it with their swords. It didn't help because they weren't hitting his heart. He was throwing them around like they were rag dolls. I think he might have even killed one of them. It's how the massina got that big scar on her leg. The vampire dug his nails into her and tore her leg wide open before throwing her into the trees. He had Dacia pinned up against a tree and was about to tear her throat open with his nails when the massina just limped up behind him with blood gushing out of her leg. She shoved her dagger into his back and right through his heart. He burst into ash and the other women started freaking out but the massina didn't. It was like she knew what a vampire was and how to kill it even though the other women didn't."

"Maybe she's from your world," Silas said slowly as a light bulb went off in his head.

"She isn't," Lutan said. "She's from this world."

"How do you know for sure?" Silas asked.

"A few of the women I've slept with have told me she is," Lutan said.

"Maybe they were lying."

"Why would they?" Lutan gave him a puzzled look.

Before Silas could reply, Vida popped up from the water and reclined against the back of the tub. He grinned happily at Silas, his fangs gleaming in the candlelight. His blue skin was back to its smooth appearance and he radiated an aura of strength and health.

"You look better," Silas said grouchily. His jealousy over the thought that Quinn might be fucking Vida was overruling his idea of a friendship with the big man.

"Thank you, big human," Vida said. "I feel delightful."

Gage and the others laughed as Silas grunted in reply before quickly finishing bathing. It was stupid to be jealous of Vida. Even if the man was fucking Quinn he hadn't done anything wrong. Silas had no say in what Quinn did. It wasn't like she was his damn girlfriend or something.

*Maybe she glows for Vida.*

Jealousy reared its ugly head again and Silas glared at Vida. The man gave him a cool look in return. "Is there something wrong, big human?"

"No," Silas said. He was tempted to try and force Vida to tell him if he was fucking Quinn, but he had a feeling it was a battle he would lose and lose quickly. Lloyd had said that Vida was a pacifist but who knew what he would do if pushed to anger.

The door to the bathing room opened and a small and slender woman entered the room. She glanced at the men in their tubs and turned a brilliant shade of red before beginning to glow so brightly that Silas had to squint against the light.

One of the guards spoke sharply to her and she blushed again before looking at the floor. As her glow dimmed she spoke quietly to the guard closest to her. The guard nodded and with a final glance at the bathing men, the woman left the room.

"Danens," the guard approached the tubs and

pointed to Silas and Vida, "hurry and finish bathing and then follow me."

"Why?" Silas asked.

"You're dining with the queen tonight."

༄ ༅

Quinn paced nervously in the large dining room of the castle. The queen had sent her a message instructing her to bathe and dress for dinner with her. She ran her hands nervously over the blue silk of her gown. It hugged her full breasts and flowed over her hips to brush against the floor. She knew it fit her well but she wished she was wearing her usual battle outfit. She felt uneasy wearing the dress and she missed her sword. She touched the comforting bulk of her dagger hidden in the pocket. She was never unarmed around the queen. It was foolish not to be.

She continued to pace and wondered why the queen requested her presence. There was a time when she dined nightly with the queen but over the last few years that had gradually ceased to once or twice a month. She stared at the flickering flames in the giant fireplace that dominated the room. She should have murdered the woman then. Their dinners together were often just her and the queen while they discussed the day-to-day running of the clan and battle strategies, and it would have been the perfect opportunity. The queen was growing older but so was she and many mornings there were aches in her body that weren't there even two years ago.

*You haven't done it because you don't want Kila*

*to hate you.*

Her back was aching miserably and she rubbed at the bruised and swollen flesh. She loved Kila and thought of her as her daughter. It was foolish to deny that she was worried Kila would hate her for murdering her mother. Of course she would hate her. The queen was cruel and that cruelty often extended to her own daughter but she was still Kila's mother.

*What about Kevin? You loved him too, remember? The queen slit your husband's throat without a second thought and you're worried that Kila will hate you for avenging his death? Who fucking cares? Kila is not your daughter and never will be. Besides, not two days ago Kila told you she hated her mother. Do what you vowed to do nearly a decade ago and kill that bitch.*

She took a deep breath. Her inner voice was right. She needed to take her revenge now. If she didn't, the queen would take Silas and she would never –

*So now this is about Silas instead of Kevin? Garna, Quinn, what is wrong with you? Kevin was your husband and Silas is some guy you fucked once. Get your fucking priorities straight.*

Her stomach churned. She was killing the queen for Kevin, not to stop her from fucking Silas. Still, she couldn't help but wonder if she could convince Silas to leave with her once she killed the queen.

*Leave? Why would you leave? Kill the queen and take her place as ruler.*

She laughed bitterly. She had no desire to be

queen. It was Kila's reign to take, not hers. Besides, the chance of walking out of here alive after murdering the queen was slim. Her own clan might fear and loathe her but not even they would take the murdering of their queen lightly.

*Are you sure? This queen took the throne through violence and murder.*

That was true but Quinn wasn't interested in slaughtering all those who opposed her. She wanted the queen's death but not the chaos it would undoubtedly cause if she stuck around after. No, it was best to murder her and then slip quietly away. She would live in the forest until an orb appeared. She would let the light take her to another world and forget completely about this one.

*You would forget Kila and Naveen? Silas?*

The door opened and she stared in surprise when Silas and Vida walked into the room.

"Quinn? What are you doing here?" Silas asked.

"What are *you* doing here?" She replied.

"Dining with the queen, apparently," Silas said.

"Hello, massina. How are you feeling this evening?" Vida asked. He stepped closer to her and she groaned inwardly when Silas noticeably stiffened.

"Fine," she said shortly. She was lying. Her back was really throbbing tonight. She had skipped her dose of pain medicine. While it helped with pain it also made her feel a bit dull and slow-witted. There was no way in hell she was taking it when she was going to be around the queen.

"You're pale," Vida said.

"I'm fine," she repeated.

The door opened again and Kila and the queen entered the room. Quinn automatically dropped to one knee as Vida did the same beside her. After a moment, Silas followed.

"Rise," the queen said.

She studied the three of them before smiling. As always the smile didn't quite reach her eyes. "Come, let us sit together."

They followed her to the large table. She sat gracefully at the head of the table as Kila and Quinn sat on her left and her right. Vida took the seat beside Quinn and Silas frowned before sitting next to Kila.

She gave him a tentative smile. "Hello, danen."

"Hello, princess," he said politely. "How are you this evening?"

"Very well, thank you."

Five women entered carrying large platters of food. They set them on the table as a sixth woman poured wine into their glasses. When they retreated, the queen lifted her glass. "To a successful clan, healthy children, and," her cold eyes travelled over Silas' face, "new breeders."

The others dutifully lifted their glasses before drinking the wine. Quinn took a tiny sip before setting her glass down. The wine on this world was very potent and she needed to keep her wits when with the queen.

"Tell me, danen," the queen said as they began to eat, "are you enjoying your new life?"

"Yes," Silas said. He winced – Quinn had the feeling that Kila just kicked him - and added, "my

Queen."

"Good. You have been treated well by the clan?"

"Very well, my Queen."

"We are the largest clan in the province. You are lucky that we took you from the orb," the queen said.

Silas didn't reply and the queen smiled at Vida. "You are looking well, Vida."

"You grow more beautiful by the day, my Queen," Vida said.

She laughed, a cold sound that sent shivers down Quinn's back. "Thank you, Vida. Are you trying to earn a place in my bed this evening?"

"It is a great honour to be in your bed, my Queen," Vida replied.

The queen studied him. "You do please me well when we are fucking." Her gaze slid to Silas. "Of course, I am eager to see what the new danen will do for me."

Quinn's hand tightened around her knife and she stared grimly at her untouched plate of food. She knew the queen would take Silas but to hear her say it sent waves of jealousy over her.

"What do you think, danen? Would you like to fuck me?"

Silas glanced at Kila and the queen arched her eyebrow at him. "You think ill of me for speaking of such things in front of my daughter?"

"No, my Queen," Silas replied.

"You do. I can see it. Kila may be young but she knows well of my appetite for sex. It is not something to be hidden or ashamed of. Is it, my child?"

"No, mother," Kila said.

"Perhaps I will give you to Kila for the claiming ceremony, danen," the queen said thoughtfully. "It is her first claiming ceremony and I'm sure she would enjoy having a danen like you between her legs for her first time."

Kila flushed and cleared her throat. "That is kind of you, mother, but I believe I would prefer someone," she paused, "smaller for my first time."

Her mother laughed. "Perhaps that is wise. I would imagine the danen's cock is as big as the rest of him."

She touched Kila's hand in a loving caress. "May I suggest you do not choose Vida then. His cock is the largest I've ever seen."

She smiled at Vida who said, "You flatter me, my Queen."

"Have you decided who you will bid on, child?" The queen asked Kila.

Kila shrugged. "Not yet." She glanced quickly at Quinn. "Maybe I will try one of the new breeders."

The queen frowned. "That may not be wise, child. They are untested. You want your first time to be memorable. Perhaps go with a breeder who has been proven to please a woman."

"Perhaps," Kila said noncommittally.

"Quinn, you're quiet this evening," the queen said.

"Just enjoying the delicious meal, my Queen," Quinn said.

"How is your back?"

"Nearly healed, my Queen," Quinn lied.

"I doubt that, massina. Akia was brutal in her punishment. But you deserved it. Did you not?"

"Yes, my Queen."

"You never did thank me," the queen said.

A muscle ticking rapidly in her jaw, Quinn cleared her throat. "Thank you, my Queen, for showing me the error I made in disobeying you."

"You're welcome, massina," the queen said. They ate in silence for the rest of the meal. Quinn forced a few bites past the pinhole her throat had become. When the castle servants returned to clear their plates, she threw her napkin over the uneaten food and took another small sip of wine.

The queen held up her glass and studied the red liquid in the candle light before smiling at Silas. "Did you have a mate or young ones in your world?"

"No, my Queen," Silas said.

"Naveen tells me that you provided a large sample of seed. Why did you not breed in your world?"

"I hadn't found anyone I wanted to breed with," Silas said.

The queen laughed. "In this clan it matters not if you want to breed. You are mine to do as I wish and I wish for you to breed. Do you understand?"

Silas stared at her for a long moment and Quinn was just about to give him her own kick under the table when he nodded and said, "Yes, my Queen."

"Good. Tell me, do you please women when you're fucking them?"

"I haven't had any complaints," Silas said

shortly.

Quinn put her hands in her lap and clenched them into tight fists as the queen said, "I am very particular, danen. Perhaps I will take you to my bed tonight and see what you can do."

"My Queen," Quinn said in a low voice, "the rule is to wait for the claiming ceremony."

"I am well aware of that, massina," the queen said in an icy voice. "But I am the queen."

"You are," Quinn said, "and your people look to you. What will they think if you do not follow the same rules that govern them?"

The queen slammed her fist down on the table and Kila made a low noise of fear as her mother snarled, "I am the queen and I will do what I want. Do you hear me, Quinn?"

Quinn stared steadily at her, the muscle still ticking in her jaw. "If a queen does not follow the rules that she has put in place, why should she expect her people to follow them?"

"Massina, stop," Kila said in a horrified little voice as the queen rose to her feet.

"Do you seek further punishment, massina? Is that it?"

"No, my Queen," Quinn said.

The queen turned and threw her wine glass into the fire. It exploded and Kila flinched as her mother stared into the flames. After a few seconds the queen relaxed and returned to her seat. She smiled serenely at Quinn. "Perhaps you are right, massina. Perhaps a queen rules best when she follows the same rules as her people."

Quinn's head would have spun at the queen's

mood swing if she had not witnessed it many times before over the years. The queen was a sociopath and a person never knew what would set her off.

*You knew trying to stop her from fucking Silas would set her off! What were you thinking?*

She touched the dagger in her pocket before taking a small sip of wine. It was dangerous to disagree with the crazy bitch but she had spoken out loud before she could stop.

*She's going to take Silas and there's nothing you can do about it. Garna! Get it through your thick skull before you get yourself and Silas killed!*

"Come," the queen said, "let us sit by the fire and get acquainted with one another."

ॐ ॐ

Quinn stalked angrily down the wide hallway of the castle. Silas trailed silently behind her. A guard standing at the end of the hallway smiled at her. "Good evening, massina. I will return the danen to the breeders' quarters."

"I will do it myself," Quinn snapped at her.

The woman recoiled and Quinn forced herself to smile at her. "I'm sorry, Belda. I did not mean to snap. I will return the breeder to his quarters. Stay at your post, please."

Belda nodded and watched silently as Quinn and Silas turned the corner into another empty hallway.

*Garna, Quinn. Get a hold of yourself.*

After dinner, the queen forced Silas and Vida to sit on either side of her. She spent most of the evening running her hands all over Silas' body and glowing lightly. With every touch Quinn's jealousy and anger grew. She was acting foolish and dangerous but it was driving her crazy watching the queen touch him.

*It could have been worse. She could have taken Silas tonight.*

That was true and, honestly, she was surprised the queen hadn't. She broke the rules by keeping Vida with her for the night – he wasn't supposed to be a breeder this month – but she sent Silas back to the breeders' quarters.

"Quinn?" Silas said in a low voice.

"What is it?" She answered without slowing her pace.

"What's wrong?"

"There's nothing wrong. Keep moving, danen."

"I am," he said patiently. He caught up to her and tugged absentmindedly at the collar around his neck. "Why are you so angry?"

"Stop asking me questions," she retorted.

He laughed. "You might be forcing me into some type of breeding program but you can't force me to shut my mouth."

Her temper snapped and she grabbed his arm before opening a door and shoving him into the room. It was one of the many bedrooms in the castle and she ignored the very tempting urge to push him onto the bed. Instead she pushed him up against the wall and glared at him. "Are you deliberately looking to be punished?"

"That depends," he said cheekily, "are you going to spank me?"

She bit back her laughter and scowled at him. "You're trying my patience, danen."

"Tell me what's wrong?" He said. "Is it your back? I saw you wincing a few times tonight."

"Did you enjoy the queen's touch?" She asked suddenly.

He blinked at her. "What?"

"The queen was touching you all evening. Did you enjoy it?" She hated the jealousy she could hear in her voice.

"Of course I didn't."

"You weren't stopping her," she said waspishly.

"What's going on with you?" He said. "Of course I didn't stop her. I assumed she'd be pissed if I did."

She stepped closer to him, her nostrils flaring angrily. "So now you're afraid of a woman?"

"Are you going crazy, Quinn? Is that what's happening?" He said.

"No," she said. She folded her arms across her torso and a twinge of lust went through her belly when Silas' gaze dropped to her breasts.

"You're jealous," he said.

"I am not jealous," she hissed at him. "Let's go."

He grabbed her arm before she could leave and pulled her against his body. "You are jealous," he said. "I like it."

"My jealousy will get us both killed," she said sullenly.

He touched her dark hair before running his fingers through the soft strands. "I like your hair tonight and I like your dress."

He ran his rough fingertips over her exposed collarbone and she shivered violently. It sent a throb of pain through her back and he frowned when she winced.

"How bad is your back, Quinn?"

"It'll heal," she said. "We have to go, danen."

"In a minute," he whispered. He put his arm around her, being careful to rest it against her ass and not her lower back, and squeezed her hip. "Are you going to bid on me tomorrow night?"

"You know I can't," she said.

"Can't or won't?"

"Does it matter?"

"Yes."

"I can't," she repeated.

"Why?" He dipped his head and tasted the tender skin of her throat. She moaned and squeezed his arms, digging her fingers into the hard muscles.

"Why?" He asked again before sucking on her earlobe.

"Silas," she whispered.

"Quinn," he muttered before pressing his mouth against hers. They kissed hungrily as he pushed his hand into the bodice of her dress and cupped one full breast. He kneaded it before tugging her nipple into a hard little bud. He sucked on her bottom lip sending shockwaves of desire through her entire body. She wanted him so much it hurt and she didn't object when he used his other hand to unbutton the back of her dress.

She waited for him to push her dress down but instead he turned her around and spread her dress open.

"Silas, what - "

"Oh my fucking God," he said in a horrified whisper. "Jesus Christ, Quinn, your back – it isn't any better."

She tried to pull away but he hooked his arm around her waist and held her in a tight grip. "Fuck," he said.

"It's better than it looks," she said.

"I fucking doubt that," he said. "How are you even standing let alone walking around?"

"I have a high pain tolerance," she said impatiently. "Danen, are we doing this or not?"

He shook his head before pressing a tender kiss against one of the purple blotches on the back of her shoulder. "Not with your back like this."

She sighed impatiently. "I told you, it isn't that bad. Silas, I want to fuck you."

"I want to fuck you too, Quinn, you know I do. But I can't with your back like this. There's no way I won't hurt you."

"We have to be fast and quiet," she said, ignoring his last comment. "Can you do that?"

"I'm tired of fast and quiet," he said before pressing another light kiss against her bruised back. "Wouldn't you like to see what it's like when I take my time?"

She shuddered all over before shaking her head. "No."

"Liar," he whispered. "Bid on me tomorrow night, Quinn, and I promise I'll show you."

"The queen will take you tomorrow night," she said dully. "No one will have the chance to bid on you."

He sighed and buried his face in her hair and she squeezed his arm. "Fuck me right now, Silas. Please. It's our last chance."

"It isn't," he said. "You can bid on me at the next claiming ceremony."

He quickly buttoned her dress as Quinn stared at the floor. He turned her around and pressed a kiss against her mouth. "Your back will be healed by then, Quinn."

"Aye," she said in defeat. She couldn't tell him that once he'd been with the queen she would never see him the same way again. It wasn't his fault but she couldn't imagine having him between her legs after he'd been with the queen. Not after everything that bitch had taken from her.

*So now you're just going to roll over and let her take Silas from you too?*

She closed her eyes as Silas pressed another brief kiss against her mouth. "Maybe she won't choose me tomorrow night."

"Maybe not," Quinn replied.

"If she doesn't, promise that you'll bid on me," he said.

"Sure," she replied. He smiled happily at her and she forced herself to return his smile. It was easy enough to agree to something that would never happen.

"Let's go, danen. We have lingered too long," she said.

"Quinn, what about the women who were with us? Are they okay?"

She studied him carefully. "Are you dating one of them?"

"No," he said patiently. "We just haven't seen any of them and I'm worried."

"They all live," she said. "They've been working in the kitchen and doing housework in the women's quarters."

"Are your people being nice to them?" He asked.

"I would imagine they are. The one named Veronica is making it difficult. She's a spoiled brat and if she doesn't learn to hold her tongue she'll be punished."

"Like you were punished?" He asked.

She nodded and he sighed. "Maybe if you let me talk to her I can convince her to keep her mouth shut."

"You'll see her at the ceremony tomorrow night," Quinn said. "The breeders are allowed to visit with all of the women the night of the claiming ceremony."

"Will we be chained?" He asked.

"No," she replied. "Do not think of escaping, Silas. You will be given your freedom tomorrow night but only to a certain extent. If you try to escape, you'll be punished."

She eased open the door and looked up and down the empty hallway as Silas said, "What's the worse they can do? Beat me?"

"The queen doesn't like to harm the breeders, you're too valuable" Quinn said absently as she checked the hallway again. "Most likely she'll make you watch as she mutilates one of the women that came with you."

"Mutilate?" Silas said.

"Yes. She'll cut out their tongue or maybe one of their eyes," Quinn said solemnly. She stared up at him before touching his face. "The queen is neither stupid nor blind, Silas. You would do well to remember that. All right?"

He nodded and kissed her again before she could

stop him. "Remember your promise, Quinn," he said. "If the queen doesn't choose me tomorrow night you have to bid on me."

A look of fleeting sorrow crossed her face. "Aye, I remember, danen."

*Chapter Fourteen*

"Gage!"

Silas and Gage turned to see Angela and Veronica pushing their way through the crowd of women and children.

"Gage, I'm so happy to see you!" Angela cried before throwing her arms around him.

Gage hugged her before gently pushing her back. "Hi, Angela."

"Hi? That's all you've got?" Angela said before trying to put her arm around his waist. He stopped her and she gave him an odd look. "I didn't even know if you were alive. They wouldn't tell me."

"I'm good," Gage said. "How are you?"

"Fine," Angela said as Veronica put her arms around Silas' waist and squeezed.

"Hi, Silas.

"Hi, Veronica. Where are Paula and Gemma?"

"They were chosen to work in the kitchens tonight making the food for the ceremony," Veronica said. She sighed and rested her head on

Silas' broad chest. "It's been so terrible, Silas. They make me clean every day and the other women are so mean."

"They're not mean," Angela said. "You won't even talk to half of them."

"Why should I?" Veronica said. "I'm not staying in this horrible place. As soon as I figure out a way to escape I'm out of here. I'm not going to be a stupid maid for the rest of my life."

"There's no way to escape," Silas said. "Don't try, Veronica. You'll be punished."

Veronica shuddered delicately and pressed closer against him. "Like that horrible woman who captured us was? Frankly, she deserved to be beaten that way. She - "

She squealed and jumped when the handle of a sword was poked into her back. Quinn was standing behind them and Veronica paled as Quinn studied her.

"Hands off the breeder," Quinn said.

Veronica gave Silas a quick look. "They – they said we could visit with our friends tonight."

"You can visit but do not touch," Quinn said shortly. "Or I'll chain you in your room and leave you there for a day or two."

Veronica dropped her arms from Silas' waist and took a step back. "You're a real bitch, you know that?"

"Veronica, be quiet," Silas said.

He waited for Quinn to either beat the crap out of Veronica or drag her away but Quinn simply smiled at her. "Aye, I know. Keep your hands to yourself."

She turned and walked away, sheathing her sword. She was dressed in the leather bustier and the blue cotton skirt again. Glimpses of her tanned thighs could be seen through the strips of her skirt and Silas' stomach tightened. God, he wanted her. His gaze rose to the top of her back visible above the bustier. The bruising was just as bad as last night and he gritted his teeth against the anger rising in him. He could kill that bitch Akia for what she did to Quinn.

"I hate that Xena wanna-be," Veronica said sullenly. "She's the reason we're in this mess."

"If it hadn't been for her we'd be dead," Silas said absently. He was still staring at Quinn and Veronica poked him in the side.

"What the hell, Silas? Do you have a thing for her?"

"No," he said before frowning at her. "I'm just smart enough to know that we got lucky in being picked up by this clan."

Angela was giving Gage a pensive look. "Gage, have you missed me?"

"Sure," Gage said distractedly. He was staring into the crowd and Angela followed his gaze. Kila, dressed in the same outfit as the other warriors in the queen's guard, was standing with Fionn and Barkha. She gave Gage a quick smile before turning her back to them.

"Yeah, I bet you have," Angela said bitterly.

Gage gave her a guilty look. "Angela, I'm sorry, but I – "

"Don't, Gage," Angela said. "I'm not stupid. You are for thinking you're going to have some kind of relationship with her. Forgetting that you're going to be used by hundreds of different women for your goddamn sperm, she's the queen's daughter. Remember?"

"I remember," Gage said. "I really am sorry, Angela."

She just shook her head and walked away. She joined a group of women standing near the long tables of food. One of the women put her arm around Angela's shoulders and squeezed before giving her a warm smile. Angela rested her head on the woman's shoulder and Veronica snorted.

"Angela thinks these women are her friends," she said. "She's given up completely on going back home and so have Paula and Gemma. Gemma's already talking about trying to join their stupid army for God's sake."

"You should try and make friends," Silas advised. "There isn't any way to get back home, Veronica."

She gave him a look of anger and horror. "You don't know that for sure. Just because you're looking forward to banging a bunch of different women doesn't mean I should just give up and accept my new life. Asshole!"

She stalked away, joining Angela and the group of women. Silas sighed as Gage shook his head. "She's going to get herself killed."

"Probably," he said shortly. "Why are you being so rude to Angela?"

"I wasn't rude," Gage protested. "There's just no point in pretending we'll ever be more than friends now."

"Because of how you feel about Kila?" Silas asked.

Gage nodded. "Yes."

"Gage, you can't have a relationship with her. You know that, right?"

"Yes. Just like you know you can't have a relationship with Quinn."

Silas glanced around nervously. "I don't want a relationship with Quinn. Keep your voice down."

Gage grinned at him. "Oh please, Silas. You're my brother and I know you better than anyone. I see the way you look at her."

Silas sighed again. "We're both fucking idiots."

"Yup," Gage said solemnly.

Silas took a sip of wine. The party had started nearly two hours ago and it was the first time that he and Gage hadn't been surrounded by women. All of the men were very popular but he as well as Gage and his friends were obviously the most admired. Although the women had mostly just looked and not touched, he'd had his ass grabbed more than once. The party was taking place in the courtyard just in front of the castle and while hundreds of torches were lit, they were hardly needed. Almost all the women had a soft glow and their combined light kept the darkness away.

Gage took a quick glance around before lowering his voice. "Kila said she was bidding on me tonight. Is Quinn bidding on you?"

"If the queen doesn't choose me, yes," Silas said.

Gage flinched. "God, I hope she doesn't. How weird will it be if you're banging my girlfriend's mother?"

"Kila is not your girlfriend," Silas said. "Stop thinking that she is, Gage."

Gage just shrugged and for a moment Silas wanted to try and smack some sense into his younger brother. "Gage, if the queen knows that you've got a thing for Kila she'll use it against you. Don't you get that? You can't let her - "

"Boys! What do you think of the party?" Lloyd approached them. He was carrying a boy of about three and he placed an affectionate kiss on the boy's cheek. "This here is one of my boys, Lloyd Junior."

"Lloyd Junior?" Gage said.

"Well, his mama actually named him Rardin but what the hell kind of name is that?" Lloyd said with a laugh. He kissed the boy's cheek again and the little boy stared solemnly at him for a moment before bursting into tears.

Lloyd winced and awkwardly jiggled him before patting him on the back. "Don't cry, little man."

A woman appeared and held her hands out for Rardin. Lloyd handed him over and the woman smiled briefly at him before disappearing into the crowd with the crying boy.

"He don't know me real well," Lloyd said. "What do you think of the party?"

A woman stopped next to them with a tray full of glasses of wine. He grabbed one and winked at her. She blushed and glowed before staring at Silas. Her glow brightened and Lloyd held up his hand to block the light before laughing and drinking the wine in one large gulp.

"What I tell you? You're real popular, Silas."

"A glass of wine, danen?" The woman said shyly.

"Thank you," Silas said. He took a glass and smiled at her. The light beamed out of her and another woman laughed before taking the woman's arm and leading her away.

"So, what do you think? These gals sure know how to throw a party, don't they?" Lloyd said.

"Yes," Gage replied. He was staring at Kila again and Lloyd nudged him.

"You hoping the princess will pick you for her first time?"

Gage just shrugged and Lloyd grinned. "She's a pretty little thing. I'm hoping she'll pick me sooner or later. Probably will. I ain't much of a looker but the ladies love me because I'm just so damn good in bed."

He pumped his hips, laughing again when a few of the women around them glowed brightly. Silas rolled his eyes as a young woman stopped in front of them. She was light purple in colour and she had small sharp fangs. There was no doubt that she was an offspring of Vida and he smiled politely at her when she looked him up and down.

"Hello, danen."

"Hello," he said.

"Tonight is my first claiming ceremony," she announced. "I'm going to bid on you. I would enjoy having you between my thighs."

She walked away before Silas could reply.

"If she wins you'd better treat her right," Lloyd said. "Otherwise the big blue smurf will have your head on a pole."

"Who my daughter chooses to breed with is no business of mine."

Vida stood next to Silas and stared silently at Lloyd. Lloyd flushed a little. "Hey, just because your kind doesn't care about your kids doesn't mean the rest of us don't. I'm gonna go grab another glass of wine and something to eat. The games are starting soon."

He ambled away as Silas nodded to Vida. "How are you?"

"Tired," Vida said. "The queen was very demanding last night."

Silas gave him a sympathetic look and Vida shrugged. "You will find out soon enough."

"Vida?" A blonde-haired woman holding the hand of a blue-skinned boy tapped hesitantly on his broad back.

"Hello, Asina," Vida said politely.

"I have brought Broden to say hello to his father," she said.

Vida crouched and smiled at the boy. "Hello, Broden."

The boy - he looked to be about seven - hid his face in his mother's leg. She squeezed his shoulder. "Say hello to your father, Broden."

"Hello, father," the boy mumbled.

"You are looking well," Vida said. "Are you obeying your mother and doing well in your studies?"

The boy nodded and Asina gave Vida a proud smile. "He is very clever, Vida. He is at the top of his class."

"Well done, Broden," Vida said.

There was a moment of awkward silence and then Asina smiled again at Vida. "It was good to see you again, Vida. I will be bidding on you this evening."

Vida stood. "I hope you win, Asina."

"As do I," she said. She looked over his broad body and glowed before stroking Broden's hair again. "Come, my son. We will have something to eat before the games begin."

"Yes, mama," Broden said.

They walked away and Gage gave Vida a curious look. "Do you spend much time with your children, Vida?"

Vida shook his head as regret crossed his face. "Not as much as I'd like." He paused as another troubled look flickered over his features. "In my world, there is a ritual that must be performed between a father and their offspring. If it is not performed within a few days of birth the child will not bond with the father no matter how much time they spend together."

"What kind of ritual?" Silas asked.

"The father and the child exchange takenas," Vida said.

"What are takenas?" Gage asked.

"You do not have them on your world?" Vida said.

"I don't think so," Gage replied.

"Takenas are not an object but more of a," he paused, "living essence within us. Our young are born with their takena already bonded to their mother's. It happens in the womb. But a father, no matter how much he might love his child, has no hope of his child's love unless he bonds his takena with the child's during the ritual."

"They wouldn't let you do the ritual," Silas said.

Vida shook his head. "I asked repeatedly with every baby but the queen refused to allow it. The massina went to the queen on my behalf and tried to convince her but she still refused. The babbling idiot is wrong. I love my children very much but they will never love me. It is impossible for them to do so."

He stared moodily across the crowd. "If they had allowed me to perform the ritual with even one of my children, there would be a reason for me to stay. But they have not and now my children will never see me as anything more than a stranger."

"I'm sorry, Vida," Silas said. He couldn't imagine having a child who wouldn't love him no matter what he did.

Vida grunted in reply before pointing toward the foot of the castle where the women were beginning to congregate. "The games are beginning."

Two of the queen's guards approached them. "It's time, breeders. Follow us."

∂≈ ≪

Her stomach in knots, Quinn scanned the breeders. Silas was standing next to Vida at the back of the group. He smiled briefly at her and she scowled before looking away. She turned to the queen who was sitting in a lavishly-decorated chair beside her.

"Are you ready to begin, my Queen."

"Aye, massina."

Quinn whistled piercingly. The large crowd quieted and stared expectantly at her. "Welcome to the claiming ceremony, my friends."

There was a loud cheer and Quinn waited patiently for them to quiet again. When they were quiet she said, "The games will begin. Those of you who wish to participate in this month's claiming ceremony have given your choice of breeder to Zeeda and she has paired you against another to fight."

Quinn studied the crowd. "You know the rules. You must fight whoever Zeeda has paired you against. If you win you will move up in the rankings. As always, you may ask another to fight on your behalf."

The crowd cheered again and Quinn held up her hands. "Before we begin the claiming ceremony let us give thanks to our queen for her kindness in sharing her food and drink with us this evening."

"Thank you, my Queen!" The crowd shouted.

The queen waved her hand at them before crooking her finger at Quinn. Quinn bent and the queen whispered into her ear. For the briefest of moments Quinn's hands clenched into tight fists before she straightened and smiled at the crowd.

"Our queen has chosen a breeder for this month's claiming ceremony."

The crowd cheered as Quinn walked toward the group of men. Her stomach was churning and her hands were ice cold but she kept a look of vague disinterest on her face as she stopped in front of Silas.

"Come with me, danen," she said.

A look of anger and frustration crossed his face but he followed her toward the queen. There were loud groans of disappointment and a flurry of movement as the women who bid on him hurried to Zeeda to amend their choice.

"Your breeder, my Queen," Quinn said. She pushed on Silas' shoulder and he kneeled in front of the queen.

"Such a handsome danen," the queen said happily. "Sit at my feet, breeder."

Silas sat stiffly on the ground at the queen's feet. Her hand stroked and tugged his thick hair. When she pulled sharply he lifted his head obediently.

"Are you looking forward to fucking me tonight, danen?"

"Yes, my Queen," he said woodenly.

"I am looking forward to it as well," the queen said. "Although I doubt your cock is as big as Vida's so you will have to work hard to impress me. Do you understand?"

"Yes, my Queen," Silas repeated.

The queen laughed before glancing at Quinn. "Massina, do you think the breeder will be as good at fucking as Vida?"

"I wouldn't know, my Queen," Quinn said.

"No, I suppose you wouldn't," the queen replied. "You would never lower yourself to fuck a breeder, would you?"

Before Quinn could reply, Zeeda waved at her and Quinn shouted, "Are you ready, my sisters?"

There were loud cheers from the crowd and

Zeeda clapped her hands irritably before scanning the paper in front of her. "The first fight is for the breeder Lutan!"

The women screamed with delight as Lutan stepped into the middle of the courtyard and waved before stripping off his shirt. There was a pulse of light as nearly all the women glowed brightly. Lutan winked and flexed his arms before Quinn pointed her sword at him and motioned for him to return to the other men.

"There are six who wish to claim him," Zeeda shouted. "Yolan, come forward!"

A small woman with red hair and freckled skin slipped out of the crowd. She crossed her arms nervously as Zeeda scanned the paper again. "Yolan will fight Belda!"

There were groans of disappointment and a few shouts that it wasn't fair. Zeeda glared at the crowd. "I draw the names randomly. You know that!"

Wearing her battle outfit, Belda grinned fiercely at Yolan. "Are you ready, Yolan?"

Yolan shook her head before staring at the crowd in desperation. "Fionn! Will you fight for me?"

Fionn ran into the courtyard as the women cheered. "Aye, Yolan. I will."

Belda laughed as another woman handed wooden swords to her and to Fionn. "You will not defeat me, Fionn. It has been months since I've had a man between my thighs and my dry spell ends tonight."

"We'll see about that," Fionn replied before

lifting her sword.

The crowd quieted and stared at Quinn. She studied the two women in the middle of the courtroom before shouting, "Begin!"

Quinn watched as the two women fought. She was feeling jittery and angry and her gaze fell repeatedly to Silas sitting at the queen's feet. She was resting her hand on the top of his head like he was a dog and Quinn's stomach twisted. She knew the queen would choose Silas so why was she so bitterly disappointed?

There was a loud cheer from the crowd and her head snapped up. Belda had knocked Fionn's wooden sword from her hand. With an excited shout, she shoved Fionn to the ground and pressed the blunt end of her wooden sword against Fionn's throat.

"Do you yield, Fionn?"

"Aye," Fionn said in disgust. Belda laughed and stepped back as Fionn climbed to her feet.

"I'm sorry, Yolan," Fionn said.

"That's all right," Yolan replied with obvious disappointment. "Thank you for trying, Fionn. You did better than I would have."

Lutan was standing at the edge of the crowd and Belda ran up to him and grabbed his ass. She squeezed it tightly as she glowed and Lutan grinned at her as Zeeda pushed her away.

"You still have others to fight," she reminded Belda. She scanned her paper before calling two more names. "Darra and Fina, come forward and fight for the breeder Lutan!"

Two women slipped out of the crowd. They

were two of the castle staff and Quinn watched as they both picked up wooden swords and held them clumsily. Quinn stared at the queen's hand again, idly picturing herself chopping it off at the wrist, and jerked when Zeeda called her name. She stared at the old woman who frowned at her. She realized that Darra and Fina were waiting patiently in the middle of the circle of women and she cleared her throat.

"Begin!"

The two women began to fight, their swords smacking against each other with hollow thuds. Quinn studied Silas' hands. They were clenched in tight fists. When he took a quick glance at her she immediately looked away. The crowd roared happily. Darra had already knocked the sword from Fina and she pointed it hesitantly at her.

"Do you yield, Fina?"

Fina lunged for her fallen sword and Darra kicked it out of the way before smacking Fina on the back with the broad side of the sword.

"Ow, Darra! That hurt!" Fina said.

"Do you yield?" Darra repeated. She jabbed Fina in the butt with the sword and Fina yelped before rubbing her ass.

"Yes, I yield."

Darra screamed excitedly and the crowd screamed back as Fina stalked away. Zeeda herded Darra to Belda and the two stood at the front of the crowd as the old woman called, "Denia and Pelza come forward!"

Quinn sighed. It was another gross mismatch. Pelza worked in the nursery and Denia was one of her best warriors. She waited for Pelza to ask for someone to fight for her and blinked in surprise when Pelza picked up the wooden sword and held it unsteadily in front of her.

Denia gave her a curious look. "Will you not ask another to fight for you, Pelza?"

Pelza shook her head. "No, Denia. I have been practicing."

"Have you now?" Denia said with a small grin. "Then let us begin."

They both glanced at Quinn who shouted, "Begin!"

She flinched when Denia immediately knocked Pelza's sword from her hand. The warrior allowed Pelza to pick it up again and even gave her the opportunity to take a couple of swings at her before she knocked the sword away for a second time. She gave Pelza a playful poke in the stomach with the tip of it. "Do you yield?"

Pelza scowled at her and glanced at her fallen sword before her body slumped. "Aye, I yield."

She started to walk away and Denia pulled her into a friendly hug. "You did well, Pelza. Keep practicing and some day you can join the queen's guard."

"Do you think so, Denia?" Pelza said.

"I do," Denia said. "Come see me tomorrow and we will practice together. If, that is, I'm not too tired from fucking the breeder."

Pelza smiled happily at her before disappearing into the crowd. Zeeda cleared her throat. "Belda and Denia will fight and Darra will fight the winner. Are you ready?"

Belda ran out and picked up Pelza's sword. "Aye, I'm ready."

"Denia?" Zeeda said.

Denia nodded and raised her sword. The two warriors grinned at each other as the crowd quieted.

"Begin," Quinn said.

With a shout of excitement Denia rushed Belda. Their swords clashed repeatedly as they circled each other, lunging and jabbing as the women screamed and shouted encouragement.

Quinn smiled at Kila when the young woman slipped out of the crowd and stood next to her. "Have you put in your bids, sandora?"

"Aye, I have, massina," Kila said. Her gaze drifted to Gage and Quinn elbowed her in the side.

"Tonight is a very special night," the queen said. "My child becomes a woman."

She pulled hard on Silas' hair, twisting his head until he was facing Kila. "Are you sure this breeder is not to your liking, my child?"

"I'm sure, mother," Kila replied.

"Perhaps it is for the best," the queen replied. "Taking a danen's cock as your first may not be wise."

Kila blushed and the queen laughed. "You will lose your innocence soon enough, Kila. I will let you know how this danen is in bed and whether he's worth bidding on at the next claiming ceremony."

She stroked Silas' hair affectionately. Quinn gritted her teeth and forced her gaze to the women fighting. Belda was tiring and she tripped and fell when Denia feinted to her right before moving left and slamming her sword down on her arm. Belda

grunted in pain as her sword fell from her hand.
She reached for it and screeched when Denia
shoved her facedown onto the ground and planted
one foot on her back.

"Do you yield, Belda?"

Belda squirmed violently and Denia put more of
her weight down. "Do you yield?"

"Aye! I yield! Get off me, for garna's sake!"
Belda retorted.

Denia released her and held out her hand. After
a moment Belda took it and allowed the woman to
help her up. "You fought well, Belda."

"Thanks, Denia," Belda said glumly. She gave
Lutan one last look of longing before joining the
other women in the crowd.

"Darra, are you ready?" Zeeda said.

Looking pale and more than a little nervous,
Darra stood next to Denia and grasped the sword
she handed to her.

"Will you choose another to fight for you,
Darra?" Zeeda asked as Darra gave Denia an
anxious look.

Denia gave her a predator's grin and Darra
paled further before scanning the crowd. Her gaze
fell on Quinn and she shouted, "Massina, will you
fight for me?"

The crowd bellowed laughter and Darra flushed
bright red. Denia patted her on the shoulder. "You
should have chosen another, Darra. The massina is
injured and will not fight on your - "

She was interrupted by Quinn's low voice.
"Aye, Darra. I will fight for you."

The crowd gasped in surprise as Quinn stepped

forward. She took the sword from Darra and nodded to Denia.

Denia frowned at her. "Massina, you are injured."

"I am fine," Quinn said. "Begin."

Denia hesitated. "Massina, I - "

Quinn raised the wooden sword and Denia instinctively did the same. "Are you certain, massina?"

"Aye, I am. Begin," Quinn said again.

Denia shrugged and attacked.

## Chapter Fifteen

Silas shifted uncomfortably. The fighting for the breeders had been going on for hours and his ass was sore and his back hurt from sitting on the hard ground. He glanced at Quinn and snorted to himself. He was whining about his back being sore when she had to be in excruciating pain.

As if she heard his thoughts, she shifted herself and a grimace of pain crossed her face. Her hand reached behind to touch her back before she caught herself and dropped it back to her side. She took a few deep breaths before her face cleared and she watched as the two women fought.

The crowd had thinned out a bit. The women with babies and children left first, followed by those who were too young or too old to participate in the claiming ceremony. There was a shriek of happiness as one of the women fighting lost her grip on her sword and it fell to the ground. Panting heavily, Kila tapped her on the shoulder with her sword and the woman nodded wearily before trudging off into the darkness.

The torches were low and with some of the women gone darkness had crowded in on them. Silas searched for Gage in the gloom. His was the last claiming fight and the last two left to claim him were Kila and Akia.

Kila had bid on Steve as well as another breeder whose name he didn't know. Silas wondered if he was the only one who suspected that Kila deliberately lost her previous fights. He guessed that Quinn knew, at least the tightening of her mouth had indicated she did. Of course, that could also be pain and weariness. He studied her again, noting the lines of pain at the corners of her eyes and the way she continually shifted her weight from one foot to the other. She had fought in nearly every claiming fight tonight. After the first woman called on her to fight and she agreed, many more asked her to fight on their behalf. She accepted each one. If the crowd's reaction was any indication that was extremely rare.

He couldn't understand why she kept agreeing to fight. Vida was very popular and over twenty women bid on him. Quinn fought on the behalf of another three women alone in the claiming for Vida. She'd only had a brief rest before Dora asked her to fight in the claiming for Evan. It was obvious that she was in pain and her last fight she had nearly been defeated. But it was only her pain and weariness that allowed Barkha to almost defeat her. He was sure of it. He was completely fascinated with watching Quinn fight. Her skills and her abilities were unmatched by everyone else.

*Fascination? Is that all it is? Watching Quinn*

*fight makes you so horny you can barely think straight. Admit it, Silas.*

Fine. He could admit that watching Quinn fight was a huge turn-on for him. He had no idea why but the contrast between the Quinn who commanded the queen's army and the Quinn who submitted so sweetly to him in bed made him ache to have her again. Not that it would do him much good. He'd be in that bitch of a queen's bed tonight and if he couldn't get an erection she'd probably lop off his head.

*So think about Quinn when you're in the queen's bed. It's the only way you'll get through the night.*

That was probably true but he didn't think there was any way in hell he could pretend the queen was Quinn.

*If you don't, you're a dead man.*

"Last fight of the night!" Zeeda shouted. The smaller crowd cheered, although there was a hint of apathy to it. Silas watched as Kila bit at her bottom lip nervously when Akia stepped into the light. Kila was good but Akia was better. Just watching the two of them in the claiming ceremony had made that more than obvious.

Kila glanced at Gage. He gave her an anxious look and she bit at her bottom lip again before staring at her mother.

"You've done well, child," the queen said. "But you still have one fight remaining if you wish to lose your innocence tonight."

"Are you ready, princess?" Akia asked.

"I…" Kila trailed off, staring hesitantly into the

crowd before her desperate gaze fell on Quinn.

"Massina, will you fight for me?" She almost whispered the words and Silas and everyone else turned to stare at Quinn.

Quinn nodded and walked slowly toward Kila and Akia. "Aye, Kila, I will."

Kila gave her a grateful look. "Thank you, massina."

"You're welcome, sweet sandora," Quinn said. She smiled at Kila but little lines of fatigue were apparent on her face.

"I'm sorry," Kila murmured.

"Do not be," Quinn said. She squeezed Kila's shoulder affectionately before smiling stiffly at Akia.

"Are you ready, Akia?"

"Aye, I am, massina," Akia said. She grinned smugly as Quinn took the wooden sword from Kila.

"Go on, sandora."

Kila joined her mother. The queen gave her a look of disapproval. "You ask the massina to fight for you?"

"I cannot defeat Akia," Kila said.

"Because you are weak," the queen replied.

Kila flushed bright red and her mother scowled at her. "If I see you show such weakness again in front of my people I will have you punished. Do you understand?"

"Yes, mother," Kila said.

The queen took her wrist in a tight grip and squeezed. "We can not afford to show weakness, Kila. Ever. I will forgive you for it this time because I know of your desire to lose your innocence. Fail me again and I will not be so forgiving. Do you hear me?"

"Yes," Kila said before ripping her arm loose of her mother's grip. Her face still red and her eyes shiny with unshed tears, she stared resolutely ahead as her mother studied her with a cold look.

"Good. Now let us see if the massina can win one more fight."

"She will," Kila said.

"She has fought many tonight and she does not hide her pain as well as she thinks," the queen said. "I don't know what has come over her tonight. She is acting very oddly. Wouldn't you agree, Kila?"

"The massina enjoys fighting," Kila said.

"Aye, she does," the queen replied. "Fighting but not fucking. Sometimes I wonder if her brains are addled."

Kila didn't reply and the queen clapped her hands before smiling at Akia and Quinn. "The night grows long and my people are tired. Begin your fight!"

Silas tried not to flinch when Akia and Quinn clashed swords. He leaned forward, watching anxiously as the two women circled around each other. Despite her exhaustion it was quickly apparent that Quinn was better than Akia. They fought for long moments, their swords banging against each other as the crowd watched with bated breath. Silas frowned as Akia danced away. It was obvious the woman was using Quinn's fatigue against her and drawing out the fight for as long as she could. When Quinn stumbled and fell, Kila made a sharp noise of worry. Sweat pouring down her face, Quinn quickly rolled away from Akia's sword and stood. Before she could turn to face her opponent, Akia slammed the flat edge of her sword against Quinn's back. Quinn's shriek of pain was drowned out by the cries of outrage from the crowd. Shouts of 'cheater' and 'unfair' were thrown into the cold air and Akia gave the crowd a dirty look as Quinn staggered away. She was panting harshly, her arms and legs shaking wildly, and there was no colour at all in her face.

"Mother," Kila said. "Akia is cheating and does not deserve to - "

"Taking advantage of an opponent's weakness is not cheating," her mother interrupted. She stood and glared at the still booing and hissing crowd. "Hold your tongues!"

They quieted down as Quinn glanced quickly at him. Silas tried to give her an encouraging smile. Truthfully, he believed there was no way Quinn would win this fight. She was too weak and in too much pain.

Quinn turned to face Akia. Her chest heaved as she gulped in air and Akia smiled at her. "Do you yield, massina?"

"I do not," Quinn said. She raised her sword. "Begin again, Akia."

Silas squinted at Gage. His younger brother was standing still with his hands clenched into tight fists. His gaze flicked back and forth between the fighting women and Kila. His eyes widened and Silas turned back to the fight just in time to see Quinn charge at Akia. The women cheered as Quinn swung and slashed her sword at Akia in a frenzy of controlled elegance. Akia was the one sweating now. Her cheeks were red with exertion and she did her best to defend against Quinn's assault. It was pointless. A switch seemed to have been thrown in Quinn and she fought like a mad woman, swinging her sword so quickly it was just a blur of movement.

There was a shout of pain from Akia as Quinn slipped past her blade and slashed her wrist with her own sword. The wooden swords were blunt and no blood flowed but Akia dropped her own sword as a bright red blotch appeared on her skin. Quinn kicked her legs out from under her before dropping on top of the smaller woman and pinning her to the ground. She pressed the end of her sword against Akia's throat.

"Do you yield, Akia?"

"Never!" Akia hissed at her. "Get off me, massina, before I - "

Silas flinched when Quinn punched her in the face. Blood flowed from Akia's lip and she screamed in pain and outrage when Quinn punched her again.

"Yield, Akia, or I swear I'll break your jaw," Quinn snarled before punching her for a third time.

Akia's head rocked back, slamming against the ground, and she gave Quinn a dazed look.

"Yield!" Quinn shouted and slapped Akia viciously across the face.

Blood trickled from Akia's nose and she whispered, "I – I yield."

Kila screamed triumphantly as Quinn heaved her body off of Akia's. She dropped her sword and walked stiffly to Kila. Kila threw herself at Quinn and wrapped her arms around her. Quinn winced and Kila gave her a stricken look. "Massina, I'm sorry."

"It's fine, sandora," Quinn said. She touched Kila's hair with a trembling hand. "Enjoy your evening with the breeder."

"Thank you, Quinn," Kila whispered before squeezing her hand.

"Kneel before me, massina," the queen demanded.

Quinn dropped to her knees in front of the queen. She was very close to Silas and he wanted to touch her but he kept his hands folded in his lap. He stared at the ground as Naveen slipped out of the crowd and joined them.

"You have done well, massina," the queen said.

"Thank you, my Queen," Quinn replied.

"You fought so bravely for so many this evening and yet you will not receive your reward." She leaned forward and placed her fingers under Quinn's chin, tipping her head up until Quinn's gaze met hers.

"Is there really no one you wish to claim, massina?" The queen said.

Quinn's gaze flickered to his face. It was nothing more than a fleeting glance before she was staring at the queen again but a cruel smile crossed the queen's face.

"You want the danen," she said.

"I do not," Quinn replied. "Please, my Queen. It has been a long day and I am very tired. If you will excuse me, I would - "

"Do not lie to me, massina," the queen said as her fingers tightened on Quinn's face. "You desire to have the danen for yourself."

She glanced at Silas before dropping her hand from Quinn's face and rising gracefully to her feet. "My sisters, your massina has fought well this evening. Has she not?"

"Aye, my Queen!" The crowd shouted.

The queen turned her cold gaze to Silas and he shuddered inwardly at the cruelty that shone from them. "She deserves her just rewards for fighting. Does she not?"

"Aye, my Queen!"

"She will have it," the queen said. "The massina will take the danen for the month. He will warm her bed and perhaps she will find herself with child. A child who will grow to be as strong and courageous as her mother."

The crowd cheered as Silas stared wide-eyed at Quinn. She refused to look at him and kept her gaze on the ground as the queen placed her hands on each of their heads. "Am I not a kind and generous queen, my sisters?"

"Aye, my Queen!"

"Quinn, do you agree?" The queen asked.

"I do. Thank you, my Queen, for your generosity," Quinn said through clenched teeth.

The queen laughed before patting both their heads. "Go. Get out of my sight, the both of you."

Not completely sure what was happening, Silas stumbled to his feet as Naveen helped Quinn to stand. She shook off his hand and without looking at either of them started toward the castle.

"Come, danen," Naveen said in a low voice. He gripped Silas' arm and the two of them followed Quinn through the crowd. The women were grinning at Quinn and reaching out to squeeze her arms as she pushed through them. She ignored all of them and Silas breathed a sigh of relief when they were finally free of the women and walking down the dark street. The castle loomed ahead of them and he nudged Naveen.

"Has that ever happened before?"

"Never," Naveen muttered. "The queen takes what she wants when she wants it. I don't know why she – massina!"

Ahead of them, Quinn was weaving unsteadily. As she crumpled to the ground Silas rushed forward and caught her. She cried out and he winced before shifting his arm away from her back.

"I'm sorry, honey."

Her eyes rolled up in her head and she went limp in his arms.

"Naveen!" Silas shouted.

Naveen was already holding Quinn's wrist and he pressed his other hand against her forehead. "She has passed out from the pain. Can you carry her, danen?"

Silas nodded and carefully cradled Quinn in his arms. She moaned in pain and he pressed a kiss against her smooth cheek.

"Quickly, danen," Naveen said.

Silas was surprised when instead of leading them to the breeders' quarters Naveen took a sharp right. They hurried toward the small stone building to the right of the castle and he followed the old man into the home. Naveen quickly lit the candles on the wall using flame from his fingers before hurrying Silas through the house.

"Naveen, aren't we supposed to go to the breeders' quarters?" Silas asked as Naveen opened a door.

"No. The queen and the princess take their breeders in the castle and the massina takes hers at her home."

"How many breeders has Quinn taken?" Silas asked as he placed Quinn on her stomach on the bed.

"None before this night," Naveen said. He unhooked the leather bustier Quinn was wearing and eased it from her body.

"Fuck," Silas muttered under his breath.

"It's getting better," Naveen said as he probed at the bruised flesh.

"Bullshit."

"It is," Naveen replied. He pulled a cloth bag from somewhere deep in the folds of his cloak and opened it. It was filled with a grey-coloured salve that he rubbed into Quinn's skin.

"What is that?" Silas asked as he sat on the bed beside Quinn.

"It's the same mixture that was in the poultices," Naveen said. He finished spreading it across Quinn's back before placing the bag on the floor beside the bed. He stood and gave Silas a cautious look.

"What?"

"If I leave, I am trusting that you will not harm the massina while she is unable to defend herself,"

Naveen said.

Silas scowled at him. "You know I won't hurt her, Naveen."

"Aye," Naveen said as he leaned over Quinn. He shook her shoulder before slapping her lightly on the cheeks. "Massina, open your eyes."

Quinn groaned and Silas squeezed her hip as her eyelids fluttered open. She gave Naveen a blurry, confused look. "Naveen? Where am I?"

"You are home, massina," Naveen said. "You fainted from the pain."

Quinn's eyes widened and she struggled to sit up. "In front of her?"

"No, massina," Naveen said as he pressed her back onto the bed. "There was no one but the danen and me when you fainted."

"Garna," Quinn said. She twisted her head to stare at Silas.

He gave her a small smile. "Hey."

"What have I done?" She whispered. She gave Naveen a look of panic. "Naveen, what have I done? She'll use this against me, you know she will! I have to return him to her. I can't – I can't keep him."

"Whoa, slow down," Silas said. "I'm not a dog you can just return. Besides, I'm not going to the queen. She said you could have me for the month, remember?"

"Naveen," Quinn was clutching the old man's arm, "why the fuck did she do this?"

"I don't know, massina," Naveen said gravely, "but you need your rest. Take this."

He produced a packet of the yellow powder and

Quinn opened her mouth obediently. He poured it onto her tongue before reaching for the wooden cup of water on the nightstand beside the bed.

"Drink, massina."

She drank and made a face as she swallowed the powder. She gripped Naveen's arm when he stood. "Where are you going?"

"The danen will stay with you tonight, massina," Naveen said. "Send him over if you need me."

Silas waited for Quinn to argue but she simply nodded and closed her eyes. "I'm so tired, Naveen."

"I know, massina," Naveen said. "Sleep. The danen will keep you safe."

"Will he?" Quinn mumbled.

"Yes," Silas said before pressing a kiss against her shoulder. "Sleep, Quinn."

He followed Naveen down the narrow hallway to the front door. Naveen handed him another packet of powder. "Give this to her if she wakes in the night."

"I will," Silas replied.

Naveen hesitated. "Danen, I know the purpose of the breeders is for fucking but the massina is injured. She is in no shape to - "

"I'm not going to try and fuck her while she's unconscious for God's sake," Silas snapped. "Jesus, Naveen, what kind of guy do you think I am? I know she needs sleep and to heal."

Naveen regarded him silently for a moment. "Good night, danen. Come get me if Quinn needs me in the night."

"I will," Silas said. "Good night, Naveen."

He closed the door behind Naveen and returned to the bedroom. Quinn's breathing was slow and even and he removed her boots before sliding her skirt down over her hips. He stripped off his clothes and climbed into the bed beside her.

He rubbed the back of her neck, frowning when she tried to shift to her side to face him. She groaned in pain and he pressed on her neck. "Stay still, honey."

"I want to sleep on my side," she mumbled sleepily.

He helped her turn to face him. He was stupidly happy when she snuggled up against him and he stroked the strands of hair that had loosened from her braid. She rested her head against his chest and he kneaded the back of her neck again.

"Good night, Silas," she whispered.

"Good night, honey." He pressed a kiss against her forehead before blowing out the candle.

## Chapter Sixteen

"Danen, move your arm."

Silas squinted at Naveen in the early morning light. He was lying on his back in Quinn's bed with Quinn sprawled across him.

"Move your arm," Naveen repeated patiently.

Silas lowered his arm. It had been resting against Quinn's lower back and he strained to see around Quinn's head. If he made the bruising worse he would never forgive himself.

"Did I hurt her?" He asked.

"No," Naveen said absently. He had the grey salve out again and Silas wrinkled his nose against the smell.

"Did she wake in the night?"

"Yes. I gave her more of the powder."

"Good."

As the old man rubbed the salve into Quinn's back, Silas stroked her hair back from her face. Her nose crinkled and she frowned before blinking sleepily at him. Naveen dipped his hand back into the bag of salve as Quinn smiled at Silas.

"Silas," she sighed before pressing her mouth against his thick neck. She licked him and his hips twitched helplessly. She giggled – God, a sleepy, mostly-drugged Quinn was adorable – before kissing him. Her tongue stroked across his lips and she traced her fingers down his ribs.

"Kiss me, Silas," she said as she reached for his rapidly-hardening cock.

He caught her hand. "We're not alone."

"What?" Despite the pain and being drugged, she was sitting up in an instant. He had a quick glimpse of her full, firm breasts before she whirled around. Her arms caught Naveen in the chest and knocked him to the floor. He muttered a curse and Quinn groaned in pain before sliding out of the bed.

"Naveen! I'm so sorry."

"It's fine, massina," Naveen said as she helped him to stand.

She winced, her hand touching her lower back delicately. Silas sat up as Naveen said, "Get back into bed."

She nodded and turned to climb back into bed. She raised her arms, instinctively covering her naked breasts when she saw Silas sitting in her bed.

"Wh-what are you doing in my bed, danen?" She asked in confusion as pain clouded her eyes.

"The queen gave the danen to you last night, massina," Naveen said. "Do you not remember?"

Quinn closed her eyes. "Aye, I remember now. I think."

"It's the drug. It makes you slow-witted," Naveen said. "Lie down so I can finish putting the salve on your back."

With a cautious look at Silas, Quinn slid into the bed and lay on her stomach. She flinched a little when Silas gathered her long dark hair in one hand and held it out of the way so Naveen could rub the salve into her upper back.

"Did we fuck last night?" She suddenly asked.

Naveen laughed. "If you cannot remember, then the danen has much to learn."

Silas gave him a mock scowl and Naveen grinned as he smoothed the salve over the bruising.

"Did we, danen?" Quinn asked.

"I'm not in the habit of having sex with unconscious women," Silas said dryly.

Her body relaxed a little and he leaned over so he could stare at her. "Did you really think I would do that, Quinn?"

She shook her head. "No, I just," she glanced at Naveen, "never mind."

"What's your pain level on a scale of one to ten?" Silas asked.

Naveen was giving him an odd look but Quinn said, "Five."

"Can she have more powder?" Silas said to Naveen.

He nodded and finished smoothing the salve into Quinn's lower back. "Aye."

"I don't need it," Quinn said.

"Don't be stubborn," Silas said.

"My senses can't be dulled around her," Quinn said to Naveen. "You know that."

"Aye, I do," he said gravely. "But you are to remain in your home today."

Quinn started to protest and Naveen frowned at

her. "Be quiet, massina. I am the kalan, not you, and you are to stay in bed. You set back your healing by participating in the claiming ceremony last night. Why did you do that?"

Quinn just shrugged and Silas stroked her hair. "You shouldn't have fought so much, Quinn."

"If I hadn't you would not be here with me," she said.

"Point taken," Silas replied.

"Open, massina," Naveen said. He poured more of the powder into Quinn's mouth. She chased it down with a glass of water before burying her face in her pillow.

"Stay in bed," Naveen said. "I will come by at noon to check on you and bring you something to eat."

"I can keep an eye on her," Silas said.

"Afraid not," Naveen said. "You need to return to the breeders' quarters for breakfast and then work. I believe you're on pit cleaning duty today."

"Shit," Silas muttered.

"Yes," Naveen said with a grin.

"He isn't," Quinn's voice was muffled and both Naveen and Silas leaned closer.

"What did you say, massina?" Naveen asked.

Quinn raised her head. "He isn't on pit cleaning duty. I had Belda switch him yesterday morning."

Silas leaned over her again and gave her a loud and wet kiss on the forehead. "Thank you. I owe you big time."

Her lips curved up in a rare smile. "You're welcome, danen. Although considering it's my bed you're sleeping in tonight it's benefiting me just as much."

He pressed a quick kiss against her lips before whispering in her ear, "I like sleeping in your bed."

He nipped her earlobe then slid out of bed and dressed. Naveen squeezed Quinn's shoulder. "Get some rest. I'll be back later."

ન્જ જ્ન

He had barely stepped into the common room when Lloyd appeared beside him and clapped him on the back. "Silas! You fucking lucky bastard! Come sit beside me at breakfast and give me all the details about fuckin' the massina."

"No," Silas said shortly.

He walked away from Lloyd as the man gave him a disappointed look and followed him toward the long tables. "C'mon now, don't be shy. Give us the details. What are her tits like? Did she keep you chained up while you were fucking?"

Lloyd nudged Steve as he sat next to him. "I could see the massina keeping him chained. She likes control, that one."

Silas ignored him completely. Kyle was sitting across from him and he tapped him on the arm. "Okay, Kyle?"

Kyle nodded. "Yeah, it was fine, man."

"You sure?"

He nodded again. "I'm sure. My girl was nice and it wasn't as," he paused, "awkward as I thought it would be. We, uh, talked for a while before."

"Aw, you talked. Ain't that sweet," Lloyd said before grabbing a hunk of pork. "Did you rub her feet and braid her hair?"

"Shut up, Lloyd," Steve said.

"How was it with Dora?" Lloyd asked Evan. "You have trouble gettin' your willy to work when you could see her face?"

"No," Evan said coolly. "Dora's sweet."

Lloyd rolled his eyes as Silas searched the long tables. "Where's Gage?"

"Still with the princess," Lloyd replied. "Probably takin' a while to break her in. Christ, I don't know if he's the luckiest or unluckiest guy in the whole damn place. Sure, he gets to be the first fuck for the princess and dollars to donuts her cunt is as tight as a - "

A large blue hand fell on his shoulder. Lloyd winced when it squeezed. "Jesus, Vida let up."

"I think it would be best if you sat at another table this morning, my friend," Vida said in a low voice.

Lloyd stared at the others. They were all giving him looks of disgust and he shook off Vida's hand before standing. "Fine. I don't need to be around a bunch of pantywets like you anyway."

He stuffed a final piece of pork in his mouth before sauntering to the other table. Vida sat down and studied Silas. Silas returned his look unblinkingly until Vida nodded to him and helped himself to some food.

❧ ❧

Silas muttered a curse and pulled off his leather glove. His thumb was bleeding and he sucked away the blood as he tossed the weed into the wooden bucket beside him. This world's weeds seemed to have an inordinate amount of thorns but weeding the garden was still better than cleaning out a pit of human shit.

He looked up as there were a few catcalls from the other men weeding. Gage was being led into the garden by a guard. He was handed a bucket and a pair of gloves. He took both before following the narrow path between the carrots and a yellow plant that gave off a cilantro-like smell to where Silas was standing.

Lutan was weeding a few feet away and he grinned at Gage. "Enjoy your time with the princess, Gage?"

Gage just waved at him before pulling on his gloves and squatting next to Silas. "Hey, Silas."

"Hi, Gage."

They pulled weeds for a few moments before Gage said in a low voice, "Is Quinn okay?"

Silas nodded. "Her back is pretty beat up but Naveen is giving her pain meds. She's resting today."

"Good."

"How did it go last night?" Silas asked a bit awkwardly.

Gage blushed slightly. "It was good. Really good." He paused in pulling out a weed. "I tried to be, uh, gentle."

"I don't need details," Silas said with a small grin.

"Right, sorry," Gage replied. "I really like her, Silas."

"I know you do."

"Did you and Quinn uh…"

Silas frowned at him. "Of course we didn't. She's

injured, Gage."

"Yeah, I know. I also know how much you like her," Gage replied before pulling a weed.

"Why weren't you at breakfast this morning?"

"The queen made me have breakfast with her and Kila."

"How was it?"

"Truthfully? Terrifying," Gage said. "That woman is a psychopathic bitch."

"Keep your voice down," Silas said with a glance at the guard standing at the end of the row.

Gage shrugged. "Kila told me that everyone hates her mother. I think even Kila hates her. I know she's afraid of her."

"Really?" Silas asked.

Gage nodded. "She won't admit it but she is. She loves Quinn though. She says everyone does, with the exception of Akia. Kila says that Akia hates her because she wants to be the massina."

"Why?"

Gage shrugged again. "The power I guess. Personally, I think she's nuts. The less you have to do with the queen the better."

"Sleeping with the princess isn't exactly having less to do with the queen."

"I didn't have a choice," Gage said. "Kila won me at the claiming ceremony, remember?"

"I remember," Silas said.

"It's fucking weird, isn't it? To be just handed over to a woman without any say in the matter?"

Silas nodded. "Yeah, it is."

"Oh well. At least I got to be with Kila," Gage said.

"For a month," Silas replied. "Don't forget that it's

only for a month, Gage."

A dark look crossed Gage's face. "I haven't. But Kila has already said that she'll bid on me again."

"Is that smart?" Silas asked. "You don't want to draw the queen's attention."

Gage sighed. "I want to be with her, Silas."

"I know you do but this world isn't like ours. We have to follow their rules. If this queen is as fucked up as everyone says she is, you'll want to fly under her radar. I know you like Kila but you have to be smart, Gage. You need to be prepared that you can't date Kila. At least not like you would have in our world. You can't - "

"I know, Silas," Gage said irritably. "Give it a rest, would you? At least let me enjoy my month with Kila, okay?"

"I just want to keep you safe," Silas said.

"I know and I appreciate it," Gage replied. "But I'm not a little kid anymore. I can take care of myself."

"I don't think you're a little kid but your feelings for Kila are clouding your judgement. It's dangerous to – "

"I *know*," Gage retorted. He stood and stepped over the row of carrots before moving further down to weed.

Silas gave him a troubled look as the guard standing at the end of the row said, "Danen, continue weeding or I'll send you to the pit to clean."

Silas sighed and bent back to the weeds.

ॐ ॐ

Quinn nibbled at some cheese before pushing

aside the piece of pork on her plate. After years of pork being the main meat source, she was more than a little tired of it. She stood and paced nervously in the small kitchen of her home. Silas would be finished his dinner with the other breeders soon and then one of the guards would bring him to her.

Her stomach twisted and she abruptly threw the rest of her dinner into the garbage. He wouldn't like what she had to say but she had to do it. She couldn't let him stay with her, simple as that. Tomorrow she would speak to the queen. She would thank her for her generous offer but make it clear that she had no interest in Silas. She had no choice.

*Not fair! He's ours! She gave him to us.*

She shook her head in disgust. It had taken nearly a decade but she was finally starting to think like the other women in this world – like men were nothing more than objects for them to use. Shame and self-loathing permeated her body. Silas didn't belong to her. He was a human being with his own wants and needs and not her toy to play with for the month.

*He wants to play with you.*

A little shiver of lust went through her. Yes, he did, and she wanted to play with him. Garna, did she want to play with him. But it was too dangerous. The queen would use him against her if she thought Quinn had feelings for him. She needed to prevent that.

*It's too late. You saw the look on her face last night.*

Quinn cursed and slammed her fist on the table.

It sent a vibration of pain through her back and she winced. Her back was actually feeling much better than it did even this morning. She suspected it was a combination of the salve and the drugs that Naveen kept plying her with.

She should never have participated in the claiming ceremony fights. But seeing Silas sitting at the queen's feet and knowing that he would be fucking her made her angry. Fighting was a way to work off that anger and so, like an idiot, she had thrown herself into the fights. She rubbed her lower back. Both Barkha and Akia nearly defeated her. It was only luck that allowed her to beat Barkha. As for Akia – her intense dislike of the woman and her desire to win for Kila was what made her final push to win so effective. If Akia had taken Gage it would have crushed Kila.

She lit the candles in the kitchen and built up the fire. It was going to be a cold night and the stone houses were drafty. Her mind nagged and worried at her as she did the simple tasks. She should have had better control last night. What was she thinking even looking at Silas? She wasn't, that was the problem. Tired and in so much pain she could hardly think straight, her glance at Silas had been completely involuntary.

*Was it, though? You were insane with jealousy over the thought of Silas being with the queen. Admit it.*

There was a knock on her door and she froze as her stomach twisted with nerves and anticipation. Her heart thudding in her ears, she walked down the narrow hallway and opened the door. Kila stood on her doorstep and Quinn smiled weakly at her.

"Sandora, what are you doing here?"

"I wanted to check on you. I'm sorry, I should have come by earlier but I was," Kila's cheeks turned a delicate shade of rose, "resting for most of the day."

She stepped into the house and hesitated only briefly before giving Quinn a gentle hug. "How is your back?"

"Better." Quinn led her into the kitchen. "Are you hungry?"

"No. I ate with mother. I can't stay long. They'll be bringing Gage to me soon and the danen to you," Kila said as she sat at the small wooden table.

Quinn joined her and reached for Kila's hand. "How are you feeling?"

"Good," Kila said. "A little sore but Gage was very sweet and gentle when we fucked last night."

She suddenly grinned at Quinn. "Mother went on and on about not having a large cock for my first time so I decided not to tell her that Gage's was very large."

Quinn smiled inwardly. The women on this world were incredibly open about their sex lives. It wasn't uncommon to overhear them comparing notes on the different breeders and suggesting tips on how to help a breeder improve his lovemaking skills.

"I'm glad you enjoyed yourself, sandora."

"I did," Kila said enthusiastically. "Fucking is so much fun, Quinn. I mean, I assumed it was based on what the other women said but it's so much better than I ever imagined."

She squeezed Quinn's hand. "Gage ate my pussy twice last night. His tongue was so soft!"

Quinn laughed as Kila glowed so brightly the kitchen was washed in light. "Sorry, massina."

"For what?"

"I probably shouldn't share such intimate details with you but I didn't want to speak to the other women about it. I know it doesn't sound like it but I feel like what happened with Gage is special and not their business."

Quinn smiled at her. "You can share whatever you'd like, sweet sandora. I am not easily embarrassed."

"Tonight I'm going to try sucking Gage's cock. I wanted to last night but he said he wanted to make it all about me last night," Kila said. "Isn't that sweet?"

"Very," Quinn said.

"I was so nervous," Kila confessed. "But Gage said we could stop at any time and that we didn't even have to fuck last night if I didn't want to. Wasn't that kind?"

"Yes," Quinn said. Her opinion of Silas' brother was growing by the minute.

"I decided to just go for it and I'm so glad I did," Kila said happily. "It didn't really hurt that much the first time and, garna, each time after that was better and better. I finally truly understand why the women go on and on about it and are so excited when they win a breeder."

She hesitated before smiling at Quinn. "I'm so glad that mother gave you the danen for the month."

The smile dropped from Quinn's face and Kila gave her an alarmed look. "Massina? What's wrong?"

"Nothing," Quinn said abruptly.

There was another knock on her door and Kila stood. "That will be the danen."

Quinn followed her down the hallway and stood back as Kila opened it and smiled at Silas. "Hello, danen."

"Hello, Kila. How are you?"

"Good. I was just leaving." Kila kissed Quinn on the cheek. "Good night, massina."

"Good night, sandora," Quinn said.

Kila followed the guard into the dark night. Silas closed the door and locked it. "How are you feeling?"

"Better."

"Are you sure?"

"Yes." Quinn paused awkwardly before turning and walking to the kitchen. Silas followed her and she poured herself some steaming liquid from a clay kettle. "Would you like a drink?"

"Sure."

She poured him one and they sat at the table as Silas sipped cautiously at it. "It tastes a bit like tea."

She didn't reply and he smiled at her. "Tea is a warm drink in my world. It's brewed from leaves."

She just nodded and took her own sip. "Danen, we need to talk."

"All right."

"Tomorrow morning I'm going to tell the queen that I appreciate her generous offer but I do not want you for the month."

Hurt flashed across his face. "Why?"

"The reason is not important," she said.

"I think it is."

"It isn't. Just know that it would be very dangerous for you to spend the month with me."

"You're going to have to give me more of an explanation than that," he said.

"No, I don't," she retorted. "Why I do what I do is none of your business."

"It is when it affects me," he replied. "If you give me back," he said the words with a hint of disgust, "the queen will take me for herself. Right?"

Bile rose in her throat but she nodded.

"Which means that then I'll have to fuck her, right?"

She didn't respond and he leaned closer. "Am I right, Quinn?"

"Yes, you're right," she said angrily.

"What happens if I won't?"

Anxiety crept into her stomach. "You have no choice."

"Of course I do."

"No, you don't," she said. "Silas, when the queen takes you to her bed you have to fuck her. I'm sorry but you have no choice."

He shrugged and said again, "What happens if I don't?"

"She'll kill you!" Quinn shouted. She forced herself to take a deep breath. "If she doesn't outright kill you, she'll hurt you until you wish you were dead. You have to have sex with her, Silas."

"I don't want to," he said.

She gave him a look of frustration. "It doesn't matter what you want in this world. Don't you understand that by now?"

"I get it," he said, "but it doesn't mean I have to do what the queen wants."

"That's exactly what it means!"

"Do you remember the night of the testing, Quinn?" Silas asked suddenly.

"Yes."

"Then you remember that I didn't get an erection until after I knew it was you in the room with me."

"So?"

"So, apparently, I can't get an erection unless it's you I'm with," Silas said almost cheerfully.

Her mouth dropped open. "You can't be serious."

"Totally serious," he said. "I don't know why and I'd be lying if I said it wasn't a little alarming but it's the truth."

"Silas," she said desperately, "you need to get over this."

He laughed and she clenched her hands in frustration. "This isn't funny."

"I know it isn't," he said. "You think I like being this obsessed with you? I'm on a different world, I've lost everything except for my brother and I can't stop thinking about you. I'm all sorts of fucked up."

"You're not obsessed with me," she said.

"I kind of am," he replied. "Just like you're weirdly obsessed with me."

"No, I'm not."

"Liar," he said with a grin. "Fucking me is all you can think about. Admit it, Quinn."

"No."

He laughed again. "Chicken. My point is – you can hand me back to the queen like I'm a pet you've lost interest in, but if you do, you're basically signing my death warrant. I won't get a stiffy with that bitch."

"You – you can think about me," she said desperately. "Just close your eyes and pretend it's me."

"Tried that the night of the testing. Didn't work," he said.

"Try harder," she hissed.

"It won't work," he said with maddening patience. "Trust me, Quinn."

She slammed her mug on the table and the liquid splattered across the top of it. "Danen, you can't stay with me!"

He didn't reply and she stood and paced the kitchen. "If the queen thinks you mean something to me she'll use it against the both of us. I can't let that happen."

"It's too late," Silas said, "and you know that. I saw the look on her face when you looked at me."

"It isn't," Quinn said. "I can convince her it was a moment of madness and nothing more."

"You can't," Silas replied. "The damage is done, Quinn."

She sagged against the wall in defeat. Silas was right. The damage was done and it was entirely her fault.

Silas stood and hurried over to her. "Quinn, are you okay?"

"No," she whispered. "I'm not okay at all."

He pulled her into his embrace, pressing her head against his broad chest and rubbing just below her back. "We have a month to be together. That's a good thing."

"When the month is over?" She asked dully. "What then?"

"We'll figure it out," he said. "For now, let's just enjoy our time together."

She raised her head and stared silently at him. It wasn't his fault that he truly didn't understand how dangerous the queen was, but she was too tired to keep arguing. Besides, he was right. Giving him back to the queen tomorrow would do nothing to convince the woman that Quinn didn't want him. She had made a mistake in never sleeping with a breeder, she realized that now. She should have done the opposite – she should have slept with as many as possible so that the queen believed she felt nothing for anyone. By choosing Silas after so many years of denying herself a breeder she caused the problem with the queen.

"I'm sorry, danen," she whispered.

"Don't be," he said. "I want to be with you, Quinn. Even if we only have a month."

He leaned down and kissed her. She put her arms around his broad shoulders and returned his kiss, moaning when his tongue touched hers. Unlike his previous kisses which had been overshadowed with a sense of urgency, this one was delightfully slow. He took his time, tasting and licking her mouth before sucking on her lower lip.

She pressed her pussy against him, rubbing against his erection and ignoring the brief flare of pain in her back. She was wearing a loose cotton shirt and a pair of pants and he squeezed her ass before cupping her right breast through her shirt.

She moaned again before pressing a kiss against the line of his jaw. She could see lines of dirt in the creases in his neck and he smelled strongly of the earth and the crops he'd been weeding.

"Silas, wait," she whispered.

He groaned but dropped his hand and took a step back. "I'm sorry. I know your back needs to heal."

"No, it isn't that," she said. "You're dirty and you kind of smell."

He laughed before glancing at his big body. "I asked them to let me bathe before supper but they said I could bathe in the morning."

He rolled his eyes. "The bathing schedule for the breeders makes no sense."

"Most of the women don't care about the way the breeders smell," Quinn said. "Unless they've been cleaning the pit."

He made a face and she smiled briefly before holding out her hand. "Come with me."

He took her hand and she led him down the hallway and past her bedroom. She opened the door to the bathroom and he made a grunt of appreciation at the sight of the large metal tub. "This is nice."

One of the first changes she made when she first became massina was to have her own tub installed in the bathroom. The previous massina had continued to bathe with the other women in the mornings and Quinn knew the women found it odd when she added the tub. It required some work to dig a drain through the dark earth but it was totally worth it in her opinion. The communal bathing that the other women enjoyed never appealed to her.

"If you'd like to use the tub, you can," she said. "You'll just have to haul water to heat first."

He nodded immediately. "That would be great."

As she slipped past him into the hallway, he said, "God, what I wouldn't give to have a shower."

She laughed as she walked away. "Sorry, danen. No running water means no shower."

Her back was to him and she didn't notice the way he twitched in surprise or the thoughtful look he gave her.

"Are you coming, danen?" She called over her shoulder.

He nodded and hurried after her.

ल ल

Silas groaned in pleasure as he sank into the hot water. Quinn was standing in the bathroom and he smiled at her. "Join me."

She hesitated and he moved back in the tub. "It's big enough for both of us and the warm water will help your back."

She bit at her bottom lip before winding her long dark braid around her head and pinning it in place. She slid her pants down her legs. She wasn't wearing panties and he stared appreciatively at the dark curls at the apex of her thighs as she stripped off her shirt. She climbed carefully into the tub and sat down. He used his hands to cup water and poured it over her shoulders and back. He tugged on her arms until she was leaning back against him.

"Does that hurt your back?"

She shook her head and he reclined against the back of the tub. They sat silently in the steaming water for a little while before she reached for the soap. He took it from her and lathered his hands before running them over the top of her shoulders and down her arms. Her back arched a little when he cupped her breasts with his soapy hands. He pulled on her nipples and she moaned. He kissed her cheek before washing her flat abdomen. When his hand disappeared into the water she widened her thighs. He made a low chuckle. She flushed but couldn't stop her hips from rising when he slid his hand between her thighs. He cleaned her gently and she scowled in frustration when he moved on to washing her thighs.

She lathered her own hands with soap and washed his thighs before turning to face him. She washed his chest and shoulders then unbuckled the collar around his neck and tossed it on the floor.

"Thanks," he said.

She cleaned his thick neck before running her hands over his six pack. "You have an amazing body, danen."

"So do you," he said.

He closed his eyes and his own hips arched when she gripped his cock. He was already hard and she cleaned him quickly but couldn't resist rubbing her thumb over the head of his dick. He groaned and arched his hips again, forcing water over the side of the tub and onto the floor.

"Danen," she whispered.

"Yeah?"

"Let's go to bed."

He hesitated and she gave him an impatient look. "What?"

"You probably need more time to heal," he said.

She stood and he stared at her naked, gleaming body in the candlelight.

"Will you deny me what I want, Silas?" She asked.

He shook his head before leaning forward and pressing a kiss against her dark curls. She shivered with pleasure before carefully climbing out of the tub. He followed and they dried each other's body with slow, measured strokes before she took his hand and led him to her bedroom.

She laid down on the bed, trying not to wince as the pressure sent waves of pain over her body. He frowned and lay on his back beside her. "Straddle me, Quinn."

She didn't want to. She wanted the feel of his hard body on hers, pinning her down and holding her captive. Just thinking about being trapped under him made her pussy wet. She resisted when he tried to tug her into a sitting position.

"It's fine, danen," she said.

"It isn't," he replied. "Straddle me now."

His tone sent her scurrying to obey him as more wetness coated her. When she was sitting on him, he reached up and cupped her breasts. She made a soft noise of excitement when he pinched her nipples and he grinned at her. "Lean down."

She did as he asked, crying out when he sucked on her right nipple. It was beaded into a hard, throbbing point and her body jerked uncontrollably when he nipped it. She ignored the pain in her back as he soothed the sting of his bite with slow licks. He moved to her left nipple, giving it the same treatment until she was whispering his name.

He cupped the back of her neck and guided her mouth to his. As they kissed she stroked his broad chest and rubbed her pussy against the hard length of his cock. The head bumped against her clit and sent shivers of pleasure up and down her legs. She ground herself against him. Shamefully, she was already close to coming and she moaned in disappointment when his hands cupped her hips and forced her still.

"You don't get to come yet, Quinn," Silas said.

"I need to," she replied before trying to wiggle out of his grip.

His fingers bit into her flesh, giving pain and pleasure. "Not until I say you can."

A little thrill of excitement went through her. God, she loved the way he took control.

"Put my cock in your pussy," he suddenly demanded.

She rose up on her knees, grasping the base of his cock and guiding it toward her entrance. The blunt head speared her and sent tingles of pleasure down her spine. She was wet but it was still a tight fit. She rocked against him, trying to force her body to take more. Her inner walls stretched to accommodate the invasion but she still had to stop short of a couple of inches.

"All of it," he said.

"I can't," she panted.

"All of my cock or I won't fuck you, Quinn."

She scowled at him and he pinched her nipple hard. "Be a good girl."

She rocked again, bracing her hands against his chest as he said, "You've taken all of it before."

"I *know*," she said grumpily.

He made a low chuckle. She squealed in a decidedly undignified manner when his rough fingers grazed her clit. "Do you need some help?"

"Yes," she moaned.

"Yes, what?"

"Yes, please."

He stroked her clit firmly. It brought on a surge of wetness and she made a happy little moan when she took the last of his cock.

"That's my good girl."

She shivered all over at the approval in his voice as he raised his knees.

"Lean back," Silas demanded.

She did what he asked, resting her hands on his knees and using them for leverage to raise her body up and down. She ignored the few twinges of pain in her back.

Silas cupped her thighs and thrust upward. It sent a surge of pleasure through her body and she cried out. He grinned up at her before using one hand to caress her nipples. She moved a little faster. He stopped the motion of his hips and watched as she bounced on his cock. She moved her hand to her swollen clit and he shook his head before taking her wrist in a tight grip and holding it at her side.

"No."

She scowled at him and tried to touch herself with her left hand. He laughed and took that wrist, pinning it down easily. Her lust skyrocketed the moment he restrained her and she moaned.

"I said no, Quinn." Silas said.

She gave him a pleading look and he squeezed her wrists. "Your pussy and your orgasms belong to me. I decide when you get to come."

His words brought on another almost painful throb of lust through her lower body as well as a feeling of relief. She wholeheartedly embraced the loss of control as Silas said, "Put your hands on my shoulders and don't move them."

She leaned over him and clutched at his shoulders as he cupped her ass and fucked her hard and rough. She couldn't come this way, there wasn't enough pressure on her clit, but she welcomed that too. Knowing she could do nothing as Silas used her body for his own pleasure sent an almost embarrassing wave of excitement through her.

She closed her eyes and lost herself in the sensation of Silas' hard body beneath hers and the hard rhythm of his driving cock. His warm breath panted in her ear and the low groans of his pleasure fed her desire. She dug her nails into his shoulders as he drove in and out. Her sensitive nipples rubbed against his coarse chest hair and she squeezed his narrow hips with her firm thighs.

His hand snaked between their bodies and he

rubbed at her clit. She cried out as her entire body arched and her orgasm rushed through her. She climaxed all over his thick cock, her pussy squeezing him in a tight grip. He moaned and made two more hard thrusts before warmth flooded through her. She collapsed against him and he stroked her ass as their breathing slowed.

Silas pressed a kiss against her throat. "Did I hurt your back?"

Her back was aching but she shook her head. "No."

"Lie on your stomach," Silas said.

She moved gingerly off his body and tried not to wince. He frowned and studied her back in the candlelight before reaching for the salve on her nightstand. "Hold still, honey."

He rubbed the salve into her bruised back. When he was finished, he blew out the candle and settled on his side next to her. He stroked the back of her neck. "I shouldn't have been so rough."

"I liked it." Her voice was muffled by the pillow.

"I did too," he admitted, "but I should have been gentler."

"I'm not a fragile little doll," she said.

He laughed. "Yeah, I know."

She eased to her side to face him. He stroked her face and kissed her. "Are you tired?"

"A little."

They faced each other silently for a few minutes. She ran her hand across his chest and he cupped her ass and pulled her closer against him.

"What world are you from?" He asked

suddenly.

"This one," she lied.

"You're not."

"I am."

"The women from this world glow. You don't glow," he pointed out.

"They only glow when they're horny," she said.

He laughed. "You're telling me you weren't turned on just now?"

"Not enough," she said. She waited for his look of hurt but he just laughed and kissed the top of her breasts.

"If this is you only slightly turned on I can't wait to see what it's like when you're really horny."

She blushed as he rubbed her ass and said, "Your pussy was like a damn vice around my dick. Especially when I held you down and wouldn't let you come."

"Go to sleep, danen," she said. Embarrassment was starting to creep in.

"Why are you embarrassed by that?"

"I'm not."

"You are, I can hear it in your voice," he said.

Alarm threaded through her. She had known Silas for less than three weeks. There was no way he should be able to read her emotions that well.

"Tell me why it embarrasses you to give up control in bed," he said.

She sighed. "I'm not embarrassed by it. More worried I guess."

"Why?"

"I command the queen's army, danen. The women look to me when there is danger and when they're uncertain. If they knew that I enjoy letting you take control they would lose their confidence in me."

He considered her words for a moment before shaking his head. "I don't think so, Quinn. I know I haven't been here very long but it's more than obvious that the women here respect you. Just because you're submissive in bed doesn't say anything about your ability to lead them."

She didn't reply and he pressed a kiss against her forehead. "Is this why you haven't slept with any of the breeders? You don't want them knowing you're submissive?"

"No. I wouldn't have shown them my – my submissive side if I had slept with them."

He stroked her arm. "Why did you let me see it?"

She didn't know how to answer that, mostly because she didn't really know why. After a moment he squeezed her arm. "I'm not the kind of guy who kisses and tells, Quinn. Okay?"

She made a low laugh. "I know you're not, danen, but thank you for saying it."

"So is the queen the main reason you haven't slept with any breeders?"

"Yes."

"Do you like being massina?"

"Yes."

"So you like protecting a woman that you hate?"

She hesitated. "It is my duty to protect the queen."

"You didn't have a choice in becoming massina, did you?"

"The former massina failed and the queen appointed me as the new one. It was an honour to be chosen," Quinn replied.

She decided it wouldn't be wise to tell Silas that she didn't give a rat's fuck about the honour. Becoming massina had been an integral part of her plan for revenge.

"So for the last decade you've been saving the queen's ass?"

"Yes."

"Is the queen batshit crazy?"

"Yes."

"Is Naveen gay?"

"Yes."

"Are you from my world?"

"No."

He paused and Quinn poked him in the chest. "I am from this world, Silas."

"You don't glow."

She sighed. "Who cares whether I glow or not? You turn me on and we both know it. Not every woman from this world glows. All right?"

"How many times have you nearly died?" He asked suddenly.

"Many," she replied shortly. "I'm tired and my back is hurting. Are you finished with your questioning, danen?"

"Yes. I'm sorry, Quinn."

She turned away from him and gingerly wiggled back until her back was resting against his chest. He put his arm around her and cupped her breast. "Does it hurt your back to lie this way?"

"No," she said. "Your body heat feels good on

it."

She wasn't lying. The stone houses were sturdy but cold and it felt good to have Silas' warmth in her bed. She waited for the guilt about having another man in her bed and was a little surprised when there wasn't any.

*It's been over ten years. There's nothing to feel guilty about. Kevin is dead and he's never coming back.*

She shuddered all over and Silas pulled her closer before kissing the back of her neck. "Good night, Quinn."

"Good night, Silas."

## Chapter Seventeen

"How is the danen in bed?"

Quinn set down her spoon and smiled politely at the queen. "He is adequate, my Queen."

"Adequate?" The queen raised her eyebrow. "Does he have a large cock?"

"Large enough, my Queen."

The queen scowled at her. "I would think after all these years alone, massina, you would have more to say about a breeder in your bed."

Quinn didn't reply and the queen gave her an irritated look. "Perhaps I will take the breeder back if you do not find him pleasing."

"Your gift of the breeder was very kind, my Queen, and I am grateful," Quinn replied. "However, I am more than happy to return him to you if that is what you wish."

The queen studied her for a moment before smiling bitterly. "Aye, I'm sure you would, massina."

Quinn returned the queen's gaze unblinkingly as she clenched her hands into fists beneath the table.

She willed herself not to look away or show any emotion on her face. After a long tense moment, the queen turned to Kila.

"Are you enjoying your time with your breeder?"

"Yes, mother," Kila replied.

"Does he please you in bed?"

"Yes, mother."

The queen waited and when Kila didn't elaborate, she snorted angrily. "Akia, since neither the massina nor my daughter are in a talkative mood today perhaps you will keep me company after lunch."

"It would be an honour, my Queen," Akia said before smiling smugly at Quinn.

Quinn could barely stop from rolling her eyes. The queen had summoned the three of them to join her for lunch and Akia was the only one genuinely happy to be in the queen's presence. As Akia smiled at the queen, Quinn forced herself to eat another spoonful of soup. Akia wanted to be massina and had been trying for years to win the queen's favour. No doubt she considered the invitation to keep the queen's company this afternoon as a sign that she was making progress. She had yet to learn that the queen would use her in whatever way she wanted.

"Come, Akia. I have lost my appetite," the queen said abruptly.

She stood and left the room with Akia at her heels. Quinn set down her spoon and rubbed at her forehead as Kila let her breath out in a shuddering sigh.

"Are you okay, massina?" She asked anxiously.

"Yes, sandora," Quinn replied.

Kila glanced at the open doorway. "Mother keeps hounding me for details of sleeping with Gage. I refuse to share them and she's growing angrier each time."

She stared into the half-eaten bowl of soup in front of her. "She's already made a few comments about sleeping with Gage once she is finished with the danen."

Quinn groaned inwardly as Kila said, "What is wrong with her, Quinn? What kind of mother would even want to fuck the man that her daughter has fucked?"

"Sandora, your mother is…complicated," Quinn replied.

"She's crazy," Kila said. "Most of my life I have tried to convince myself that she was normal but she isn't."

She glanced at the doorway again before lowering her voice. "She hardly sleeps anymore, Quinn. Last night she was lurking outside of my bedroom door while I was with Gage."

"Are you certain of that?" Quinn asked with a frown.

"Aye," Kila replied. "I went to get us some wine after we finished fucking and I startled her in the hallway. It isn't the first time I've found her wandering the halls of the castle in the middle of the night."

Kila pushed away her bowl of soup. "I will not allow her to fuck Gage, Quinn. He is mine."

"Kila," Quinn said in alarm, "the breeders are

shared. You know that."

The young woman stood and shook her head. "I don't care. I'm not sharing Gage. If she wishes to challenge me at the next claiming ceremony for him, she can. But if she tries to just take him for her own she'll be sorry."

"Sandora, do not - "

"I have to go," Kila interrupted. "Mina had her baby last night and it was a boy. I haven't seen him yet."

She left the room and Quinn, anxiety growing in her belly, followed her.

ঔ ঌ

"Move it a little to the left," Silas said. "Perfect. Hold it steady, Belthor."

He leaned over the shelving unit and pounded three nails into the wood before straightening. "Okay, that should do it. Let's pick it up."

Belthor nodded and the two men lifted the shelving unit. They pushed it up against the wall as Zeeda gave Silas an admiring look.

"You are very good at this, danen."

Silas just shrugged as Belthor scratched absentmindedly at his ass. He and Belthor were brought to the large stone building just after breakfast. Belthor told him it was a store of sorts. The traders brought their goods here and haggled with Zeeda over the grinding of their grain. He studied the large room they were standing in. It was filled with bolts of fabric and piles of fur. They had passed two other rooms on their way to this one and he had taken a quick peek into them. One had large barrels lined up in neat rows on the floor. Belthor had told him they were filled with salted fish the women caught in the river. The second had rows of shelving with hundreds of jars filled with strange coloured salves and liquids. When he had questioned Belthor about that room, the man shrugged and told him they were medicines.

"It's so straight," Zeeda said as she ran her hand over the shelves.

The other shelves in the room were all poorly built and Silas eyed them thoughtfully. "We could probably fix these other shelves. Straighten them out so it's easier to put your fabric and furs on them."

"Aye, I imagine you could. You're very good with your hands," Zeeda said before running her hands over his broad chest. A soft glow emanated from her and Silas hid his grin. Zeeda had to be pushing seventy and she was maybe four feet tall.

"Zeeda." Quinn's low voice made Zeeda snatch her hands away from his chest and she turned and gave Quinn a guilty look.

"Hello, massina. I was just speaking with the breeders. What can I do for you?"

"I'm in need of a small, soft fur. Mina's baby was born last night and he is on the small side. He requires extra warmth."

"Of course," Zeeda said hurriedly. "Let me find the perfect one."

She moved deeper into the room, searching the shelves as Silas smiled at Quinn. "Good afternoon, massina."

She gave him a cool look of disdain before

studying Belthor. "Barkha tells me she caught you trying to escape by climbing the wall the day before yesterday."

Belthor paled and took a step back, bumping up against the newly-built shelving unit. "I, no, massina."

Quinn stepped closer. "You call Barkha a liar, Belthor?"

"No, no, of course not," Belthor stammered. "I meant that I was not trying to escape."

Silas watched in utter fascination as Quinn drifted closer and the blood drained from Belthor's face. He was a few inches shorter than Quinn but he was solidly built and heavily muscled. It didn't seem to matter. He was obviously afraid of the woman standing in front of him and he cleared his throat nervously when Quinn studied him coldly.

"Do I need to remind you what happens to the breeders who try to escape, Belthor?"

"N-no, massina," Belthor said. "I wasn't trying to escape, I swear it."

"Breeders are forbidden to go beyond the wall. You have been here long enough to know that," Quinn said as she glanced behind her at the doorway.

"Aye, I know. I was only planning on going to the river, massina."

"For what, Belthor?"

He swallowed heavily. "There is a plant that grows at the water's edge. The muskina plant. It's used for - "

"I know of it," Quinn said. "What I don't know is why you are in need of a plant that is used to smooth a woman's skin."

"It has other uses, massina," Belthor said hurriedly. "It heals other, uh, ailments."

"What ailment do you have?" Quinn asked.

"I," Belthor glanced at Silas before mumbling, "I have a rash, massina."

"From what?"

"I accidentally, um, brushed up against some pinacker plants."

"Why did you not go to Naveen?" Quinn asked before glancing at the doorway again. To Silas it appeared like she was biding her time, waiting for something or someone to walk through the door.

"I was embarrassed," Belthor admitted.

"Show me the rash," Quinn said.

"I'd rather not, massina."

Quinn folded her arms across her chest and stared at Belthor. He flushed and cleared his throat again. "It is, uh, in an embarrassing spot."

"Show me, Belthor." Quinn said.

He sighed and turned around. He dropped his pants and Silas was unable to stop himself from saying, "Holy mother of God."

Belthor's ass and the back of his thighs were covered in large red bumps. His skin was bright red and irritated looking and a few of the bumps were bleeding.

"How long have you had the rash?" Quinn asked.

"Over a week, massina," Belthor said as he pulled up his pants and buttoned them.

"When you're finished here you are to go directly to Naveen. He will give you some muskina salve. Do you understand?"

"Yes, massina," Belthor said.

"In the future, Belthor, I would advise that you watch where you're sitting and do not wait such a foolishly long time when you require medical treatment."

"Yes, massina."

Quinn's gaze flickered to Silas and he gave her a flirty little grin. "You look lovely today, massina."

"Hold your tongue, danen," she said icily. Belthor was watching them and she raised her eyebrow at him. "Is there something else you wish to say, Belthor?"

"No, massina," he said.

"Good. Both of you get back to work," Quinn replied.

She walked away and Belthor said in a low voice, "I know you're sharing the massina's bed but you should not speak to her unless she speaks to you first."

"Why?" Silas asked.

"You just shouldn't," Belthor said. "Trust me."

"Why are you afraid of her?"

"I'm not afraid of her," Belthor said.

"Could have fooled me," Silas said as Zeeda returned and hurried to Quinn with several furs in hand.

"I'm not," Belthor repeated.

"Is she cruel to the breeders?" Silas asked.

"Of course not," Belthor replied. "But angering her wouldn't be wise. You might be big but she's strong and quick for a woman. You have only seen her fight in the claiming ceremony and that's nothing compared to when she's actually fighting. She - "

"I've seen her fight," Silas said absently. A man had entered the room. He was short with a big belly and he was dressed entirely in furs. Silas could smell him from where he was standing across the room. "Who's that?"

Belthor shrugged. "One of the traders. Help me put the fabric on the shelf."

Silas bent and picked up a pile of fabric from the floor as he continued to watch Quinn. She had chosen a small fur and she smiled her thanks at Zeeda before moving toward the door. She nodded cordially to the trader. Silas frowned when the man slipped her a piece of paper as she passed him. She hid it beneath the fur she was holding and left the room without speaking to the trader or Zeeda.

ช∘ ๑

"I am troubled as of late, Akia."

"What troubles you, my Queen?" Akia leaned forward in the chair and stared intently at the queen.

They were sitting in the common room next to the fireplace and the queen stared at the flickering flames for a moment. "The massina hides something from me."

Akia didn't reply but a flickering flame of excitement lit in her belly. The queen studied her. "Can I trust you, Akia?"

"Aye, my Queen. With your life."

"There is no need to put my life in your hands, Akia. Although I know how capable you are. You crave the position of massina, do you not?"

"I want to protect my Queen in whatever way I can," Akia replied.

The queen laughed. "Quinn is my fiercest warrior. She can best you even when she is injured and tired."

Akia flushed. "Being the best warrior does not mean she is the best massina, my Queen."

"Does it not? You think you would be better?"

"I do," Akia said.

"Why?"

"Quinn is too soft-hearted."

"Some would call it being fair," the queen replied.

Akia snorted with derision. "A soft-hearted massina is a massina who cannot do her job. You need a warrior who keeps her people in line."

"Your sisters respect Quinn," the queen said. "They have no quarrel with her."

"Aye, they do respect her," Akia said. "There are some who say she is more respected than even you."

"Is that what they say?" The queen snarled at her. She withdrew a dagger from the folds of her skirt and examined it in the light of the fire. "They respect the massina more than their queen?"

Akia chewed at her bottom lip nervously. "I do not respect her, my Queen."

"That is obvious," the queen snapped. "But you sit here and tell me that my people show the massina more respect than they do me. Did you expect that to please me?"

"No, my Queen," Akia said. "But my respect

for you demands me to be truthful. Quinn has wormed her way into the hearts of your people and I do not believe that is a good thing."

"Nor do I," the queen replied. "I need a favour of you, Akia."

"Anything, my Queen," Akia said.

"I want you to watch the massina carefully over the next few weeks. You will report to me on a daily basis of her activities."

"Yes, my Queen," Akia said.

The queen turned to stare at her and Akia's blood ran cold at the look in her eyes. "If she discovers you are watching her, Akia, I will cut your eyes from your head and feed them to the pigs."

"She won't."

"Make sure she does not," the queen said. "I grow tired. Leave me."

She turned her gaze back to the fire as Akia stood and bowed. "Thank you, my Queen."

❧ ❧

"You did a good job on the shelves in the trading store today," Quinn said as Silas joined her in her bedroom. He had just finished bathing and hadn't bothered to get dressed. She stared at his naked body and tried valiantly not to drool.

"Didn't think you had noticed," he grunted. He was grumpy and quiet when Fionn brought him to her home after dinner. When Quinn suggested he bathe, he heated the water in silence and didn't ask her to join him in the tub.

She sighed. "Tell me what's wrong, danen."

"Silas," he said. "I have a name, okay?"

"Tell me what's wrong, Silas."

"You mean besides the fact that you were kind of a dick to me earlier?"

She stood and walked to where he was standing in the middle of the bedroom with his arms folded across his chest. "Da – Silas, I cannot show you any affection in public."

"I get that but what about common courtesy?"

She tugged on his arms until he dropped them and then pressed a soft kiss against his chest. "It's better if the others think I dislike you."

She sucked on one flat nipple and he inhaled sharply as he cupped the back of her head. She had unbraided her hair and he threaded his fingers through the long dark strands as she licked his collarbone. "I will not be nice to you in public, Silas, nor will I apologize for my actions. It's the way it has to be. I am, however, willing to make it up to you now."

"What did you have in mind?" He asked.

She smiled at him. "Whatever you want."

An unmistakeable look of lust flickered across his face. "Take off your shirt."

She immediately swept her nightshirt over her head and dropped it to the floor. She was naked beneath it. Silas gave her a long appreciative look that made her nerve endings tingle.

He reached out and traced her bottom lip with his thumb before pushing it between her lips. She sucked at his thumb as his left hand cupped her breast and he rubbed her hard nipple.

"On your knees," he said as he pulled his thumb

free of her mouth.

She knelt on the floor in front of him. His cock had hardened and he stroked it with one large hand as his other curled into her hair.

"Hands on your thighs, Quinn. If you move them, I'll spank you. Understand?" Silas said.

She nodded as a hard rush of excitement went through her. The thought of being spanked by Silas drenched her pussy. She pressed her legs together and ignored the brief flare of pain in her back.

"Quinn," Silas said.

She quickly placed her hands on her thighs and stared up at him. He cupped the back of her skull and drew her toward him. He traced her lips with the head of his cock. "Suck."

She took his cock into her mouth with eager abandonment. She sucked hard, flicking her tongue against the sensitive ridge as he moaned.

"That's right, honey. Keep sucking," he groaned as he pushed her hair out of her face. He gripped it tightly before curving his hand under her chin. "Keep your mouth wide open, honey."

He held her head in a firm grip and pumped his hips back and forth. She kept her hands on her thighs and her eyes on his face as he forced her to take more of his cock with every thrust.

"Wider," he said. "You can take more of my cock in your hot little mouth, Quinn."

She opened wider for him, her eyes watering as he pushed his hard length down her throat.

"Fuck!" He whispered before retreating and pushing again.

She sucked firmly, swirling his tongue around

his thick shaft as he pushed in and out. She gulped in air when he retreated and sucked with renewed vigor when he returned. His hand tightened in her hair and the slightly salty taste of his precum coated the back of her throat.

He muttered another curse and pulled out of her mouth. He wiped away the saliva and the precum coating her mouth before yanking her to her feet. He hurried her over to the bed and she balked at the side of it.

"Silas, my back."

"I know," he grunted. "Get on your hands and knees, Quinn."

She dropped to her hands and knees, gasping when Silas shoved her thighs apart and clamped his hands around her hips. He dragged her back to the edge of the bed and pushed again at her thighs until she was spread wide open.

"Such a pretty pussy," he muttered.

She cried out when he shoved his cock deep into her aching warmth. He pushed steadily and she tried to ease away from the invasion.

"No," he growled. He leaned forward, being careful not to touch her back, and cupped her throat. He held her immobile as he pushed forward until his entire cock was sheathed. She wiggled against him and he slapped her sharply on the ass.

"Hold still, Quinn."

She forced herself not to move as he rubbed and caressed her ass.

"Ready?" He asked hoarsely.

"Yes, oh God, yes," she moaned.

He plunged in and out of her aching pussy as

she gasped and pleaded for more.

"Touch your clit," Silas demanded.

She rubbed frantically at her clit as Silas made a low growl of need. The intensity was growing, her legs beginning to shake and pleasure unfurling in her belly.

"Silas! I'm going to come," she gasped.

"Yes!" He shouted as his entire body stiffened and he drove into her a final time. Her orgasm shot through her like an arrow, lighting up all of her nerve endings and pulling a scream from her throat. She arched, the pain in her back dim and meaningless as Silas' hands clamped down on her hips. He pumped rapidly, groaning as her pussy squeezed him rhythmically. She was trembling violently beneath him and he pulled out of her and helped her ease onto her side before collapsing next to her.

"Jesus, that was good," he said.

She smiled as he cupped her breast and tugged at her still-hard nipple. "Yes, it was."

They lay quietly for a while before Silas kissed the top of her shoulder. "How was your day?"

"It was fine. Zeeda asked if you could come back tomorrow and work on the shelves," she said.

"Oh yeah?"

"Yes. She was impressed with the shelving you built today."

"It was easy. I've worked in construction for most of my life so building some shelves was no problem."

"What did you build on your world?" She asked.

"Houses mostly. I own a small construction company. We did the framing of the houses, that sort of thing."

"Did you enjoy it?"

"Mostly. I hated the admin side of it but I have a pretty good accountant and admin person. They handled a lot of the day-to-day stuff. Of course, with me just disappearing the whole company will probably fold."

He sighed heavily and she squeezed his hand. "I'm sorry."

"I had some good guys on my crew. They'll be out of a job now," he said. "They had families to feed, you know?"

She turned to face him and stroked his jaw. "It's not your fault, Silas. You didn't know this would happen."

He laughed bitterly. "That's for fucking sure. To tell you the truth, I'm still not entirely certain I wasn't hit over the head by a 2x4 and this isn't some weird coma-induced dream."

She kissed him on the mouth. "It's real, Silas."

"The ironic thing is, I almost didn't go out with Gage. I was tired, the weather was terrible and he was just using me as a wingman to get his friends laid."

She smiled at him. "Did it work?"

"We were sucked into that orb of light before we even made it to the bar."

He touched a few strands of her dark hair. "If I hadn't gone with him, Gage would have just disappeared and I would have never known what happened to him. As much as I wish I was still on my own world, being without Gage and being completely alone would have been horrible."

"Your parents?" She asked.

"Killed in a car crash when Gage was ten," he said.

"Garna, I'm sorry," she said.

"I was in university to get my degree in architecture. I returned home and after the funeral I quit school and started working construction to pay the bills and keep us fed."

"Oh, Silas," she said, "I really am sorry."

He shrugged. "I have some regrets but Gage was what mattered, you know?"

"I do."

"Do you have siblings?"

"No."

"Parents?"

"Not anymore."

That wasn't a complete lie. She had been missing for nearly fifteen years and she would never see her mother or her father again. For all she knew they could be dead. She felt the familiar dull ache of missing them and buried her face in Silas' thick throat.

"You okay?"

She nodded and stiffened when he stroked her hair and said, "Aren't you going to ask me what a car is? Or a university?"

She forced herself to relax. "I know what they are. That idiot Lloyd explained many things from your world."

"You talk a lot with Lloyd?" He said skeptically.

She shook her head. "No, but I listen when he talks with others. It's hard not to. The man never shuts up."

He laughed. "That's true."

She snuggled in a little closer as Silas stroked her hair. Lying with him in the dark, talking about their day made her nearly dizzy with happiness. God, she missed being in a relationship.

*You're not in a relationship. Don't start thinking you are. In three weeks, Silas will be in the queen's bed and you'll never have him in your bed again.*

Dismay coursed through her and she started to push away from Silas. What was she thinking? Cuddling with him, learning more about him was madness.

"What's wrong?" Silas held her a little tighter.

"Nothing is wrong," she said before wiggling against him. "Let me go please, danen."

He shook his head. "No."

"Danen," she warned.

He squeezed her ass. "Silas. Out there you might be in charge but in your bed you'll do what I want."

Desire and anticipation flowered in her belly and he gave her a wicked grin. "Do we have an agreement, Quinn?"

She nodded and he smacked her lightly on the ass. "Say it."

"I'll do what you want in bed, Silas," she whispered as he cupped and caressed her breasts.

"Good," he said with another wicked grin. He brushed his mouth against hers but pulled back when she tried to deepen the kiss.

She frowned at him and he shook his head. "No more for tonight."

"I want more," she said.

"I do too but not until your back heals."

"It's much better," she said.

"It doesn't look much better," he replied.

She started to protest and he squeezed her ass again. "You need to rest, Quinn. No arguing."

"I'm not tired," she said.

He laughed. "Fine, we'll talk some more. What was that piece of paper the smelly trader gave you earlier today?"

"I don't know what you're talking about," Quinn said stiffly.

"I saw him give you a piece of paper. I'm just curious what it was," Silas said.

"He didn't give me anything," Quinn insisted. "You're confused."

"I'm not."

She turned in his arms and pulled up the bedcovers. "You're right, Silas, my back is sore and I'm more tired than I said. Good night."

"Quinn – "

"Please," she said, "can we just sleep?"

There was an odd vulnerability in her voice and Silas paused before leaning over her and kissing her. "Yes. Good night, Quinn."

She lay quietly, staring into the darkness long after Silas had fallen asleep. Her mind wouldn't stop worrying at her. She knew she was playing a dangerous game by allowing Silas to mean something more to her than just a warm body to fuck.

*If you would just fucking kill the queen already we could have Silas for ourselves,* her inner mind grumbled at her.

*It's not the right time.*

*It hasn't been the right time for the last ten years. Jesus Christ, Quinn, it's time to shit or get off the pot. If you don't kill her, she's going to take Silas from you just like she took Kevin. Is that what you want?*

*You know it isn't.*

*Then kill that stupid bitch and claim Silas as yours.*

*And then what? Just expect to live happily ever after? I'll have to leave the clan after I kill her and Silas would never agree to go with me. Not without his brother.*

Her inner voice stayed silent for once and she sighed inwardly. If she killed the queen she'd never see Silas again. But if she didn't kill her, Silas would be in her bed in less than a month's time. She had never been more stuck between a rock and a hard place in her life.

*Kill her and take the throne,* her inner voice whispered slyly.

She shook her head. Silas snorted softly in his sleep and eased a little closer to her. Quinn pressed her hand against his, closed her eyes and tried to sleep.

# Chapter Eighteen

"Your back is looking much better, massina," Naveen said happily.

Quinn shrugged into her shirt and buttoned it. "It feels much better."

"You should keep putting the salve on it at night."

Quinn made a face as Naveen handed her another bag of the smelly salve. "I know your back is better but it's only been a week. You still need the salve."

"It's been almost two weeks," she corrected him.

He thought back before nodding. "Aye, I guess you're right. How is fucking the danen?"

"Naveen," Quinn said, "you know I'm not going to talk to you about that."

Naveen laughed. "At least tell me if his cock is large, massina."

"It is," Quinn replied.

"Lucky girl," Naveen said with a wink. "No wonder you seem so happy as of late."

"I'm no happier than I was before," Quinn replied.

"You are," Naveen said. "You enjoy being with the danen."

"I enjoy fucking the danen," Quinn corrected.

"It's more than that."

"It isn't," she insisted.

Naveen frowned at her. "Why do you refuse to admit you enjoy the danen for more than just his big cock?"

She sighed. "Because I'm married, Naveen. It's bad enough I'm sleeping with him, I can't have affection for him as well."

"No, massina, you are widowed," he said, "and have been for many years. It is time for you to move on. Affection for the danen is not a bad thing."

"I don't feel guilty about my...affection for him," Quinn said abruptly. "I keep waiting for the guilt and there's nothing. Does that make me a terrible person, Naveen?"

"It does not," Naveen said. "Your husband has been dead for over a decade. It's time to move on."

"Move on?" Quinn said with a bitter laugh. "I have no interest in fucking a different breeder each month. I know it's the way of this world and I understand that but it isn't what I want. It's why my affection for Silas is so dangerous. Already the thought of him sleeping with the queen – cf sleeping with anyone else – fills me with jealousy."

"Oh, massina," Naveen said. "I am sorry."

"Aye, so am I," Quinn said.

"Perhaps you should start distancing yourself

from the danen," Naveen suggested.

"I cannot," Quinn said. "It's too late for that. I want him for myself and in two weeks I'll have to give him to the queen."

She gave Naveen an anxious look. "The danen says he won't fuck her."

Naveen's eyes widened. "He has to, massina."

"I know."

"If he doesn't, she will - "

"I know better than anyone what she will do, Naveen!" Quinn shouted at him.

He didn't reply and she took his hand and squeezed it. "I'm sorry. I shouldn't have yelled at you."

"Massina, you must convince the danen that he has to fuck the queen. It will only be for a month and after that you can claim him at the next ceremony. There is nothing that says you can't fight for him each time he is available. I know it isn't ideal but it's the best you can hope for here. You know that."

"Is it?" She said. "We could leave."

"And go where?" Naveen asked in alarm. "You would not survive on your own outside these walls and joining another clan wouldn't allow you to keep the danen."

Quinn sighed and Naveen took her hand. "You could take the throne for yourself."

"I have no interest in ruling," Quinn said.

"But you do wish to kill the queen."

She gave him a startled look. Naveen was her closest friend on this world but she had never spoken of her plan to murder the queen. It was too dangerous for the both of them to speak of it.

"Keep your voice down," she said with a nervous look at his front door. "I am loyal to our queen and it is my job to protect her."

Naveen lowered his voice. "Aye, that is what you say but your heart speaks differently."

She opened her mouth to argue but nothing came out.

Naveen gave her a solemn look. "You must be careful, massina. The queen is still powerful."

She leaned down and kissed his wrinkled cheek. "I should get going. Have a good evening, Naveen."

"Are you not having dinner with the queen?"

Quinn shook her head. "No, there was no request from her for dinner."

Naveen gave her an odd look. "I received a request as did Akia."

Quinn didn't reply and Naveen said, "Massina, it is worrisome that she invited Akia and not you."

"Perhaps," Quinn said.

"Perhaps? Akia has wanted to be massina for many years. If she is worming her way into the queen's good graces…"

Naveen trailed off and gave Quinn a nervous look. "You have been the massina for a long time. I'm not trying to insult you but you're not getting any younger."

"Aye, nor is the queen," Quinn said.

"It is not the queen you would have to worry about," Naveen said. "I know you can still beat Akia in combat but her fighting skills grow more advanced by the week. She is preparing to become massina. You know that, do you not?"

"Aye, I do," Quinn said calmly as she headed for the door. "She will eventually challenge me for the position."

Naveen trailed after her. "What will you do when she challenges you, massina?"

"Kill her," Quinn said bluntly.

ॐ ॐ

"Good night, danen," Dacia said as she stopped in front of Quinn's home.

"Good night, Dacia," Silas replied. She walked away and he let himself into Quinn's home without knocking. He supposed he should have knocked but after only two weeks Quinn's home felt like his as well.

"Stupid and dangerous to think that way," he muttered as he slipped off his shoes.

He was a little early which suited him just fine. The more time he had to spend with Quinn, the better. Over the last few days she had begun to relax around him. He still refused to fuck her more than once a night even though the swelling on her back was gone and the bruising had faded to yellow. It left plenty of time for talking. She didn't actually talk about herself at all but she asked plenty of questions about him. He had told her about his childhood and his job. Hell, he had even tried his best to explain how awful it was when his parents died. How afraid he was that he had failed Gage and his worry that his brother would somehow realize that a small part of him was resentful about quitting university.

He walked silently down the hall toward the kitchen. Quinn was a good listener and there was no judgment on her part when he confessed he was bitter about never finishing university. In fact, she had –

He stopped abruptly and cocked his head as the sound of Quinn's singing floated down the hallway. She had a nice voice but it was the song she was singing that made his heart pound with excitement.

≈ ≪

Quinn cut up more cheese before laying it on the plate next to the carrots and the pork. She popped another piece of dranina into her mouth. The purple fruit tasted vaguely of pears and was her favourite from this world. She did a little shimmy before breaking out into song again. Silas would be brought to her in half an hour or so. Despite her conversation with Naveen she was feeling happy and, she grinned wryly to herself, horny as hell. Her back was finally better and she was certain she could convince Silas to fuck her more than once tonight.

She sang the chorus of the song and did another hip shimmy. God, she couldn't wait to –

"Big Rolling Stones fan, huh?"

She shrieked and whirled around. Silas was standing in the doorway grinning cheekily at her. She returned his grin and said, "Yeah, my mom had a huge crush on Mick Jagger. When I was a kid we listened to them all…"

She trailed off as his grin widened.

"Fuck," she said.

"You're from my world," he said.

She turned back to the plate of food. "I suppose it's too late to convince you that Lloyd told me about the Rolling Stones."

He laughed and strode forward to wrap his arms around her waist. He kissed her on the neck. "Way too late. Why didn't you want me to know?"

"Most people in the clan believe I'm from this world. I want it to stay that way."

"Why?"

"It's just easier."

"Does the queen know?"

"She knows I'm not from this world but beyond that she has no interest in where I come from."

"You've been here for over a decade, right?" He asked curiously.

"Yes," she replied.

"Jesus," he said. "You don't miss our world?"

"I used to," she said. "But it's been a long time."

"You don't want to try and get back?"

She turned in his arms. "Silas, there is no way to return to our world. You need to understand that. There is no guarantee that an orb would take us back to our own world."

"It might," Silas said. "You don't know for certain that it wouldn't."

"If it didn't?" She said. "What then? You start all over on another world? What if it was worse than this one? We have a breeder who came from a world that was being overrun with vampires. Real vampires, Silas. One came through with the breeder. It killed Patina and would have killed more of us if I hadn't realized what it was and stuck my dagger through its heart. Would you want to live in that world?"

Her voice was rising and Silas rubbed her lower back. "Okay, Quinn. Okay. I get your point."

She rubbed wearily at her forehead and Silas pressed a kiss against her mouth. "Eat your dinner, Quinn, and we'll talk about our world, okay?"

"I'm no longer hungry," she said. "I'm going to have a hot bath. Can you help me heat the water, Silas?"

He nodded and gave her a troubled look as she left the kitchen.

ॐ ◌

"Are you sure your back is good for this, Quinn?" Silas asked. He had helped Quinn heat water for her bath and at her insistence joined her in the tub. They bathed quickly before she took his hand and led him to her bedroom.

She was lying on her back on the bed and he studied her naked body as she cupped her breast and pulled lazily at one hard nipple. "Yes. Come to bed, Silas."

She spread her thighs invitingly as he approached the bed. He smiled and kneeled between her legs before leaning over her. He kissed her, tracing her tongue with his. She stroked his naked back and tried to pull him down onto her body.

"Patience, Quinn," he said.

"I need you," she whispered.

"Soon, honey," he replied before tracing her

295

collarbone with his tongue. He kissed his way to her breasts and traced each tight nipple with the tip of his tongue. She moaned and clutched at his head, urging him with breathless cries to suck on them.

He sucked hard on each nipple and bit them gently before laving them with his tongue. She arched her back and dug her nails into his back. She rubbed her pussy against his erect cock. "Please fuck me, Silas."

"Not yet."

She glared at him. "Don't tease me."

He laughed. "Honey, I haven't even started to tease you yet."

He kissed her flat stomach before nipping at her ribs. She inhaled sharply and squeezed her thighs around his waist. "Silas, please."

He licked a slow path to her navel and circled it with his tongue before blowing lightly. She shivered and tugged on his thick hair as goosebumps rose on her skin. He nibbled at her hipbones before sliding back and lying on his stomach between her thighs. He kissed the tender skin of her inner thigh and she moaned.

He pushed on her thighs. "Wider, Quinn."

She let her legs drop open and he stared at her glistening pussy before leaning forward and slowly licking the entire length of her pussy. She cried out, her fingers digging into his scalp. Her clit was swollen and peeking out from between her lips. He parted her lips with his thumbs and licked the swollen bud. She arched her back and he sucked experimentally at her clit. Her hands pulled painfully at his hair and he tugged them away before pinning them at her hips. She strained to free herself and he nibbled at her pussy lips until she was crying his name.

With slow deliberateness, he licked and sucked her clit until she was writhing on the bed and her thighs clamped around his broad shoulders. He lifted his head and growled, "Keep your legs open, Quinn."

Her entire body shuddering, she spread her thighs wide and he kissed the dark curls at the top of her pussy. "I want you to come for me, honey."

"Yes," she moaned. "Yes, Silas."

He smiled and buried his face into her pussy again. Less than a minute later she was arching up off the bed, her hands clenching and unclenching helplessly as her orgasm swept through her. When she collapsed on the bed he released her and straightened. His cock was painfully hard and precum dripped steadily from it. He pressed the head against her tight opening and slipped inside of her easily.

He took her wrists and lifted her arms over her head, pinning them to the bed. She stared up at him as he slid in and out of her with long, powerful strokes.

"This is what you want, isn't it, honey?" He said.

She nodded and he leaned down to kiss her. She returned his kisses eagerly, her hips rising to meet each of his thrusts. He drove in and out, watching the way her breasts moved with every thrust. She pulled experimentally at his hands and he shook his head before tightening his grip on her wrists. Excitement and lust flickered across her face. He kissed her again, sucking hard on her tongue before nipping at her bottom lip.

"Oh God," she moaned. "Silas, oh God…"

Her pussy squeezed around him as her body shook. He slanted his mouth over hers, swallowing her loud scream of pleasure. He thrust wildly as his balls tightened and the base of his spine began to tingle. He tore his mouth from hers and made a low roar of pleasure as he climaxed. He collapsed against her body, releasing her hands and burying his face in her throat. She stroked his back and pressed kisses against the top of his head as he waited for his heartbeat to return to a normal pace.

"Heavy," she whispered before pushing at him.

He rolled off of her and she curled up on her side, resting her cheek on his chest. He stroked her dark hair and said, "Is your back okay?"

She nodded and kissed his chest. "It's fine."

They lay silently for a while before she sat up and smiled hesitantly at him. "Do you – can we talk about our world?"

He smiled at her. "Yes, I'd like that."

❧ ❧

"Facebook," Quinn said again before popping a piece of cheese into her mouth. "Honestly, it just sounds really stupid to me."

Silas laughed. "I know but trust me, it and Twitter are very popular."

"Twitter," she repeated. "That's the program people use to insult other people in 140 characters or less, right?"

Silas laughed again. "Close enough."

"God, so many things have changed. You really can just do a video chat with people using your cell phone?"

He nodded and she shook her head in disbelief. "Crazy."

"Where is my cell phone and wallet, by the way?" Silas asked.

"Naveen would have given them to the queen," Quinn said.

"What does she do with them?"

"Nothing. She has a remarkable lack of interest in the technology from other worlds."

"Does that seem strange to you?" He asked.

"The queen is far from normal," she said.

"What happens in two weeks?"

"What do you mean?"

"You know what I mean," Silas said. "In two weeks the queen will take me for herself. Will you bid on me at the next claiming ceremony?"

She looked away and he cursed before pushing back the covers.

"Silas, wait!" She grabbed his arm and pressed her naked body against his. "Let me explain, okay?"

"What's there to explain?" He said. "You don't want me as much as I want you."

"That isn't true," she said.

He sat back in the bed. "Then why aren't you going to bid on me?"

She pulled the covers around her and sat cross-legged on the bed. "When I came through the orb I wasn't alone. There was a man with me. His name was Kevin and he – he was my husband."

"Holy shit," Silas said.

"We were captured by the current massina. Her name was Dahlia. She and the other members of the queen's guard brought us back here. Kevin was taken to the breeders' quarters and I was put to work in the kitchens. It was only a week since the last claiming ceremony so we had three weeks to try and adapt to what had happened. I pleaded on a daily basis for them to allow me to see Kevin but they refused. I caught occasional glimpses of him working in the gardens but I wasn't allowed to speak to him."

She studied her hands for a moment before continuing. "Kevin was a big man. Not as large as you but tall and muscular. The night of the claiming ceremony the queen chose Kevin. He refused to sleep with her and she slit his throat. He bled to death on the floor of her bedroom."

Silas took Quinn's hand. She was pale but dry-eyed and she squeezed his hand. "I wasn't at the claiming ceremony. I was chosen to stay in the kitchens and make the food for the ceremony. I didn't find out that Kevin was dead until the next morning when Naveen told me. He took pity on me and let me see Kevin's body before they buried him."

"I'm so sorry," Silas said.

"I was devastated. Not only was I on some weird new world but the person I loved most was dead. Killed because he honoured his vows to me."

She swallowed before whispering, "So many times I wished that I was there that night. I would have – have somehow conveyed to him that it was okay, you know? That it didn't matter. That I knew how much he loved me and he had to do what he needed to survive."

Silas rubbed her thigh and she stared briefly at him before lowering her gaze again. "Standing next to Kevin's dead body, I made a vow that I would kill the queen for what she had done. I wanted revenge. Do you understand, Silas?"

He nodded and she sighed. "I think I went a little crazy the first year or so. I joined the queen's army and learned how to fight. I was terrible at it at first. I had no natural talent for it and I was afraid of dying. I shouldn't have been. There was nothing left for me on this world and if I died, I would have been with Kevin again. But I was afraid. I was weak and afraid."

"Being afraid doesn't make you weak," Silas said.

"Does it not?" She said.

"Are you still afraid?" He asked.

She shook her head. "No."

He waited for her to elaborate but she said, "When the warkins attacked us and Dahlia panicked, I knew that was my chance. If I were to have any hope of killing the queen, I needed to be the massina. Only the massina was given unguarded access to the queen. I took control of the queen's guard and destroyed the warkin clan that was attacking us. I even saved the queen's life when a group of them made it into the castle. The queen is very good at fighting and is extremely dangerous but she was outnumbered. Without me there she would have been killed. The queen abhors weakness of any kind. When the fighting was over she killed Dahlia and named me the new massina."

Silas didn't say anything and Quinn sighed heavily. "I am not a monster, Silas. The queen would have killed Dahlia regardless of what I had done."

"I know," he said.

She took his hand and held it. "That is why I can't sleep with you after you've been with the queen. She took everything from me and I hate her. The thought of being with you after you've been in the queen's bed, it…"

She trailed off and then whispered, "I'm sorry, Silas. Truly I am."

When he didn't reply, she squeezed his hand. "Say something, Silas. Please."

"What do you want me to say?" He said woodenly. "You're still in love with your dead husband, you won't go near me again in two weeks' time and you're planning on murdering the queen. It all seems pretty clear and simple to me."

She shook her head and crawled into his lap. She cupped his face and made him look at her. "I am not still in love with Kevin, Silas."

"It's fine," he said bleakly. "I understand why you - "

"I'm not!" She insisted vehemently. "I will always love and miss Kevin but he has been dead for over a decade."

She brushed her mouth against his and then threw caution to the wind. "I could fall in love with you, Silas. Very easily. There's something special between us, is there not? You feel it too."

"Yes," he said in a low voice. "I feel it too."

She hugged him, sighing with relief when he returned her hug and pressed a kiss against her throat.

"This is why you must sleep with the queen when she takes you to her bed," Quinn said. "I – I don't want to lose you either, Silas."

"If I sleep with her I'll never be with you again," Silas said.

"But you'll be alive," she replied.

"Some life," he said. "I'll spend it having to fuck God knows how many women when the only woman I want won't have anything to do with me."

"Silas, I - "

"Why haven't you killed the queen?" He asked abruptly. "You've been the massina for nearly ten years."

"At first it was because I needed to gain her trust. I will never have it fully, she has survived this long precisely because she doesn't trust anyone, but she at least believes that I am loyal to her."

She laughed bitterly. "Do you have any idea how difficult it has been over the years to protect a woman that I hate?"

He kissed her throat again and she stroked his thick hair. "Once she believed in my loyalty, I began to plan my revenge in earnest. I was going to murder her in her sleep. Cowardly, I know, but I needed to make it look like an assassination. If the others knew that it was me who killed her they would have killed me despite their fear and dislike of the queen."

He rubbed her lower back as she said, "As the queen aged she grew more and more paranoid. A few years ago, she requested guards to stand outside her bedroom while she slept. I lost my chance to kill her in her sleep."

"Why didn't you do it before that?" He asked

"I found love again," she said.

He stiffened against her. "With who?"

She cupped his face and kissed him until he relaxed. "As the massina, my job is not only to protect the queen but her child as well. Kila was almost eleven when I became the massina. She was a sweet child. Kind and loving and the exact opposite of her mother in every way. I tried to ignore her at first but she found her way into my heart. I love her like she is my own child, Silas, and she loves me. When I kill her mother that love will turn to hatred."

"Gage says that Kila is afraid of her mother," Silas said. "He thinks she even hates her."

Quinn sighed. "Kila is afraid of her mother but she doesn't hate her. She is a horrible woman but she is still Kila's mother and she will always love her."

"Are you sure about that?"

"Yes," Quinn replied. "My love for Kila has made it more difficult to do what I swore I would do. I'm no longer afraid but I'm still weak."

He didn't know what to say to that so he pulled her closer and rubbed her bruised back lightly. She nestled against him and they sat silently for a few moments.

"What will you do after you kill the queen?" He

asked.

"Leave, if the others don't capture me and kill me first."

"You keep saying that leaving the safety of these walls would get you killed."

She didn't reply and he leaned back so he could look at her. "I'll go with you. I'll help you kill the queen and we'll leave together."

"It is a death sentence, Silas," she said. "I won't do that to you."

"But you'll let yourself die?" He said angrily. "Quinn, we have a better chance of surviving outside the walls with two of us."

"No," she said, "we don't. Men are precious in this world and having you with me will only bring the other clans after us in greater numbers."

"We can live in the forest," he said. "We can - "

"What of your brother?" She asked. "You would leave Gage? You would never see him again, Silas."

Shame coursed through him. He wanted to be with Quinn and he hadn't given a single thought to his brother. What was wrong with him?

"Quinn, I'm sorry," he said hoarsely.

She cupped his face and smiled at him. "Do not feel bad, Silas. You should stay with your brother here behind the walls where it is safe. I will kill the queen and leave this place and you will forget me. It's what needs to happen."

"There's one little detail you're forgetting," he said morosely.

"What?"

"I can't seem to fuck anyone who isn't you."

Fear crossed her face and her hand tightened on his jaw. "You have to, Silas.

"It's not that simple, Quinn," he said.

"It is!" She insisted. "Have you not heard a word I've said? She will kill you if you don't sleep with her. I don't – I can't stand the thought of losing you like that. You don't have a choice."

"What if I did?" He asked. "What if there was another choice?"

"There isn't," she said impatiently.

"The orb," he said slowly. "We could use the orb to go to another world."

"I already told you – that's just as dangerous as living beyond these walls."

"Maybe, maybe not," he said. "We could be taken back to our world or we could find a different world that isn't as awful as this one."

"Or we could find one that's worse," she said.

"I'm willing to take that chance if it means I can be with you."

She stared silently at him. "And what of Gage?"

"I'll convince him to come with us."

"Will you? He already cares deeply for Kila."

"I know but I can convince him," Silas said. "He barely knows Kila and I'm his brother."

"Even if you could convince him and even if we could escape without the queen finding out, we don't know when the next orb is coming," she said desperately.

"Don't lie to me, Quinn. I know about the majii, remember?"

She scowled at him. "There may not be another

orb for months or years."

"Or there could be one next week," he said. "Lucky for us, we'll know exactly when it's going to happen. This could work, Quinn."

"Another world could be far worse than this one," she said again.

"It could be," he said steadily. "But we'd be together."

"This plan of yours would only work if there's going to be another orb within the next couple of weeks. Plus, it would have to be an orb that takes not gives," she said.

"That's true," he said.

"Silas, the odds of that happening are astronomical."

"Probably," he said. "But what if it did happen? Think about it, Quinn. This solves our problems. You don't have to kill the queen and we can be together."

"I want to kill the queen," she said.

"You did," he replied. "Are you still so certain now? Can you live with Kila hating you forever?"

She hesitated and he squeezed her waist. "Can you talk to the majii? Can you find out at least if she knows yet when there will be another orb?"

"Aye, I could," she said.

"Then do it. What harm is there in asking?"

"Plenty if the queen were to find out," she said.

He didn't reply and she tried to ignore the small trickle of hope that was filling her belly. The majii was in her debt and had been for many years. Quinn had never called in the favour but now...

*Quinn! Have you gone mad? You can't leave*

*this world. Just kill the queen and take the throne.*

*Kila will hate me. I'll lose her forever if I kill her mother.*

*You'll lose Silas forever if you don't.*

"Quinn?" Silas touched her arm. "This could work. We can be together and away from that crazy bitch."

She smiled bitterly at him. "I will talk to the majii, Silas. But do not get your hopes up. The odds of another orb happening is very low."

He suddenly grinned cheekily at her. "It's time for my luck to change, Quinn. This will work. I know it will."

He cupped her breast and rubbed his thumb over her nipple. "How's your back feeling, honey?"

"Fine," she whispered.

He trailed kisses down her throat and licked a path over her collarbone.

"Silas," Quinn tugged on his hair until he was looking at her, "promise me if this doesn't work that you will sleep with the queen."

"I don't have to," he said before nipping at her earlobe. "It will work, Quinn."

"Silas - "

He slanted his mouth over hers and kissed her before threading his hand through her dark hair. "Enough talking for tonight, honey."

He pushed her onto her back on the bed and covered her body with his own. She moaned when he pulled her thighs apart and rubbed his erect cock against her pussy. She squirmed beneath him. Shamefully she was already wet and she cried out with pleasure when Silas pushed into her with one hard thrust. As he began a slow, deep rhythm, she closed her eyes and clung to him.

## Chapter Nineteen

"You want to leave this world," Gage said blankly.

"Keep your voice down, Gage!" Silas stared nervously at the man a few rows down in the garden.

"You really want to leave this world in the hopes of getting back to our world?" Gage said in a low voice. "When everyone here tells us that's impossible?"

"I know we probably won't make it back to our world but we can't stay here, Gage," Silas said.

"It's not going to work," Gage said. "We'd have to know when the orb is coming."

"Have you listened to anything I've just said to you?" Silas asked impatiently. "Quinn is going to speak with the majii and find out when the next orb is. Once she knows we will sneak out and head to the orb."

"What about Kila?" Gage asked.

"You can't be with her, Gage. At least not the way you want to be," Silas said.

"She's going to fight for me every claiming ceremony."

"What happens the first time she loses?" Silas asked. "She only won you this time because of Quinn. What happens when she doesn't win and you have to sleep with another woman?"

"That's not going to happen," Gage said stubbornly. "Kila is a good fighter."

"It will happen. It's only a matter of time," Silas said. "Gage, I know you care about Kila and I understand that but we can't stay in this world. The queen is crazy and - "

"No, *you* can't stay in this world," Gage said. "Kila told me that the queen will pick you again once the month is over. You don't want to sleep with her because you're in love with Quinn."

"I don't want to sleep with her because she's batshit insane and just as likely to kill me as she is to fuck me," Silas said tightly.

Gage didn't reply and Silas yanked out a few weeds before saying, "I'm sorry, Gage, but you're coming with us."

Gage stared at him in astonishment. "You think that you can just tell me to jump and I'll ask how high? I'm at adult, Silas, and I can make my own decisions. If you want to leave me for some woman you just met, go ahead and - "

"That is not why I'm leaving!" Silas snapped.

"Okay, fine, I know it isn't. But don't try and deny that you care for Quinn. There's a part of you that wants to leave because you know that's the only way you can be with her. I feel the same way about Kila. Why can't you understand that?"

"Gage, I…"

Silas trailed off. This was going badly but he didn't have a clue how to fix it. He thought it would be simple enough to convince Gage to leave with them but he underestimated how his brother felt about Kila. God, he was a fucking idiot.

"I'm not leaving Kila," Gage repeated, "but maybe I can convince her to come with us."

"What? Gage, no! Do not speak to her about this," Silas said.

"Why not?"

"Why not?" Silas repeated in disbelief. "She's the princess. If she goes to her mother and tells her that we're thinking of leaving that bitch will kill us."

"She wouldn't tell her," Gage said.

"You don't know that for sure," Silas said.

"I do. Besides, this plan has a few holes in it. Unless there's an orb in the next few days you're going to be in the queen's bed," Gage said. "After that, who knows who you'll have to sleep with. Everyone in this goddamn place wants the chance to fuck you. You really think that Quinn can beat every one of them at the claiming ceremony?"

Silas ignored the wave of depression coursing through him. Last night while lying in the dark with Quinn's warmth pressed against him it was almost easy to believe that an orb would come in time. But harsh reality had been slowly setting in all morning. He hid his melancholy from his brother and tried to give him a confident smile.

"There will be an orb, Gage. I know there will be," he said. "If you don't come with me we'll be separated forever."

Gage shook his head. "You think I don't know that? You're asking me to choose between you and the woman I love. That's a really fucked-up thing to do, Silas."

"I know," Silas said. "I'm sorry, Gage. I wish there was another way."

Lutan was approaching them and Silas muttered, "Just think about it. Please, Gage."

Gage nodded and squatted to pull more weeds. Silas forced himself to smile at Lutan as the younger man said cheerfully, "Good morning, Silas. I have not had a chance to ask - how is fucking the massina?"

❧ ❦

Quinn knocked on Josana's door. Her heart was pounding and her mouth was dry. She felt sick to her stomach from a combination of dread and hope. There was a soft noise behind her and she whirled around with her hand on the handle of her sword. The majii lived at the far end of the community and all of the stone houses surrounding hers were empty. The queen preferred to keep her in isolation because she believed it enhanced Josana's ability. The street was empty and she scanned it carefully as the door opened.

"Massina?" Josana gave her a surprised look. "What are you doing here?"

She hesitated and looked up and down the street before saying in a low voice, "Do you bring another letter so soon?"

"No, Josana," Quinn replied. "I am here to

collect my debt."

The hopeful look on Josana's face died and she nodded in resignation. "Aye, come in then."

Quinn followed her inside, closing and locking the door behind her. She sat down next to the fireplace as Josana added more wood before easing into a second chair.

"My bones feel the chill more deeply as of late," she said.

Quinn studied the woman. She couldn't be more than sixty but she looked closer to eighty. Deep lines were etched into her face and her long, silver-coloured hair was thinning. A white film was starting to cover her left eye. When Josana caught her studying it, she smiled wearily.

"My vision is going in that eye."

"You should see Naveen," Quinn replied.

"Aye, I have. There is nothing he can do," Josana said.

"Does it affect your ability?" Quinn asked.

Josana shook her head. "The ability to predict the orb does not come from my sight, massina. It comes from within."

Quinn leaned forward and clasped her hands between her knees. "Can you see other things, Josana?"

Josana made a sound of amusement. "All these years, massina, and this is the first time you have thought to ask that question."

"Can you?" Quinn asked.

The majii shook her head. "No. There are some majiis who can predict more than just the orb's arrival but I was not blessed that way. Much to the queen's vexation. She searches for another. Did you know that?"

"What?" Quinn said in shock.

"Aye," Josana replied. "She knows I grow old and that in time my ability will grow weak and fade completely."

"You're not that old, Josana," Quinn said.

Josana laughed. "A majii's ability ages us more quickly than most. I have often thought it to be unfair."

"I'm sorry, Josana."

The majii shrugged. "I have a few more years before my usefulness to the queen diminishes. Perhaps when I can no longer predict the orb's arrival she will allow me to join the rest of the clan. It is a lonely life."

Quinn didn't reply and Josana gave her a small smile. "More likely the queen will have me killed and fed to the pigs. What point is there in keeping me if I can no longer see?"

"She won't kill you, Josana. There will always be a place for you here in the clan," Quinn said.

"The queen grows more unstable by the day, massina. She will destroy me when I no longer prove useful."

"I thought you could only predict the orb's arrival," Quinn said.

"One does not need the gift of sight to see the queen's madness," Josana said. She pulled a folded up piece of paper from a hidden pocket in her skirt and touched it lovingly. "Thank you for this, massina. It had been many months and I was starting to worry."

"How is she?"

"She is well. The bala was born without complications."

"Did she have a girl?"

"Aye," Josana said. "The father is one of the breeders in their clan that she is particularly fond of. It is the first child he has sired and apparently he is quite smitten with her. Manda brings the bala to see him often."

"Congratulations, Josana," Quinn said.

"Thank you," Josana replied. "I will never get to the see the child but the letters you bring me give me such happiness."

A twinge of guilt went through Quinn. Once she left the letters would end. She closed her eyes. No, she couldn't do that to Josana. She would arrange for Dacia to bring the old woman the letters as well as deliver Josana's letters to the trader. Dacia was quiet and, more importantly, completely loyal to her since the day Quinn saved her from the vampire. She could be trusted to keep Josana's secret.

"You are troubled, massina," Josana said.

Quinn opened her eyes and smiled at Josana. "Only tired, Josana."

"Forgive me," Josana said. "I prattle on and on."

"It's fine."

Josana sat back in her chair and studied the fire. "For nearly thirty years I have been in your debt, Quinn. I almost believed you would never ask for payment of it. Tell me what you require of me and I will do it."

"I want to know when the next orb will arrive," Quinn said.

Josana frowned. "That is it?"

"No. I want you to lie to the queen about it. She cannot know of the next orb."

"Why?"

Quinn remained silent and Josana shook her head. "Forgive me. It is none of my business."

She stood and moved toward the doorway. "Follow me, massina."

Quinn followed her down the narrow hallway. Josana opened the door to the last room and ushered her inside. The room was small and freezing cold but was lit with an eerie blue glow. The glow was coming from a basin of liquid that sat on a small table in the middle of the room.

"I have not looked yet today to see if there is an orb coming," Josana said.

She stood in front of the basin and took a deep breath. The blue light washed over her and Quinn blinked in surprise when the old woman's face changed. The deep wrinkles that were carved into her skin faded away as did the white film that covered her eye. She watched in fascination as Josana leaned over the basin and stared unblinkingly into the liquid. She began to chant in a low voice, a litany of words that made no sense to Quinn. The liquid in the basin churned rapidly and the pulse of light grew until it was so bright that Quinn was forced to squint. Josana spoke more rapidly, her voice growing in both pitch and sound as the liquid began to boil. There was another flash and the entire room was lit up in a pulse of blue light that nearly blinded Quinn. She shielded her eyes and waited anxiously as the light faded and the liquid calmed.

Josana made a grunt of satisfaction before moving away from the basin. She staggered and Quinn caught her by the arm, keeping her upright.

"Thank you, massina," Josana said tiredly. The wrinkles on her face had returned and seemed somehow deeper. "Help me to the other room, would you?"

Quinn put her arm around the majii's waist and guided her back to the living area. She helped her sit in front of the fire and threw a fur around her shoulders when the old woman shivered violently.

"Thank you."

Quinn sat down and clenched her hands together nervously. "Did you see one?"

"Aye," Josana replied. "There is an orb coming soon."

"Is it one that gives or takes?"

"Takes," Josana said.

Quinn's stomach did flip-flops and she could barely stop her urge to scream with excitement. "When will it arrive?"

"Four days from now," Josana said. "The weather will begin to turn tomorrow night."

"Are you certain?"

"Aye, I am," Josana replied. "When the rains begin tomorrow night the queen will send for me. She will want to know if it signals an orb's arrival and I will tell her it does not."

"Thank you, Josana."

"My debt is paid then?"

"Yes."

"Will you – the letters that you bring…"

The old woman trailed off and sat forward in her chair before giving Quinn a worried look.

"The letters will continue, Josana, but your debt is paid in full," Quinn said.

Josana's body relaxed visibly. "Thank you, massina."

Quinn stood. "Remember, neither the queen nor anyone else can know of the coming orb. Do you understand?"

"Aye, I do," Josana replied gravely.

"Thank you. Good bye, Josana," Quinn said.

"Good bye, massina."

ॐ ॐ

"Are you fucking kidding me?"

Quinn shook her head and couldn't help but laugh when Silas picked her up and swung in circles. "I told you it would work! I fucking told you!"

He kissed her triumphantly and she cupped his face and returned his kiss before leaning back. "Don't get too excited, Silas. We still have to sneak away from here and travel two days through the forest without dying."

He set her on her feet, keeping his arms around her waist. "I know but at least we've got a chance."

She smiled at him. "Yes, we have a chance."

"Plus it could be our world we return to. Hell, we've been lucky so far."

"Aye, it could be," she said cautiously, "but do not get your hopes up."

He grinned like a little boy at her. "I think we should celebrate with lots and lots of fucking."

She laughed again. "Fionn just dropped you off, Silas. We have all night and I'm hungry. At least let me eat first."

"Fine," he said. "But only because you'll need your strength for what I'm about to do to you."

She jumped when he slapped her playfully on the ass. "Watch your hands, danen, or I'll tie you to the bed and leave you there."

"Actually," he said with a wicked grin, "now that you bring it up I think tying *you* to the bed would be an excellent idea. Don't you?"

She shivered all over as he stood behind her and pulled her against his growing erection. She ground her ass against his cock and he nipped at her throat. "Only I definitely won't just leave you there."

"What will you do?" She asked breathlessly.

He licked the column of her throat before sucking on her earlobe. "Eat your dinner and I'll show you."

She pouted at him and he laughed and squeezed her ass before stepping away. "Eat quickly, Quinn."

"Do you want something to eat?" She asked as she prepared her dinner meal.

"No, I ate earlier with the other guys," he said as he stole a piece of cheese from her plate and popped it into his mouth.

"Do you ever wish you could just have a hamburger?" He asked as he stole another piece of cheese.

She poked him in his flat stomach and carried

her plate to the table. "All the damn time. I'm so tired of pork."

"What's the mystery meat that we sometimes get?"

"It's a creature that lives in the forest. It's called - "

There was a knock at the front door and Quinn stiffened.

"Are you expecting someone?" Silas asked.

"No," she said. She drew her sword and Silas followed her down the hallway. There was another louder knock.

"Who is it?" Quinn asked.

"Massina, it's me. Open the door. Quickly!"

Quinn yanked open the door. "Kila? What are you doing here?"

"Let me in, massina," Kila said with a nervous glance behind her.

Quinn stepped aside and her mouth dropped open when Gage followed Kila into the house. "You bring the breeder to my house? Kila, what the hell is going on?"

"We need to speak, Quinn," Kila said.

She hurried toward the kitchen and Silas grabbed Gage's arm when he tried to follow her. "What did you do, Gage?"

Gage yanked his arm free and scowled at him. "Just listen to what she has to say, Silas."

He disappeared into the kitchen and after a moment's hesitation, Silas and Quinn followed.

"Sandora," Quinn said as she sat next to the blonde-haired woman. "what are you doing here with the breeder?"

"Gage told me of your plan," Kila said bluntly.

"Gage, you didn't," Silas groaned. "You little shit. I told you not to tell her."

"I love her and I can't keep something like this from her," Gage retorted.

"Garna!" Quinn swore. "Do you have any idea what you've done, you foolish boy?"

"What I've done?" Gage said. "You've turned my brother against me and - "

"She has not turned me against you," Silas interrupted. "Gage, this is for your own safety."

"No, it's so you can be with the woman you love. I want to be with the woman I love too, Silas. It's not exactly fair for you to be the only one who gets what he wants."

"Listen to me, you silly bala," Quinn snarled. "You're going to get your brother killed. Is that what you want?"

"Of course it isn't!" Gage nearly shouted. "You're the one who's going to get him killed, not me. You don't care about anyone but yourself. You're a selfish bitch who – "

"Hold your tongue, breeder, or I will rip it from your mouth," Quinn snapped.

"I'd like to see you try!" Gage retorted.

Quinn stood and Gage flinched. Silas stood quickly and grabbed Quinn's waist. "Quinn, don't."

"He may be your brother, Silas, but I am the massina and I will not tolerate such disrespect. I will allow him to keep his tongue but losing one of his fingers will teach him respect," Quinn said.

"He didn't mean it," Silas said. "Gage, apologize."

"Like hell I'll apologize," Gage said.

"Gage, for fuck's sake," Silas said in exasperation as Quinn tried to struggle free. "Can everyone just calm the fuck down for two minutes?"

"I will calm down when I have a piece of your brother's flesh," Quinn said as she yanked her dagger from her belt.

"You're just as bad as that bitch in the castle," Gage said.

"No, breeder, I am far worse," Quinn replied. "Now be a good little boy and hold out your hand."

"Come anywhere near me and I'll - "

"You'll what? You think you can defeat the massina? I will leave you in pieces on the floor of this kitchen if you do not learn some manners."

"I don't care how tough you think you are, lady. I'm not going to just stand here and - "

"You're right about that. You will be lying on the floor sobbing like the little bala you are when I'm finished with you."

"Nice, real nice. Some girlfriend you have there, Silas. Tell me, does she have your balls in her pocket permanently or does she let you keep them during the day?"

"Gage, stop antagonizing Quinn! Quinn, stop threatening to chop Gage into little pieces!"

"Tell him to watch his tongue and I won't have to - "

"You keep telling me to watch my tongue and I'll - "

"ENOUGH!"

The three of them jumped when Kila slammed her fists on the table. She stood, her eyes blazing anger at all three of them. "You fight like spoiled children and I'm tired of it! All of you sit down and listen to me!"

They sat down with heavy thuds as Kila glared at them. "Massina, Gage told me of your plan and he was right to do so. Both of us are going with you."

Quinn's mouth dropped open again. "Kila, you cannot go with us."

"Why not?"

"It's dangerous, sandora. We have no idea what world we will end up in. It could be a thousand times worse than this one."

"Or it could be a thousand times better," Kila replied. "I wish to be with Gage and it is not fair of me to ask him to be separated from his brother. The solution is for both of us to go."

"No," Quinn said. "You're not going, Kila."

"I am," Kila said calmly.

"Sandora - "

"I am tired of the way things are in this world, Quinn. Even before I met Gage I hated the way we treat the men. They should be free to choose who they want to be with. That will never happen while my mother lives."

"You can change it," Quinn said. "When you become queen, you can change the rules. You can set the breeders free and - "

"You and I both know I will never become queen. Mother is strong and powerful and her reign is far from over. I cannot go another thirty years this way. Besides, once she is dead another will take the throne from me. I am not a good enough warrior to defeat them."

"Not yet," Quinn said. "But you will be."

Kila smiled sadly. "No, massina. I will not."

"You could die on this other world. Do you understand that?" Quinn said bleakly.

"I could die here. There's no guarantee that staying here means I live a safe and happy life," Kila said. "I am going, massina. You cannot stop me."

Quinn stared at her before nodding. "Aye, I suppose I can't. All three of us will go."

"The others too," Gage said.

"What?" Silas said.

"They're my friends, Silas, and I won't just abandon them here. We should give them the chance to come with us."

"Sure, why not. In fact, why don't we just take a poll of everyone in the clan," Quinn said. "See if there are more who would care to join us."

"He's right, Quinn," Silas said. "We have to at least give them the option."

"What happens when they open their big mouths and blab the plans to anyone who will listen?" Quinn asked.

"They won't," Silas said. "They'll know what's at stake."

"That Veronica woman is an idiot," Quinn muttered.

"She won't say anything," Silas said. "Kila, can you speak to Angela and the other women about it? I'll talk with the guys."

Kila nodded. "Aye, I will think of a reason to be alone with them without it raising suspicion."

"Vida," Quinn suddenly said.

"What about him?" Gage asked.

"If we're inviting your friends, I should get to invite mine."

"That's not a good idea," Silas said.

Quinn scowled at him. "Vida wishes to leave this world and I will give him the opportunity to do so. He will be an asset in this new world."

"Unless it's a desert," Silas said. "Then he'll wither up and die on us."

Ignoring him, Quinn took Kila's hand. "Sandora, are you absolutely sure this is what you want? We will need to leave tomorrow night in order to get to the orb in time. There will be no returning to this world."

"I'm sure," Kila said. She squeezed Quinn's hand before standing and reaching for Gage's hand. "We must return to the castle before someone discovers us missing."

At the door, she hugged Quinn hard. "This will work, massina. We will leave this world and find a better one."

"I know," Quinn said. "I love you, sandora."

"I love you too, Quinn."

She and Gage disappeared into the dark and Silas closed the door and locked it. They returned to the kitchen and Quinn stared at her untouched plate of food.

"You should eat, Quinn," Silas said.

"Aye," she replied. She picked at her food as Silas studied her.

"I think you should reconsider asking Vida to join us," he said.

"Why?"

"I don't trust him."

"I thought you two were becoming friends."

"He sleeps with the queen on a regular basis. Who knows what he would tell her."

"He won't say anything to the queen. Tell me your real reason, Silas," Quinn said.

"He wants you." Silas could hear the jealousy in his voice.

"So?"

"So, maybe once we're away from this world you'll be more than happy to give him what he wants."

Quinn gave him a look of bewilderment. "Seriously? Silas, it is you I want, no other. You know that. Vida is my friend and nothing more."

"Sorry, I'm not usually this pathetic. I swear."

She smiled in amusement before pushing back her chair and sitting on his lap. "I do not think you're pathetic. Besides, I know a thing or two about jealousy."

She kissed his neck and he cupped her breast. She moaned before kissing him until they were both panting.

"I believe you said earlier something about tying me to the bed?" Quinn said.

He grinned at her. "I remember mentioning it."

"Good." She slid off his lap and took his hand before tugging him to his feet. "Come, danen. It is time to practice what you preach."

๛ ๛

The queen stared out the window at the

darkening sky. Thunder rumbled and lightning flashed in the distance. She drew her robe closer to her body. When there was a knock at the door she moved to the fireplace.

"Enter."

"My Queen." Akia shut the door and dropped to one knee.

"Rise, Akia. Tell me what news you have."

"Quinn went to see Josana yesterday."

"Not unusual. She often goes to see her," the queen said dismissively.

Akia frowned. "Why?"

"For reasons that do not concern you. If that's all you have you can leave."

"Before they went inside Quinn told Josana it was time to pay her debt to her," Akia said.

The queen turned toward her. "Did she now?"

"Aye."

"Interesting," the queen said thoughtfully.

There was another knock on the door and the queen smiled. "Perfect timing. Open the door, Akia, and show our guest in."

Akia opened the door and blinked in surprise. Josana was standing in the hallway and she gave Akia a timid look.

"Hello, Akia."

"Good evening, Josana."

Josana entered the room and dropped painfully to one knee. "Greetings, my Queen."

"Rise, majii, and join me by the fire," the queen said.

Josana rose clumsily to her feet and crossed the room to stand next to the queen. She kept her gaze on the floor until the queen said, "Look at me."

The queen studied the old woman's face. "You grow old."

"Aye, as we all do, my Queen."

"Indeed. Soon your powers of sight will fade and then what good will you be to me?"

Josana didn't reply and the queen arched her eyebrow. "Perhaps I will put you to work in the gardens or the kitchen."

"That would be a great honour, my Queen."

"Or perhaps I will simply cast you out beyond the walls and let fate decide what happens."

Josana gave her a frightened look and cringed away when the queen petted her long hair. "You have served me faithfully for over thirty years. Have you not, majii?"

"Aye, my Queen."

"I reward my good and faithful servants. Do I not?"

"Aye, my Queen."

The queen continued to stare at her. "What news do you bring of the storm?"

"It is only a storm, my Queen. No orb appears."

"Are you certain?"

"Aye, my Queen." Josana stared unblinkingly at the queen but as the seconds turned into minutes she finally returned her gaze to the floor.

"Very well. You are dismissed, majii."

"Thank you, my Queen."

Josana walked slowly toward the door. As she reached for the handle the queen said, "There is one more thing I must ask of you, majii."

Josana turned and gave the queen a hesitant

smile. "I am at your bidding, my Queen."

"What did you and the massina speak of when she came to your home yesterday?"

Josana paled and swallowed. There was an audible click in her throat and she cleared it. "Nothing of interest, my Queen."

"Come now, majii, I do not believe that to be true." The queen nodded at Akia who took Josana's arm and yanked her back to the queen.

"I would hear the truth," the queen said.

Josana swallowed again. "She only stopped by to check on me and to have a short visit, my Queen. The massina is kind and knows of my loneliness. She – she often stops by."

"Aye, I suppose you have been lonely since your daughter died," the queen said. "How long has she been dead?"

"Thirty years, my Queen," Josana said.

"One never gets over the loss of a child. Do they, majii?"

"No, my Queen."

"I understand that pain all too well. I was blessed with a child before Kila. Do you remember?"

Josana nodded as the queen moved closer. "She died in my womb. I gave birth to a child who would never cry, never laugh, never grow big and strong. She was perfect, you know. There was no reason for her to be dead and Naveen had no explanation for why she did not breathe."

"I – I am sorry, my Queen," Josana said.

"Are you? It is my experience that liars such as you do not possess the ability for sympathy."

"I do not lie, my Queen," Josana replied. She screamed breathlessly when the queen grabbed a handful of her hair and yanked her closer. The queen produced a dagger from within her robes and held it up to the firelight. Josana watched it gleam in the light before the queen traced it across her throat.

"Do you believe me to be simple, majii?"

"N-no, my Queen."

"Are you certain?"

Josana nodded, wincing when it made her hair pull in the queen's tight grip.

"Then why do you continue to lie to me about your daughter's death?"

Josana's eyes widened and the queen smiled cruelly. "Aye, majii. I know your daughter lives. I know you and the massina faked her illness and her death when she was but a child and smuggled her out with the trader so that she could live with the clan north of ours."

"No, my Queen," Josana gasped. "My child died of illness. She did not - "

"Stop lying to me!" The queen screamed. Spittle flew from her mouth to land on Josana's face. "I know everything that happens within these walls. Everything! I know you faked her death because she is a majii. I have allowed you to keep your secrets until now but the time of your deception is done. Tell me what you and Quinn spoke of or I will have Akia leave this very instant and bring your precious daughter to me. You will watch as I cut off pieces of her one by one and feed them to the pigs. Do you understand, majii?"

"My Queen, please," Josana whispered.

"Do you understand, majii?" The queen shrieked at her. She shook the old woman by her hair before slapping her across the face. Josana fell to her knees and began to weep as the queen gave her a look of contempt.

"Tell me all your secrets, majii, or I will make your child suffer in ways you can't even imagine. I will show you the true meaning of pain."

"Please, my Queen," Josana wept. "Do not harm my girl."

"Tell me what I want to know and your daughter will remain unharmed."

"Quinn asked me to-to check for an orb. There is an orb coming two days from now. When I told her, she asked me not to tell you."

"Why?"

"I do not know. I swear it," Josana cried. "She would not say."

"Is it an orb that takes or gives?"

"Takes," Josana whispered.

The queen stared thoughtfully at her for a moment. "Rise, majii."

Josana climbed painfully to her feet and stared at the floor as the queen touched the top of her head. "Return to your home and speak to no one about this or I'll kill your daughter."

"Aye, my Queen," Josana whispered.

She turned and hobbled out of the room, closing the door behind her.

"My Queen?" Akia said. "Why would Quinn want to know about an orb that takes."

The queen gave her a look of contempt. "Are

you that stupid, Akia? If you are to be massina you will need to learn to hide your stupidity better."

Akia flushed and the queen snorted. "It is quite obvious. Quinn is planning on leaving and I would bet my rule as queen that she intends to take the danen with her."

"She has gone mad," Akia whispered.

The queen grinned bitterly. "No, she has fallen in love. Listen closely, Akia, and do exactly as I command."

# Chapter Twenty

"Massina, tell me what is wrong."

"There is nothing wrong, Naveen," Quinn replied. "I simply wished to visit with my friend."

"I am enjoying your company but it strikes me as odd that you would spend time with me when the danen waits for you in your home," Naveen said. "Go to him, massina. I know you want to."

"The danen can wait a while longer," Quinn said. She stared morosely into the fire. In just a few hours she would never see the old man again and her heart was breaking. She was very fond of Naveen, loved him in fact, and she wished she could tell him she was leaving.

*You can't, Quinn. If the queen finds out that he knew beforehand and did not tell her she will kill him.*

She bit back her sigh and forced another cheerful smile at Naveen. The plan was in place for better or for worse. Silas and Kila had spoken to the others. To Silas' surprise, only Kyle and Veronica had agreed to go with them. She wasn't surprised. For most people, sticking with the devil they knew was better than jumping into the unknown. First thing this morning she pulled Vida aside and told him of their plan. He agreed immediately as well.

"This is the second time you've visited me today, massina," Naveen pointed out.

Guilt rolled through her. Earlier this afternoon she visited his home with the sole intention of stealing some of the kyprus powder he had. Kyprus powder was a powerful sedative and both Kyle and Vida would need it to drug the women who claimed them this month. It was easy enough to distract Naveen while she took it from the cupboard.

She sighed and rubbed her forehead. Once the women were drugged, Vida and Kyle still needed to escape from the breeders' quarters. The plan was a straight-forward one. Quinn would ask the women who were guarding the quarters to join her in the common room under the pretense of speaking with them about the training exercises in the morning. While they were distracted, Vida and Kyle would simply walk out of the quarters and join Silas at Quinn's home. Once Kila and Gage brought Veronica they would leave. It was just simple enough to work.

"Massina?"

She smiled at Naveen. "I'm sorry, Naveen. I was woolgathering."

"What does woolgathering mean?" He asked curiously.

"It means," she waved her hand vaguely, "to be lost in thought."

"You do seem to be distracted this evening. Go home to your danen, Quinn. I will see you in the morning," Naveen said.

*That's where he was wrong*, she thought miserably before abruptly standing. She couldn't wallow in self-pity any longer. The decision was made and to stay just for Naveen was madness. Nor could she ask him to go. They would probably die and she wouldn't ask him to risk his life for her. Not to mention that the women here would be without a kalan. No, it was best to keep him here where he was safe.

Naveen walked her to the door and grunted in surprise when she embraced him. "I love you, Naveen. You know that, do you not?"

He laughed. "Aye, I do, massina. I love you as well." He patted her on the back with one gnarled hand. "Go to your danen."

She opened the door and stared silently at him, memorizing his face as he gave her a curious look. "What is it?"

"Nothing, Naveen. Take care of yourself, all right?"

"Aye, I always do," he said in bewilderment. "Good night, Quinn."

She blinked back the tears that were threatening. "Good bye, Naveen."

છ જ

"This feels too easy," Silas said in a low voice.

Quinn scanned the dark courtyard. They were huddled outside her home and she searched for any sign of movement. It seemed quiet but the intermittent claps of thunder and the pouring rain made it difficult to be certain. Everything was going according to plan. Vida and Kyle escaped the breeders' quarters without issue and Kila, Gage and Veronica had just joined them. All that was left to do was get through the gate without being seen and they would be well into the forest by the time their absence was discovered in the morning.

"Quinn? Does it feel too easy to you?" Silas asked.

She nodded and drew her sword. It didn't matter that it felt like they were walking into a trap. They had to continue.

"We have to move," Kila said anxiously.

"I know," Quinn replied. "I'm heading to the gate. Follow me in five minutes."

"I'm going with you," Silas said.

"No, you're not," Quinn said. "I can approach the guards on my own without suspicion. If I have you with me they'll know something isn't right."

"What if you can't knock out both of them?" Silas said heatedly. "You need me with you to - "

"I don't," Quinn said. She cupped Silas' face as water streamed down their skin. "I can do this easily, danen. Trust me."

He nodded reluctantly before pulling her against him for a brief kiss. Veronica made a loud snorting noise behind them and Kila jabbed her in the back with her fist.

"Garna! Be quiet, fool!"

"That hurt!" Veronica hissed at her.

"Keep talking and I'll abandon you in the forest," Kila snapped.

"Some girlfriend you have there, Gage," Veronica muttered as she rubbed at her back. "God, I'm freezing."

"If you don't like the rain you can go back to your warm bed," Kila said.

Veronica rolled her eyes as Quinn held up her hand. "All of you be quiet. Kila, bring them to the gate in five minutes, all right?"

"Aye, massina. Be careful."

"I will."

Quinn pulled up the hood of her cloak and walked silently across the courtyard. The castle loomed to her right, a dark shape with only a few candles glowing in the many windows. They did nothing to dispel the darkness and she skirted around the steps leading up to the castle. As soon as the guards were –

"It is miserable night for a walk, massina."

Quinn froze at the sound of the queen's voice. She turned to face the castle as there was a flare of light. Akia had lit the torch she carried and the flames hissed and flickered in the pouring rain. The queen was standing next to her, her head and body protected from the rain by a thick fur cloak.

"Why do you creep like a thief in the night, massina?" The queen asked.

"The danen is feeling ill," Quinn replied. "I'm going to Naveen's to get some medicine."

"Without even a candle to light your way?"

"It's raining," Quinn said, "and this is my home. I know it well and have no need for light."

"Indeed," the queen said. "This is your home and I am your queen. Is that not right?"

"Aye," Quinn said.

"Aye, *my Queen,*" the queen said with a hint of anger.

Quinn remained silent and the queen's nostrils flared before she snorted. "You have no need to go to Naveen's, massina. I have brought him to you."

She clapped her hands twice and the darkness was slowly driven back as torch after torch was lit. Quinn stared at the women holding the torches and blocking her path out of the courtyard. Ten of the queen's guard stood in a neat row. They were staring at her with a mixture of bewilderment and anxiety.

"Step forward, Naveen," the queen demanded.

There was a loud crack of thunder as Naveen pushed past the queen's guard. His thin hair was plastered to his head and rain dripped steadily from the end of his nose. Akia descended the steps as he walked toward Quinn.

"You need the kalan's help, massina. Here he is," the queen said.

Quinn squeezed the old man's arm before turning to the queen. "I will no longer play your games, Edina."

She spoke the queen's given name with undisguised contempt and the women behind her gasped.

The queen smiled bitterly. "After all I have done for you, massina, you seek to not only leave but take my property with you?"

"The danen does not belong to you. None of the breeders are yours," Quinn said. "They're human beings, not property."

339

"Everything within these walls belongs to me!" The queen hissed at her. "It is a shame you have forgotten that, massina. Your punishment will be harsh."

Silas walked out of the dark and stood beside Quinn. "It was my idea to leave. Punish me for it, not Quinn."

"How brave you are, danen," the queen said. "Fear not, you will be punished as well."

She turned to Akia and said, "Do it, Akia."

Quinn stepped in front of Silas and placed her hand on the handle of her sword. Akia laughed and Quinn cried out in horror when she pulled a dagger from her belt and plunged it into Naveen's stomach.

Naveen's eyes widened and he clutched weakly at the wound when Akia yanked the dagger from his flesh. She pushed him roughly toward Quinn. Quinn caught him as he fell and she sank to the ground, cradling the old man in her arms.

"Are you enjoying your punishment, massina?" The queen called mockingly.

"Massina," Naveen whispered as Silas knelt beside them.

"You'll be fine, Naveen," Quinn said frantically. Blood was pouring from his stomach and she yanked off her cloak and pressed it against the wound.

"You're going to be just fine," she repeated. "Silas, apply pressure and don't let up. All right?"

Silas nodded and Quinn eased out from under Naveen as Silas pressed his hands against the cloak. She kissed Naveen's forehead. "Stay awake, my friend. I'll need you to tell me how to sew you up when I am finished here."

Naveen stared silently at her and she kissed his forehead again. "If you die on me, Naveen, I will never forgive you. Do you understand?"

"Aye, massina," he whispered weakly.

She squeezed his shoulder and rose gracefully to her feet. The queen's face was pale and Quinn followed her gaze. Kila and the others had appeared in the circle of light and the queen was staring at her daughter.

"Kila," she said in a low voice. "What are you doing with them?"

"I'm leaving, mother," Kila said. "I love Gage and I won't share him."

"You foolish girl," the queen snapped. "You're not in love with the breeder. Join me now and I will forget this indiscretion."

"His name is Gage and I love him," Kila said steadily. "We're leaving and you cannot stop us."

The queen studied her before staring at each of the others. Her gaze lingered on Vida and he returned her look with calm defiance. The queen laughed bitterly before pointing at Quinn. "Queen's guard! Take the traitor and her friends below the castle. Their punishment will take place at first light."

The queen's guard stared uneasily at each other but didn't move. The queen frowned at them. "What are you waiting for?"

"You've gone mad," Barkha said in a low voice. "You injure our only kalan and you ask us to imprison the massina and your daughter?"

"You will do as I command!" The queen said

shrilly.

A few of the women started to move forward and Barkha held up her hand. "No, sisters. The queen has been overtaken by madness. Do not do as she asks."

The queen pinned her angry gaze on Barkha. "You will regret your disobedience when I have your hands removed."

Barkha shook her head. "Return to the castle and rest, my Queen. We will convince the others to stay and - "

"Akia!" The queen shouted. "Do you believe your sisters are right? Do you believe your queen to be mad?"

"No, my Queen," Akia said. Naveen's blood still dripped from her dagger and she wiped it away on her battle skirt before sheathing it.

"Then bring me the massina's head and take her place by my side."

"With pleasure, my Queen," Akia said.

She pulled her sword free as Barkha and the others surged forward. Quinn shook her head as she drew her own sword. "Stay where you are, Barkha."

"Yes, massina," Barkha replied.

The two women circled each other in the pouring rain. Akia smiled at Quinn. "You grow old and tired, Quinn. Your time as massina is over. Kneel before me and I will have mercy on you and kill you quickly."

"Drop your sword and I will simply banish you from the clan instead of taking your head," Quinn replied.

Akia snorted laughter. "I am stronger and faster than you think. Did you really believe I would show you what I am actually capable of?"

"Why don't you shut your mouth for once and show me?" Quinn said scornfully.

Akia made a low snarl of anger and attacked. Quinn parried her blow easily before dancing away. Akia swung at her repeatedly, attacking with a vicious determination that drove Quinn backward. She ducked when Akia swung her sword at her head and then jabbed her own blade deep into Akia's left thigh.

Akia screamed in pain and stumbled back. She touched her thigh and stared at the mixture of rainwater and blood dripping from her fingers before glaring at Quinn.

"Do you yield, Akia?" Quinn asked.

Akia bared her teeth at her and attacked again. Their swords clashed repeatedly, the dull clanking sounds echoing across the courtyard. Quinn moved swiftly around her, thrusting and jabbing her sword with deadly accuracy. Akia made a thin scream of pain when Quinn slashed her across the wrist. She dropped her sword and Quinn kicked it away as Akia dropped to her knees in the mud.

Quinn raised her sword and Akia shouted, "I yield, massina! I yield!"

Quinn hesitated before staring at Silas still pressing his hands against Naveen's stomach. Her gaze returned to Akia and she smiled bitterly at the woman. "You should not have injured Naveen."

Akia's eyes widened and there was a collective gasp from the people surrounding them when

Quinn's sword sliced through Akia's neck. Blood jetted out from the stump of her neck as her head tumbled across the ground. Akia's body slumped forward into the mud. The pouring rain quickly washed away the spray of blood as Quinn lowered her sword and stared up at the queen.

The queen's face was bloodless and she stared silently at Akia's body before raising her gaze to the rest of the queen's guard. "Take the massina prisoner," she said. "She has killed one of the queen's guard."

The women didn't move and the queen shrieked angrily as Quinn took a step toward her. "It's over, Edina. I will offer you the same deal I offered Akia. Leave the clan now and I will spare your life."

"You're after the throne," the queen spat. "Is that it? You think you should rule?"

"No," Quinn replied. "Make your decision, Edina."

"I will not give up the throne," the queen said. "I will kill you myself, massina."

Quinn stepped back and raised her sword but the queen didn't move. Her gaze flickered to Silas. "Then you would do all of this for him? You barely know him! He is nothing! You would die for a breeder you have just met?"

"Not just him," Quinn replied. "You killed my husband because he refused to fuck you. You slit his throat and watched as he bled to death on your bedroom floor. Do you even remember his name?"

The queen removed her fur cloak and dropped it in the mud. A sword gleamed at her waist and she pulled it free before starting down the steps. "I have killed many breeders over the years, massina. I doubt your mate was special enough to - "

"His name was Kevin," Quinn said. "He was a good man who loved me and I vowed to take my revenge for his death."

"Did you?" The queen said with a derisive snort as she raised her sword. "Then perhaps it is time you stop your whining and take it."

"Yes, my Queen," Quinn said. She raised her sword and stalked forward.

* * *

His stomach churning with fear, Silas watched as Quinn stalked toward the queen. He flinched when their swords struck and involuntarily pushed harder against Naveen's stomach. Naveen groaned.

"I'm sorry, Naveen. Hang in there," Silas muttered. He couldn't take his eyes off Quinn. She was good but as she and the queen fought it was becoming quickly apparent that the queen was better. Quinn was strong and fast but the queen moved effortlessly through the mud, striking repeatedly at her.

He made a harsh groan of fear when Quinn's feet slipped in the mud and she fell on her back. She rolled away as the queen thrust her sword downward. It just barely missed Quinn's head and she jumped to her feet as the queen yanked her sword from the mud and grinned fiercely at her.

"You grow tired already, massina."

Panting heavily, Quinn rushed forward. The

queen blocked her blow and turned. She sliced Quinn across the back with her sword and Silas jumped up at Quinn's cry of pain. Quinn shook her head at him. "Stay with Naveen, Silas."

"Yes, breeder. Stay with the dying old man while I kill your love," the queen taunted.

Silas started forward, his hands clenching into fists. Quinn pointed her sword at him. "Silas, stay away from her!"

He hesitated before backing away. He dropped to his knees and pressed his hands against the bloody cloak again. He had never felt more useless in his life but Quinn was right. The queen would slice him in half in an instant.

He watched helplessly as Quinn and the queen fought viciously. The queen's small size worked in her favour as they slogged through the muddy ground. Quinn was growing weary and Silas flinched when the queen's sword slipped past Quinn's and cut her across the arm. Quinn shouted in pain and backed away as the queen grinned triumphantly at her and surged forward. She attacked again, her sword gleaming dully in the flickering light. She drove Quinn backward and Silas shouted hoarsely when Quinn tripped on the steps of the castle. She fell on her ass and the queen screamed in triumph before knocking Quinn's sword from her hand. She leaned down and grinned at Quinn.

"I'm not going to kill you right away, massina. I'm going to make you watch as I cut your precious breeder into small pieces and feed him to the pigs. I'll take his hands first, then his feet. Then I'll - "

She shrieked in agony when Quinn headbutted her. Her nose broke with a loud crack and she staggered back as Quinn jumped to her feet. She punched the queen twice in the face before grabbing her wrist and twisting violently. The queen's sword fell to the ground and Quinn kicked her in the stomach. Gasping for air, the queen dropped to her knees as Quinn picked up her own sword and raised it above her head.

"Good bye, Edina," she said.

"Quinn!"

Kila's loud cry stopped the downward motion of her sword. She hesitated, staring at the bloody queen kneeling at her feet before glancing at Kila.

"Please, Quinn," Kila whispered. She shook off Gage's hand and walked toward Quinn and her mother.

Quinn's body slumped and she lowered her sword. "Leave this place, Edina. The next time I see your face I will not show you mercy."

Kila joined her and she gave the young woman a look of sorrow. "Sandora, I - "

Her words were drowned out by Silas' shout of warning. She whipped around, slipping in the mud, to see the queen standing behind her. She held her sword over her head with both hands and Quinn stumbled back as the queen screamed victoriously and Kila lunged forward. Quinn's eyes widened when the queen lurched to a stop only inches from her. The queen stared blankly at her as her sword dropped from her hands. A thin line of blood streamed out of her mouth and she stared at the small pale hand holding the handle of the dagger sticking out from her chest.

She studied her daughter standing motionless beside her before whispering, "Kila?"

Kila made a small, moaning cry and yanked the dagger from her mother's chest. The queen fell to her knees as blood poured out of her chest in a steady stream.

"Kila," the queen whispered again.

"I'm sorry," Kila said in a low voice.

The queen pitched forward, landing face-first in the mud. Her hand scrabbled weakly for her sword before growing still. Kila and Quinn stared silently at each other before Quinn knelt on one knee in front of her.

"My Queen."

The others stared in shock silence before, one by one, they knelt before the new queen.

જ્જ ૐ

"Vida," Quinn said urgently as they approached the edge of the forest, "are you certain this is what you want? It will be different here under Kila's rule. I promise you."

Vida nodded and shouted over the loud crack of thunder, "It is what I want, massina."

"I don't think you should go," Quinn said. "Any of you."

Veronica ignored her and continued forward. Kyle licked his lips nervously and cringed when the lightning flashed. The wind was picking up, whipping their hair and clothing against their bodies and the rain was a steady downpour.

"Reconsider, Vida," Quinn said as Silas left

Barkha and Dacia and joined them.

"Silas, tell him to stay," Quinn shouted over the howling wind.

"It's safer for you to stay!" Silas yelled.

Vida just shrugged before joining Veronica at the edge of the forest. She squealed excitedly. "There it is! Look!"

The others squinted in the dark. The orb was glowing in the middle of the open field. It was only the size of a baseball but it was growing steadily and wet leaves and branches from the ground around it were already being sucked into its light.

"Vida," Quinn said, "you don't know that it will take you to your world."

"I know," Vida replied, "but I cannot stay."

He glanced at Silas before leaning down and pressing his mouth against Quinn's. "Thank you for everything, massina. I will not forget your kindness."

"Be safe, Vida," Quinn said. "I hope you find your home again."

He smiled at her before turning to Veronica and Kyle. "Humans, are you ready?"

Veronica nodded but Kyle took a step back. "I've changed my mind."

Silas touched Veronica's arm. "Veronica, maybe you shouldn't - "

"Let go!" Veronica snapped. She took Vida's hand and the two of them crossed the field toward the orb. The orb was pulsing with light now and Silas guessed it had grown to nearly twenty feet wide. The light washed over Vida and Veronica and they were lifted off their feet and sucked into the orb. They disappeared in a flash of bright light and the others clung to the trees as the wind intensified. The orb pulsed again and then disappeared completely as lightning flickered across the sky and there was another loud boom of thunder.

As the wind died down and the rain began to ease, Quinn took Silas' hand. He kissed her knuckles as Barkha and Dacia joined them. Barkha grinned at Kyle.

"I'm glad you decided to stay, breeder. I really wanted to fuck you."

Kyle rolled his eyes. "My name's Kyle."

"Kyle," Barkha said with a laugh. "A strange name, but I like it."

"What do you say we get out of here?" Silas said to Quinn.

"Yes," she replied. "Let's go home, Silas."

# Epilogue

*Two months later*

"Well, what do you think?"

Silas and the others stared wide-eyed at Gemma.

"Holy shit," Steve said. "You look fucking hot in that bustier, Gemma."

"Yes, because looking hot is what I'm aiming for," Gemma said.

Evan touched the sword hanging around her waist. "You sure you really want to be in the queen's guard, Gemma? It's dangerous."

"I'm sure," she said. "Dacia says I have a knack for it."

Craig nudged Kyle. "So, are they gonna make you wear a bustier and skirt too?"

As Kyle rolled his eyes, Silas grinned widely. About two weeks after Kila became queen, Kyle asked to join the queen's guard. It had taken some convincing but Kila eventually agreed. Silas knew the other women were surprised by her decision. After years of doing everything they could to

351

protect the men, it made the women uneasy to have one fighting in the guard. But Kila had stuck to her decision and allowed Kyle to join the guard.

"Where are Angela and Paula?" Steve asked.

"Angela's with Zeeda, putting her bid in," Gemma said, "and I think Paula is at the nursery. She and Mina have become friends and she's been helping Mina with her baby a lot."

"Angela's putting a bid in?" Steve said. "I bet it's for me."

"Actually," Gemma said with a grin, "she's bidding on Lutan and Kyle."

"What the hell?" Steve laughed. "Kyle, you're participating in the claiming ceremony tonight?"

Kyle shrugged. "Now that I have a choice in participating, why not?"

Steve laughed again and threw his arm around Kyle's shoulder. "Yeah, why not, ya man whore."

"Hello, danen."

Silas turned and gave Quinn a mock scowl before putting his arms around her waist. "I have a name."

"Hello, *Silas*," she said teasingly before squeezing his ass.

"You know," Silas said, "I think you call me danen on purpose."

"Now why would I do that?" She asked sweetly.

"Because you know you'll get a spanking for it," he said in a low voice before kissing her.

She returned his kiss and smiled at him. "Sorry I'm late. I was meeting with the queen about the ceremony tonight and it went longer than I thought."

Silas nuzzled her neck affectionately. "My brother is sleeping with the queen. I could probably have got you out of that meeting, no problem."

"So there are other perks to sleeping with you than just your big cock. Is that what you're saying?"

"You love my big cock," he said cheerfully.

"Aye, I do," Quinn replied.

"How many of the men are participating tonight?" Silas asked.

"Nearly all of them," Quinn said. "It's a little surprising to me."

"Why?" Silas said. "Now that it's completely voluntary, what man wouldn't love having women mock fighting over the right to have sex with them?"

Quinn laughed. "Good point. Do you know who isn't participating?"

"Who?"

"Lloyd."

"You're kidding me."

"Nope. Apparently, he's smitten with Selda. She gave birth to one of his children - Rardin I think his name is - a few years ago. Now the three of them are living together."

"Well, good for Lloyd," Silas said.

"I'm glad most of the men are participating," Quinn said. "This has been the way of life for many years. It needed to change but the women would find it difficult if it was completely different. It was wise of Kila to come up with this idea."

Silas gave her a solemn look. "How are things

with the two of you?"

"Better than I thought they would be," Quinn said. "Most of the guilt is on my part. Kila has assured me multiple times that she did what was necessary and has no regrets but I wonder if that will change later."

"I don't think it will," Silas said. "Kila loves you."

"Aye, and I love her," Quinn replied. "How was your day?"

"Busy. Naveen coerced me into building new shelves for his medical supplies. He says he's too old and weak to do it, but, I don't know – the guy's like a hundred years old and survived being stabbed in the stomach. I think he's tougher than he lets on."

Quinn's face softened at the mention of the old man. "Aye, he is."

She pressed a kiss against his mouth again. "I need to speak with Zeeda before the games begin. I'll talk to you later, all right?"

Silas nodded before stroking her hair back from her face. "Yes. I love you, Quinn."

"I love you too, Silas."

Please enjoy an excerpt from Choosing Rose, Book Six in the Other World Series.

**CHOOSING ROSE**
(Other World Series Book Six)

"Crap, crap, crap…CRAP!" Rose banged her hands on the steering wheel of her useless car before climbing out. She slammed the door shut and locked it. A pointless gesture considering the damn thing wouldn't even start. She hurried across the parking garage toward the elevator.

She ran through the lobby of her apartment building and out to the street. It was pouring rain and she stared up at the dark sky as lightning flashed. She covered her head with her arm and stood at the edge of the sidewalk. A taxi was careening down the street and she waved frantically at it as the rain soaked her long, blonde hair.

The taxi screeched to a halt in front of her and she climbed into the back seat. The front seat was separated from the back with a thick layer of plexiglass and the driver's disembodied voice floated out of the speakers hanging haphazardly from the ceiling.

"Where to, lady?"

"The Franklin Center, please."

The driver pulled out into the street and Rose rapped on the plexiglass. "By air, please."

"It'll cost ya extra."

"I know, that's fine. I'm in a hurry," Rose said

with an impatient sigh.

She clutched at the door handle when the driver flipped a switch and there was a loud grinding noise below her feet. The car shivered wildly and lurched sideways as Rose quickly buckled her seat belt.

"Can this thing even handle air?" She wondered out loud.

"Don't you worry, lady. Baby might be showin' her age but she's still got all the tricks," the driver replied.

There was another painfully loud grinding sound and Rose made a breathless shriek when the car lurched upward. Her stomach dropped to her feet and the driver grinned cheerfully at her through the rearview mirror. "Can you handle air, lady?"

"Yes," Rose flapped her hand at him. "I'm fine."

"There's bags in the seat pocket in front of you. Use 'em if yer gonna puke."

"I'm not going to puke," Rose said. "Just get moving, would you? I'm really late and I - "

She shrieked again as the cab rose another hundred feet then took off in a burst of speed. The driver honked his horn and cursed loudly at the car hovering next to them. "Get the hell out of my way, ya miscreant!"

Rose peeked out the window and immediately wished she hadn't. The people standing on the street below them were the size of ants and her stomach made an unpleasant heave. God, she hated travelling by air in well-maintained cars. Doing so in one that looked like it might drop from the sky at any moment made her want to vomit. She didn't have much of a choice though. Her meeting started in exactly seventeen minutes and with the morning rush hour, she'd never make it by ground. She jumped when a loud crack of thunder made the car shake and a jagged streak of lightning lit up the sky. She closed her eyes as the cab made another unpleasant sway and clung tightly to the door handle.

❧ ❧

"I know, I know. I'm late," Rose said as she scurried into the lab. She hung her coat on the hook and grabbed her lab coat, slipping into it as she tucked her purse under one of the tables.

"Relax, the orb isn't due to appear for another three hours and Solomon isn't even here yet," Brody said. He was studying something under one of the microscopes and didn't notice when Rose frowned.

"He's not here yet?"

"Nope." He adjusted the dial on the microscope before typing a note on the tablet sitting next to it.

"But he left the apartment early this morning," Rose said. "He said he was going to the lab."

Brody shrugged. "Don't know what to tell you, Rosie-girl. He's not here."

Rose checked her phone. There were no messages from Solomon and she sent him a quick text before slipping it into the pocket of her lab coat. "What are you looking at?"

"Another skin sample from Subject Blue Balls," Brody said.

"Don't call him that," Rose said sharply.

Brody glanced at her. "What else should I call him? Subject 10387? If the big guy won't tell us his name, I gotta call him something."

Rose sighed. "Is there any change?"

"No. He's getting drier by the day. He keeps this up and he'll be completely dried out within the next couple of days. His internal organs are starting to show signs of shutting down."

"Crap," Rose said. "I can't believe he's been with us for a month and we still can't figure out how to rehydrate him."

Brody gave her an odd look. "We do know."

Rose blinked at him. "We know what?"

"How to rehydrate him. Figured it out the second day. Didn't Solomon tell you?"

"No, he – I had no idea," Rose said.

Brody gave her a thoughtful look. "Weren't you on holidays when the big guy came in?"

Rose nodded and he smiled cheerfully at her. "That's why you didn't know."

"But I – I specifically talked to Solomon about rehydrating him and he said they were still working on it," Rose said slowly.

"That's weird," Brody said. "We rehydrated him a few times the first week."

"How?"

"Just plain old water," Brody said. "Dunk the big guy in some water and his body starts to rehydrate. Makes sense considering the gills behind his ears. Did I tell you that Solomon had me put a piece of the big guy's flesh in the haloden liquid? I don't know why. He's crazy if he thinks we could grow another one just from the flesh. I mean, I know haloden liquid can regenerate human limbs but this guy isn't human. The haloden didn't do anything at all. Rose? What's wrong?"

Rose squeezed the lab table. "I asked Solomon if he tried water and he said yes. He said it – it didn't do anything. He lied to me, Brody."

Brody gave her an uncomfortable look. "Rose, listen – I know Solomon is your fiancé but he's also the boss. I'm sure there's lots of stuff he doesn't tell a couple of lab monkeys like us."

"He lied to me," Rose repeated.

Her head snapped up and she stared at Brody. "If he's so close to dying why aren't we rehydrating him?"

Brody cleared his throat. "I don't know."

"Don't start lying to me as well, Brody," Rose said angrily.

The short, redheaded man gave her a guilty look. "Solomon wants to see how long he can go without being rehydrated."

"Are you kidding me? He does know he's dying, right?" Rose said.

"I gave him the report yesterday," Brody said. "He looked it over and told me to leave things the way they are."

"Son of a…"

"Rosie, where are you going?" Brody called as Rose stormed out of the lab. She slammed the door shut and using her keycard, accessed the elevators that led to the lower level. She tapped her foot impatiently as the elevator took her swiftly down fourteen floors. When the doors opened, she hurried down the hall and used her keycard to open the last door on the left.

Subject 10387 was lying motionless in the bed. Both of his arms were strapped down as were his legs. He stared up at the ceiling as she approached the bed. She studied him silently. His skin was a dusty blue colour and it was so dry and cracked that she could see blood seeping through the hospital gown that covered his massive chest. She studied the small black horns growing from his temples. His thick black hair had lost its sheen and clung listlessly to his scalp. His eyes were the colour of warm amber. When his gaze shifted to her, she felt a weird almost painful cramp of pleasure deep in her belly.

His lips were a slightly darker shade of blue as were his nails. She touched his arm, wincing when flakes of skin shed away. There was a cup with a moist sponge sitting on the table next to the bed and she swiped it across his dry lips. His mouth opened a little, enough for her to see the tips of his fangs, and his tongue flickered out to lick at the sponge. She set the sponge down and poured water into a glass before holding it to his mouth. He drank eagerly and she gave him a second glass of water before returning it to the table.

She cleared her throat as he continued to stare at her with those unnerving amber-coloured eyes. When her hand tightened on his arm he winced and pain flashed across his face. She hesitated a moment longer before turning and crossing the room to the sink that was in the corner. She filled a jug with water and marched back to the bed. She hesitated only briefly before pouring the water over his left arm. His skin sucked up the moisture and she poured more, watching with disbelief as the skin began to heal.

"Holy moly," she breathed before emptying the jug over his entire forearm. She traced the now smooth skin with the tips of her fingers. "It works."

She glanced up at the silent, blue man and gave him a look of regret. "I'm sorry. I didn't know."

He didn't reply. In the month he had been here, locked up like an animal, he had never spoken a single word. She didn't even know if he spoke English or could understand a word she said to him. She talked to him almost every time she came into the room. She spent more time in here than was probably necessary but she was fascinated by the giant blue man who had appeared from the orb. The woman that was with him was human and a real pain in the butt. Solomon kept her for only two weeks and did minimal testing on her before turning her out onto the street to fend for herself. Rose wished she had thought to ask the woman if she knew the blue guy's name before Solomon tossed her out of the lab. She certainly had no problems with talking. In fact, she never shut up.

She got more water and began to sponge the man's face, paying careful attention to the cracked and bleeding skin around the horns. The relief on his face as she sponged him with water was palpable and another surge of guilt went through her.

"I really am very sorry," she said. "Solomon, he lied to me, said he didn't know how to help you. If I had known I wouldn't have let it get this far. I'm so sorry."

She sponged water over his throat and the top of his chest. "I'll talk to Solomon and we'll - I don't know - get you into a bath or something, okay?"

She brushed her hand over his cheekbone. "Is that a little better at least?"

He nodded. It was the first response she had ever seen from him and her eyes widened. "You understand me."

His eyes shifted to the sponge she held in her hand and she quickly swiped it across his throat again before sliding it under his hospital gown. She squeezed the sponge, letting water drip over his chest and he made a soft hissing sound.

"I'm sorry. I know that hurts," she said. She used her other hand to rub his arm. "Gosh, I feel so awful about this."

She brushed his hair back from his forehead and dipped the sponge into the water before squeezing it across his chest again. "Can you speak English? Will you tell me your name?"

He remained silent and she sighed before dipping the sponge into the jug. When she turned back to him, he was staring directly at her.

Her mouth dropped open when he said in a low, hoarse voice, "Vida. My name is Vida."

❧ ❧

# About the Author

Ramona Gray is a Canadian romance author. She currently lives in Alberta with her awesome husband and her mutant Chihuahua. She's addicted to home improvement shows, good coffee, and reading and writing about the steamier moments in life.

If you would like more information about Ramona, please visit her at:

www.ramonagray.ca

# Books by Ramona Gray

## Individual Books

The Escort
Saving Jax
The Assistant
One Night
Sharing Del

## Other World Series

The Vampire's Kiss (Book One)
The Vampire's Love (Book Two)
The Shifter's Mate (Book Three)
Rescued By The Wolf (Book Four)
Claiming Quinn (Book Five)
Choosing Rose (Book Six)

## Undeniable Series

Undeniably His
Undeniably Hers
Undeniably Theirs